SWEETHEARTS AND SAVAGES

EDEN ACADEMY BOOK TWO

GRACE MCGINTY

ALSO BY GRACE MCGINTY

Hell's Redemption Series

The Redeemable/The Unrepentant/The Fallen

The Azar Nazemi Trilogy

Smoke and Smolder/Burn and Blaze/Rage and Ruin

Dark River Days Series

Newly Undead In Dark River/Happily Undead In Dark River/Pleasantly Undead in Dark River

Black Mountain Mates

Hunting Isla

Eden Academy Series

The Lost and the Hunted (Prequel)/Heart of the Hounded (Prequel)

Rebels and Runaways (Book 1)/Sweethearts and Savages (Book 2)

Stand Alone Novels and Novellas

Bright Lights From A Hurricane

The Last Note

Castle of Carnal Desires

SWEETHEARTS AND SAVAGES

For November, the original Sweetheart.
Thank you for your aggressively positive attitude.
This book wouldn't have gotten done without you.
G x

Dark River Days Series

Christopher — Alpha Wolf. Adopted Son

Carmen — Beta Wolf. Adopted Daughter

Enit — Omega Wolf. Adopted Daughter

Raine — Vampire

Dark River Guys — Nico, Lucius, X, Tex, Judge, Walker, Brody

Bobby — Alpha Heir to Brody's wolf pack.

Eden Academy Prequels

Stacey — Human. Adopted Daughter. Sister to Daniel.

Daniel — Human. Adopted Son. Brother of Stacey

Layla — Demigod

Eden Family — Alistair, Micah, Locke

Eden Academy

Black Mountain Mates

Isla — Turned Lion Shifter

Black Mountain Pride — Axel, Archer, Wyatt

Bohdie — Lion Alpha. Adopted son of Isla and the Black Mountain Pride. Rightful Heir to the Chatsville Pride

Damnation MC Duet

Serendipity — Nephilim. Daughter of Gusion

Four Horsemen of the Apocalypse and Marco — Judas, Goliath, Cain, Solomon, Marco

Madoc — Nephilim. Son of Archangel Uriel and Serendipity. Adopted son of Damnation MC

Sammie — Human. Adopted Son of Damnation MC, Half brother of Cara

Cara — Human. Daughter of Marco, Adopted daughter of Damnation MC. Half sister of Sammie

PROLOGUE
ENIT

"I've written your final essay for you. I know you wanted to do it on the French Revolution, but the Russian Revolution is more relevant in today's social context."

I stared at the pretty girl in front of me, my eyebrows drawn together as I took the manilla folder she was thrusting at me.

"Stacey, I don't need you to write my essays for me," I said softly, not wanting to injure her feelings. Stacey was a genius. I don't just mean that in the casual, pop-culture sense either. She was like, legit a genius. Just a human whose brain was so unusual that she learned things at a rate that blew my mind.

She frowned. "I dumbed it down to the correct learning level. No one will know that you haven't written it yourself. You said you were worried about this essay. I've helped you."

Hell. How did I explain to her that just because I said I was worried, didn't mean I wanted her to do it for me? "It's cheating. I don't like to cheat, Stace."

She chewed her lip, one of the few unconscious habits she had. Stacey was intense. She thought and behaved like someone three times her age, but she didn't really understand social norms outside of what books told her. Some of that was due to the fact that she was rescued from an actual laboratory, which the mean kids—like stupid Teesha—whispered about whenever she was around. But most of it was that her brain wasn't thinking like ours. If a conversation were like playing chess, she wasn't thinking about the next move; she had already won this conversation and was onto the next.

It made it hard for her to make friends. But I was an Omega, which meant I could, I don't know, sense things. She radiated so much goodness that I couldn't help but be her friend. Plus, with me always came Carmen and Christopher, my littermates. Ever-present shadows, snapping and snarling at people who looked at me the wrong way. Somehow, despite the fact she inadvertently insulted them at least five times a conversation, they liked Stacey. Carmen thought she was funny as hell, and Christopher just added her into his tiny little flock that needed protection by the big, bad Alpha wolf.

I was still walking toward my History class, my feet dragging as I tried to figure out a way to not hurt my friend's feelings. If Carmen and Christopher felt protective of me, I felt that way about Stacey, whether she needed it or not. The only reason they let me walk to History by myself was because they both had P.E. this period. I did not do sports. Gross. Plus Stacey was with me, and no one was stupid enough to tangle with the adopted daughter of the Lycanthropes who ran Eden Academy.

I herded Stacey into an alcove of lockers near the girls' bathroom, and turned my softest smile in her direction, passing back the manilla folder. "Thank you, Stacey. I really appreciate you trying to help me, but some things I have to do myself—in order to feel satisfaction in the achievement, you know?"

Stacey just stared at me, her face screwed up like when she was trying to figure out an extremely complex math problem. And I mean PHD level mathematics.

Then she leaned forward and kissed me.

I stood so still, I was basically frozen. Her lips were soft, and tasted a little like the watermelon chapstick she used sometimes. I flicked my tongue out to taste it —I couldn't help myself—and then I drew away.

I was across the hall in front of the girls' bathroom in a flash. "Stacey, I... What?"

Stacey was still frowning, but there was a flush to her cheeks now. "I think I might love you, Enit."

She said it like she was coming up with a scientific hypothesis, like it was a problem she wanted to figure out. Like *I* was a problem she needed to figure out.

I was shaking my head repeatedly, a small voice in my head wondering if I was going to shake my brains up like a milkshake.

"It's just the Omega pheromones."

Stacey was shaking her head now too. "No it's not. We don't have the same physiology."

"You're too young. I'm an Omega," I said again, like it was an excuse for what just happened. It was the only excuse I had for why I'd enjoyed it. "I'm sorry, I have to pee."

Then I pushed open the bathroom door and slammed it closed, resting my back against the door. I listened intently, and after a minute, I heard the clip-clip of her shiny blue brogues. They were the only shoes she would wear, no matter if she was wearing a summer dress or jeans and a duffle. She argued that they were the perfect shoe and she had at least fifteen pairs for when they wore out.

I let out a shuddering breath and stepped further into the bathroom, stumbling over to the sinks. I stared at myself in the mirror. My cheeks were flushed and I swear, I could still see the shine of her chapstick on my lips. Holy hell, how did I look her in the face now?

How did I tell her that I couldn't return her feelings?

How did I tell her that she probably didn't even have those feelings, that she was confusing my kindness with something like love?

How did I tell her that maybe I liked the kiss anyway?

I turned on the tap, splashing water on my face as I ignored the opening and closing of the bathroom door. I was sure that if I turned to look, whoever it was would read what just happened all over my face.

My hands stilled though, as an unmistakable scent hit my nose.

Alpha. And not Christopher or Bobby, the safe Alphas.

I straightened, my heart starting to pound. *Be calm, Enit. This means nothing. Don't overreact. He might just be here to...* To fucking what? What logical reason would he have to be in the girls' bathroom?

I looked up, not meeting the Alpha's eyes. I knew him, of course; I knew all the Alphas here by scent and sight, even if I avoided all of them. Todd. Wolf Alpha, from the grade above mine. He was huge and mean, and was of the school of thought that Omegas were made for Alphas to kick around, so they could get out their aggression and better lead their Pack.

Carmen had called it bullshit, but with a few more f-words involved. Even suggesting such a thing made Christopher go into a rage.

I skittered around him. "Excuse me," I whispered, dashing toward the door. But his hand whipped out and grabbed my arm, throwing me against the wall.

"Where are you going, Omega?" he growled, and a primal fear ran over my skin as I froze. I couldn't move, except to shake.

No. I needed to run. I kept imagining Christopher's voice telling me to get out of there. Never be trapped in a room with an unknown or untrusted Alpha. And I definitely didn't trust Todd.

"History class," I whispered, and his other hand came up to wrap around my throat.

He chuckled darkly. No sixteen-year-old guy should sound so evil. But still, I couldn't move. Couldn't shout for help.

Couldn't be anything but helpless.

Todd inhaled in a lungful of my scent, the acrid stench of my fear. Then he slapped me. My head whipped to the side, and he laughed.

"Fuck, Omegas really are as pathetic as my Alpha said. Weak. You aren't even going to fight back, are you, little Omega? Not even if I do this?" He slid his hand from my neck down to my boob and squeezed.

I whimpered, screamed inside my own head to move, but still, I did nothing. He was right, I was pathetic. His hand slid lower, his fingers slipping beneath my shirt, the rough calluses on his fingers stroking my skin.

Then the door slammed open and there was a whirl of anger and fists barrelling through it.

Carmen was here.

I let the tears fall down my cheeks with relief as the sound of fists hitting flesh echoed off the tiled walls. Carmen was on top of Todd, slamming her elbow into his face repeatedly. Todd growled, rolling out from under Carmen's furious form even as she pounded her fist into his face over and over.

Todd threw a punch, connecting with her cheek in a sickening crack, and her head whipped back. But Carmen was feral, just scrabbling backwards until she had her feet back under her and launching at him again. I don't know where she'd learned to fight like that, but she was holding her own against the Alpha. She gave him a quick jab to the throat, and he began to choke as she smashed his windpipe. She didn't stop though—oh no, she was way past that.

She knocked him backwards as he grabbed at his throat, and once he was down, she lifted her foot and stomped his dick.

I swear, I heard something crack beneath his howl of pain, his body curling like an armadillo. Carmen pulled back her foot and kicked him in the head, and then he was lights out.

The door suddenly slammed back open, and Christopher was there. His eyes took in Carmen and the unconscious Alpha on the floor, then me, still shaking like a leaf. The wall was the only reason I remained on my feet. He was across to me in two strides, and he wrapped me in his arms, his Alpha presence sliding over me like a blanket. I could finally breathe again.

"We've got you, E. We always have you," he cooed and I cried harder.

Eventually, he passed me into Carmen's waiting arms, despite the fact she was still blood-spattered. She murmured reassurances and kissed my head, echoing Christopher's words about always protecting me.

But I knew they couldn't always protect me. I was weak, powerless, and one day, I would be dead.

1

ENIT - THREE YEARS LATER

I sipped my coffee and sighed, my shoulders wiggling like an over-excited terrier as the caffeine hit my system. I didn't tell my siblings that there was a triple shot of espresso in my travel mug, I just let them think my jitteriness was actually eagerness to start my time at the Academy.

It was, to an extent. I was excited to see the familiar faces, to be ensconced in the protection of Eden for a few more years.

But this year would be the start of my Omega Studies, where they'd tell me that I should be the docile, placid heart of the Pack, and everyone would finally realize I was an imposter.

I wasn't the heart of anything. I was a fucking mess.

Christopher rolled through the gates and I let out a little sigh of relief as we crossed the wards, the familiar sensation of magic coursing over my skin. As he pulled into a spot close to the doors, I downed the rest of my coffee and unclipped my seatbelt. Christopher opened my door and I slid out, straightening my long skirt and the embroidered peasant blouse that billowed around my arms but fit snugly across my stomach. I finger combed my white-blond hair.

Carmen uncurled slowly from the car, more feline than wolf, though I'd never say that to her face. My feet skittered around on the gravel parking lot, and Carmen tugged me to her side to still me.

"Calm down, Enit. You'd think we hadn't spent the last twelve freaking years here." She didn't even bother trying to hide the droll note in her voice. Carmen wasn't a fan of higher education, but it was hard to ignore the need for the Academy in a world rife with different types of touchy-as-hell preternaturals.

I gave her a bright smile that I forced to reach my eyes. "I know, but I get to finally focus on my Omega talents, and pick a career path, and there'll be all sorts of new people to meet." My enthusiasm wasn't all forced. I was excited for most of those things. The new year always brought new students, and the Academy would get an influx as preternaturals graduated out of their mainstream schools and were sent up here to Eden Academy to study preternatural politics, as well as how to blend into human society as a functioning member of the community without outing yourself.

But Carmen wasn't listening, her eyes on something behind me. I looked over my shoulder at a group of students, new ones apparently. I recognized a few of them from the diner the other day, but my eyes didn't linger as my gaze was drawn to a guy I'd never seen before. He was tall, golden, and his aura made my skin pull tight across my bones.

Alpha.

The Omega wolf that lived inside me howled, but I didn't know if it was in fear or need.

Christopher's eyes whipped to my face, and he must have seen the confused terror on my face, because he stepped in front of me and Carmen with a low growl. Christopher was an Alpha wolf, a powerful one at that, and he had a short fuse.

The Alpha's gaze was focused on me, his brilliant golden eyes locked with mine. "You have an Omega." He didn't shout it, but the words reverberated right down to my soul.

I felt Carmen tense beside me. She stepped to the other side of Christopher, both of them attempting to block the Alpha from seeing me. Uh, too late, guys.

"What's it to you?" she shouted back.

Christopher's shoulders were tense, and I put my hand on his back to soothe his Alpha so he didn't wolf out on his first day of school. Carmen cast our brother an assessing look and then she was striding away, straight into the problem. "Watch Enit," she said over her shoulder as she ate up the distance between our two groups with confident ease.

Dang it!

"Fucking hell, Carmen. Get your ass back here," Christopher hissed, but it was too late. She was saying something in a low voice to the big Alpha. The Alpha gave her a cocky smile, and I just *knew* what was about to happen.

Carmen pulled back her fist and punched the big, blond Alpha in the face.

"God fucking dammit!" Christopher cursed, and when a big tattooed guy grabbed Carmen, he was sprinting across the space between our groups, leaving me standing there like a gaping fish.

But the Alpha's eyes were on me again, and I could see his animal riding him hard. My feet moved without my permission, like I was one half of a magnet and I didn't have the strength to resist it.

I was before him like I didn't have a choice, and then I raised my hand to his chest, calming him with my touch. I dragged my eyes up to meet his golden ones. He looked down at where my hand was pressed to his pec, then back at my face. There was nothing disgusted or derisive in his face. Just absolute awe. A low rumble started beneath my palm, deep in his chest. Definitely a feline shifter then. "I'm Bohdie," he said with a voice that was more big cat than human.

Then someone was ripping my hand away, and the shifter curled his lip.

"Fuck off," Carmen growled back. "Enit, stop touching the pussy."

I frowned at the loss of the connection, which was insane. I didn't want to touch Alphas. I wanted to avoid them at all costs. My brain flashed back to a memory that I firmly pushed away.

Bohdie bowed his head low. "Omega."

He said it reverently, like I was someone to be cherished. Something rare and special. Which, I guess, I was. There were no other Omegas at the Academy. I didn't even know any other Omegas. But the way we were treated went one of two ways. We were either revered and coddled to the point of suffocation—or used, beaten and downtrodden.

There was no in between. No normality for Omegas. But the way this Alpha was looking at me was...

"It's Enit. Nice to meet you Bohdie, I mean, Alpha."

Carmen whacked my fingers before I even realized I'd lifted them again. Bohdie growled at her, but Carmen just gave him the stink eye and bundled me away. Straight into Bobby, Alpha-Heir to the Nîso Pack of shapeshifters.

Carmen had a crush on Bobby the size of Canada. And Bobby? I looked up at my longtime friend, the only Alpha I trusted who wasn't family, and shook my head softly. The connection between them burned so hot that I almost believed I could reach out and touch it. But he pretended like their bond didn't exist, and it wasn't my place to tell him he was wrong.

"Mouse. What the hell is going on here?"

I couldn't hide my small smile as she looked up at him innocently. He was the only one who could reel her in, and probably save her from the risky shit that she was always getting herself into. They both just had to wake up and smell the pheromones.

It wasn't my place to interfere; I was happy to let it play out. I would just watch from the sidelines with popcorn and a smile.

I looked back over at the big cat Alpha, and he still hadn't taken his eyes off me. A flush crawled along my pale skin, and I knew he'd see it.

Yeah, Carmen and Bobby could sort their own issues out. I had enough of my own to deal with.

OMEGAS WERE PRETTY RARE. It's why my family guarded me so closely. It was almost a curse. On the flip side, my scarcity was the reason my dad Lucius had bought me for my mom years ago. He hadn't understood that what he was doing was wrong. He'd been a vampire who hadn't really progressed mentally past his all-powerful warlord days during his glory years. Maybe gory years would be a better descriptor.

My mom had definitely mellowed him. At least, kind of. He was still spoken about with fear among the students, and at every parent-teacher conference, I could see the trepidation on the faces of my teachers as they hoped he didn't attend.

Anyway, he'd bought me—saved me—from the black market because he thought my mom would appreciate a rare shifter instead of decapitated heads.

Chocolates and flowers weren't really on his radar.

"We couldn't find anyone to come and teach you Omega Studies in person, but we have managed to secure you weekly tele-link lessons with an Omega from the States," Miss Pea said, and I bit the inside of my cheek to bring my thoughts back to where they needed to be. To my studies. To aspirations of being something more than a tool to keep a Pack in line.

I gave her a soft smile. "That's better than nothing."

Miss Pea winced. "Yeah, I'm not so sure of that. Let's just say, I'm glad your sister doesn't take this class."

I frowned slightly, but Miss Pea continued. "Apparently, we underestimated the scarcity of Omegas in general, not just in wolf shifters. They seem to run in genetic lines, but we haven't had any luck discovering which line you are from, and even if we did..."

Yeah, I'd rather chew off my paw than "learn" from anyone in my former Pack. I didn't remember much about our time in our Pack. Flashes of fists and hands, and if I closed my eyes, I could remember the starving sensation. Remember Christopher and Carmen taking my beatings for me, even at four. Being sold was the best thing that ever happened to us.

No. I definitely didn't want anything to do with my former Pack, even if it was filled to the brim with Omegas.

"I'm sure she'll be fine, Miss Pea. I appreciate it."

Miss Pea's face softened as she looked at me. "I'm going to be sad when you and your siblings graduate from the Academy."

I raised an eyebrow. "Even Carmen?"

Miss Pea shook her head. "Especially Carmen. I look forward to our frequent meetings."

We both laughed and she led me into one of the meeting rooms with a big screen. There was a little laptop off to the side, and Miss Pea indicated I should sit in one of the plush leather office chairs. Even if this was a bust, I'd appreciate the moment of silence. One where I wasn't the coveted sister, or the special Omega, or whatever everyone else wanted me to be.

The screen lit up as Miss Pea played with the laptop. Finally, a conferencing system popped up, and she taught me how to use it to connect to the other Omega.

Turia. That was her name. She was a gorilla shifter and an Omega, which apparently was an even rarer combination than wolf Omega.

The screen flickered, and suddenly there was a

woman on the screen, looking at us hawkishly. Ah. I see what Miss Pea might mean now.

She had dark hair streaked with grey piled regally on top of her head, deep brown eyes that looked me over and more gold necklaces than I could count without staring.

"Madame Turia. I'd like to extend my gratitude on behalf of Eden Academy yet again for taking time out of your schedule to help educate the next generation."

Madame Turia sniffed, but nodded regally. She looked old, and given shifter aging, she must have been nearing two hundred. But there was no way I was going to ask.

"May I introduce your student? This is—"

"She doesn't need a name. She is an Omega. We shall address each other as such. It is a title that encompasses our entire existence, Miss Pea."

The sinking feeling in my gut finally bottomed out and I felt sick. I gave Madame Turia a bright smile. "I'm an Omega, Ma'am, but I'm also a person."

I expected derision, but I didn't expect her to throw back her head and laugh. "My sweet girl, you ceased to be your own person when your designation manifested. You are an Omega, a genetic mutation. Where Alphas were mutated to lead, to be stronger, more dominant than their brethren, we were made weaker, simpler. We were made to serve. You have one purpose in life, and the sooner you come to terms with that and abandon the idea that you will—"

Miss Pea slammed the laptop shut. "What complete and utter horseshit." I could practically see the steam coming from her ears. "Stupid old bag." She muttered some less savory things beneath her breath as she clenched and unclenched her hands.

When she turned to me, she was composed again. "What that woman said was wrong, Enit. In every sense of the word, it is wrong. You are not made to *serve*. You are your own person, entitled to your own dreams and goals. Entitled to love, and a family, and a career you are passionate about. Eden will not help prepare you for whatever bullshit that giant..." She seemed to struggle for the right word.

"Turdhead?" I offered helpfully.

Miss Pea barked out a laugh. "Exactly. I won't prepare you for the life that giant turdhead suggested. I won't allow it. Your family will not allow it."

I put a hand on her arm, pushing some of my Omega power to the place where our skin touched. Miss Pea was a telepath, but she was also a shifter. I didn't know how you could be both, but Miss Pea was unique. I loved that about her.

Her face softened, and she shook her head softly. "You're so special, and it has nothing to do with your Omega designation. It has everything to do with your heart. No one can take that from you." She cleared her throat. "Head over to the library and read or something until your next class. I will find a way to help you learn about being an Omega, and if not? Well, you can write your own rulebook, Enit. Divine your own stars."

I nodded again, hefting my backpack over my shoulders. "Yes, Miss Pea."

Even as I agreed with Miss Pea, the words of Omega Turia ran through my head.

I was weak. Simple. Made to serve. Not my own person. The words resonated in my soul and they were hard to shake. But I was determined to prove her wrong.

2

BOHDIE

"**S**top gawking, Bohdie, before you get your ass kicked by a girl again," Cara whispered, elbowing me in the ribs. She didn't need to sound so freaking amused by the whole thing. My nose still ached as my bones healed slowly.

I cleared my throat and dragged my eyes from the pretty Omega as she floated across the lawn of the school to the table that contained her siblings. And I mean, she floated, like a vision or an angel or something. "I'm not gawking," I growled at Cara, who just raised an eyebrow at me.

She was my best friend, along with Sammie. When they'd showed up on Black Mountain with a fucking pack of bikers, my Pride had almost pitched a fit. Along with the bears of the Cold River Sleuth, I honestly thought there would be a fight. But then they'd promised they weren't there to cause drama, and for a tense year, we all got used to sharing a mountain with the scariest bastards I'd ever met. Well, at that point they'd been the scariest. You didn't know scary until you'd looked into the face of the Devil himself.

"Sure you aren't, Dee. Watch where you're going, you almost stepped on a junior," she hissed, hip checking me around a tiny little shifter kid who looked up at me with eyes that were way too big for her face.

I gave her a winning smile, and it made her cheeks flush. "Sorry, kid."

Cara led us to an empty spot under a tree and I flopped down onto the ground. Cara lowered herself next to me, grabbing the food off my tray and spreading it around like an impromptu picnic.

Two seconds later, I knew why. Her brother Madoc and little cousin Attica appeared, their faces beaming.

"Oh my god, Cara, you'll never guess who I met! An actual kangaroo shifter. How crazy is that?" Attica squealed.

Madoc slumped down beside me, his wings out so he could rest back against them. "She's nice too. Really pretty."

Attica scowled at him. "I want her to be my friend, Madoc, so that means you keep your 'oh hey, do you want to stroke my wings?' stuff to yourself."

I snorted and Madoc flushed, scowling at his cousin. Cara was doing a good job of keeping a straight face. "If you start being interested in girls, I'm going to have to call our parents and they'll give you the sex talk. They'll probably use words like ejaculate and menstrua—"

"Oh my god, Cara, just stop." Madoc's face was officially as red as his hair. "I'm not interested in Attica's stupid friends, okay?"

He angrily ate his pizza, and Attica looked smug. "Are you going to do the same for Bohdie? His feelings were so gross this morning when he looked at the pretty white-haired girl, I almost puked."

I pointed my apple in her direction. "I'm an adult. And you better watch yourself, Pipsqueak."

She just laughed and launched into a story about her first classes, listing literally every person in each one. Cara managed to keep up with it, but I found my mind and my gaze wandering back across the courtyard to the Omega.

Enit. It was a pretty name. It suited her.

Her Alpha brother's head turned and his eyes met mine. His lip curled and his face portrayed his thoughts well enough. He wanted me to stay away.

Bad fucking luck. I was going to get to know the captivating Enit, whether he liked it or not. So I just grinned back, my look challenging, and he took the bait like a big-mouthed bass. He stood, and I noticed that the fist-throwing beta was nowhere to be seen. Hmm.

Cara just sighed as he strode toward us, her ever-present daggers slipping from her sleeve. He was halfway across the courtyard before she threw the first one, her knife lodging in a tree beside his face. His eyes went comically wide as he looked from the dagger to Cara, who had her chin jutted out in an expression that I knew meant trouble. But this Alpha douche? He had no clue about the world of pain he was in for. His rumbling growl had the whole courtyard silencing and every head turning in our direction.

He glared at Cara, reaching up to grab the dagger from the tree, tugging it out with ease. He leaned down, sliding it into his boot, his eyes never leaving hers. But his expression promised bloody retribution.

He turned on his heel and walked back toward Enit, ushering her out of the courtyard and back inside the main Academy building. I watched her go, a plan forming in my mind.

My parents had a very strong view of how women should be treated, something strongly supported by the Bears. Women should be treated like queens, regardless of whether they were human or shifter, or anything else. They gave the world life and we needed to treat them with the reverence they deserved. And honestly, you only needed to see how my step-dads treated my mother to know it wasn't just lip service.

They adored her. They'd waited five years before they started trying for their own kids, but I hadn't been jealous, despite the fact that I wasn't really related to any of them. My bio-Mom had died in a house fire, and my bio-Dad only visited once every few years. Isla had been the only parent I'd had for so long that she *was* my mom, and the guys treated me like I was blood kin. They loved me ferociously. And I loved them, and all four of my siblings, with just as much ferocity.

So to say that they would kick my ass if I fucked around with a girl's heart—especially a damn Omega, despite them not being a big thing in lion culture—was an understatement.

It would not end well for me.

"What a fucking asshole. These are my favorite knives," Cara hissed, "and he just stole one."

I laughed, because only Cara could be outraged that someone stole her dagger after she almost put it through their eye.

The buzzer sounded, informing us that it was time for our next classes, and the kids scampered off like their tails were on fire. Cara was still muttering to herself as she loaded up all the trash onto the tray and thrust it into my arms. She stormed away without another word to me.

I bussed our tray and headed off to my next class. My parents had sent me up here, because technically, I was probably Alpha-Heir to two Prides in North America. Not that I wanted to lead a Pride. Fuck no. But I guess if I was going to navigate that death trap, being equipped with knowledge was a good idea. Plus, Cara and Sammie were here, and they made the classes worth it.

I looked down at my schedule and groaned. Alpha Studies. I was so screwed. I was definitely getting in a fight, but you know what? I could use a good brawl.

I strolled down the hall, smiling politely at the people who were gawking at me. Guess being the new kid had its downsides. I counted down the rooms until I stood outside a small auditorium. Inside, there were only ten other people, but only two with any real Alpha power. Christopher, and a tall, broad guy with jet black hair and guyliner.

He looked at me and curled his lip, and I guessed we weren't going to be besties. My nose twitched. I couldn't really get a read on what kind of shifter he was, but he was definitely Alpha. It came off him in waves.

However when he slid his eyes to Christopher, there was absolute loathing on his face. Well. Maybe we could be friends after all.

I wandered over, standing tall under everyone's gazes, and stopped in front of the emo kid. "Hey. I'm Bohdie."

"Fuck off."

"Shit, that was kind of mean of your parents. Do they call you Fuck for short?"

The guy gave me a look that would have sent any

other shifter scurrying. But I was the motherfucking king of this jungle. "I'm not going away until you tell me your name. The mutt over there already knows it."

His eyes flicked back to Christopher, who was glaring at us both with enough heat to melt the moon. "I'm King."

I snorted a laugh. "We'll see about that."

The guy rolled his eyes. "Kingston. Everyone calls me King."

I nodded, and I could feel the white hot rage coming off Christopher as we talked together in low tones. I didn't miss the glee in King's eyes.

"What did you do to piss off the trash can puppy?"

"Made a move on his sister."

King whistled low. "That would do it. But I have to warn you, Carmen is more likely to bite off your dick than suck it."

I shook my head and shuddered. "No, not her. Enit."

King's face shuttered, going completely impassive. "What's your interest in Enit?" Shit, why didn't I think other Alphas would feel the draw of an Omega? Stupid.

So I firmed my own jaw. "What's it to you? Is she yours?"

He curled his lip. "She's a person, not a fucking trophy. If you think because she's an Omega that she's yours to kick around, it's not just that puppy over there you're going to have a problem with." He said it all in a slightly bored, monotone voice, but I could sense the steel behind it.

I lifted my chin. "My intentions are honorable. I just want to date her, treat her with the reverence owed to her designation." I swallowed hard. "Plus she's so damn beautiful and there's something about her that — I don't know."

He eyed me, and then nodded. "Just know, there's a lot of shitty Alphas with some fucked up opinions who come through this school, and Enit has to deal with all of them. If I find out you are treating her with anything but respect, I will fucking smash you so fucking hard into the ground, they won't even be able to find all the parts to send back to your Pride."

I scented him again, but the smell still eluded me. Something rare then. If there was one law to live by in the shifter world, it was don't fuck with shifters whose animal you can't take in a fight. But you had to know their animal first. This guy could turn into a dragon and snack-attack me. God knew, he had the temperament of a dragon.

So I just nodded softly. "So you are interested in her?"

King snorted. "Fuck no. I would eat an Omega alive. Doesn't mean I'll let you be a dick though."

"Fair enough."

The guy hesitated. "Look. I think we get too caught

up in the shifter Alpha/Omega bullshit. I've known Enit since we were five. She's her own person, not just a damn Omega. So if you really want to do right by her, treat her as a person first and an Omega second."

Our gazes all snapped to the door as the teacher strolled through the door. He had some real big dick energy. Definitely Alpha.

King looked back at me. "Now get the fuck out of my section."

I threw back my head and laughed, drawing the eyes of everyone in the room, including the teacher. I gave King a respectful tilt of my chin and went and sat at the back in an empty section. Well, I scared another little Alpha out of the way, but he was weak. I could probably tear him apart in human form.

The teacher cleared his throat at the front of the room. "Most of you should know each other from high school, with the glaring exception of this guy. Better introduce yourself so we can get the posturing out of the way."

I'm not shy. Hell, I thrive under the scrutiny of other people, so I uncurled myself from my seat, standing tall. "I'm Bohdie. My Pride lives down in the States, near Black Mountain. I'm an Aquarius and I like candlelit dinners."

The teacher's lips twitched, but he didn't laugh. "Nice to meet you. I'm Micah. Fuck around in my class and I'll put your head through a wall."

My jaw dropped but I nodded. "Uh, sure thing, Boss. I'll keep my fuckery to myself."

Micah's eyes dropped to King and Christopher. "That goes for you two as well. Any repeats of high school and I will kick your asses to the curb."

Christopher shrugged and King tilted his chin.

Micah sighed. "Okay. Let's get this shit started. Firstly, we are discussing the hierarchy..."

I tuned him out and let my mind wander back to Enit, and a plan began to form in my brain.

I was going to woo the shit out of her, until the only name she knew was mine.

3

———————

ENIT

S oon enough, the school year settled into a pattern like every other year. I overloaded myself with classes, Christopher and Carmen hovered over me like they were dragons protecting their hoard, and I tried—and failed—to fade into the background.

But it was weird this year. I couldn't fade because for the first time in my life, I was actually seen. Every time I walked into a room that contained Bohdie the lion Alpha, my eyes were uncontrollably drawn to him. And every single time he was looking right back. If we were walking near each other, he'd wait, hold the door open for me, and after I passed through? He'd just lower his head respectfully and murmur, "Omega," in that voice that shot pleasure straight down my spine.

He didn't try and box me in. Didn't pursue me. No,

he was standing on the sidelines, watching me like a patient hunter. This week, he'd upped the ante by leaving me candy. The first time, he pressed a caramel-filled chocolate bar into my hand as I walked past him in the hallway. That was it. I'd stood there staring at the chocolate bar in my hand, still warm from his grip, and watched his huge shoulders move through the crowds of students.

It should be creepy really. But he never tried to hide the fact that it was him leaving me these tokens. Sometimes he'd walk into my class, leave it on my desk in front of me, murmur a soft greeting, then leave again. Everyone looked at me then. No fading required. And more than half the gazes were red-hot with jealousy.

I got it too. Bohdie was... sexy as fuck. His blond hair that fell over his forehead. Those big golden eyes that saw into your soul. That body that was all hard planes and broad shoulders and made me want to lick him all over. And that was confusing as hell too.

I didn't have boyfriends.

I stood in front of the elevator that would take me down to the sub-levels, and the second part of what was making this year so damn anxiety-inducing. Miss Pea had decided that until she could find a replace-ment Omega instructor, my time would be best spent in the infirmary. There weren't often many people down there, but with a school this large, there were always one or two. And if not, the infirmary doubled as a research center.

But the infirmary was Stacey's domain. Miss Pea wanted me to be her assistant for the semester.

"The doors are open," a voice said right beside my ear, and I jumped, giving a little yelp. I looked at Bohdie, who was standing there bleeding into a t-shirt. I gasped, reaching up to pry his hand away so I could have a good look, but he pulled away.

"Elevator first. I have to go down and get a couple of stitches. Went pretty deep apparently."

I stepped into the elevator, and he stepped in after me. He dropped the shirt and it looked like someone had taken a baseball bat to his head. I clicked my tongue, my brows drawn tight.

"What happened?"

"Got hit in the head with a baseball bat."

A small laugh burst from my mouth, and I slapped a hand over my lips. "I'm sorry, that wasn't funny. I didn't mean to laugh."

He beamed at me, which made the bloody gash in his head start pouring out again, so he lifted the shirt back up.

"It's okay, Enit. I'm pretty sure I'd take a hundred baseball bats to the head to hear that sound again," he said softly.

I flushed. And then realized I was in a metal box with an Alpha. My whole body went taut, like the puppet master had pulled on my strings. Except anxiety was what made me a marionette.

Luckily, the doors opened just then, and I nearly ran out. Bohdie frowned, but didn't say anything as he followed me out.

"Do you know who I see about this?"

"That would be me."

I spun around and Stacey was there. She looked at me with her big, dark eyes that made my chest feel full. Quickly on the heels of that feeling, was guilt.

Three years ago, I'd crushed her heart. She never said it, but after she kissed me, and then after what happened in the bathrooms, I'd pulled into myself. If I saw her in the halls, I went the other way, because what did I say to her?

I liked your kiss but I'm an Omega? I liked your kiss, but I don't want to think about it because it happened on the second worst day of my life and I want to forget that day altogether. I liked your kiss, but I think you're mistaking kindness for something more?

So I was a chickenshit, and I ghosted her. And for that, the guilt rode me hard.

Stacey looked at me, her eyes doing a quick sweep of my body, my face, and I knew she was cataloguing me. That was just what she did. Goddess, she was so beautiful though. Her hair was loose and sprung up in caramel curls around her head, and her eyelashes were so long and thick she didn't need mascara. She wasn't much taller than me, but her body was curvy and strong, in an entirely human way. Shifters didn't get those truly soft curves. And her lips...

"Hello Enit."

I snapped my eyes to hers and gave her a soft smile. "Hey Stace. This is Bohdie."

She nodded. "Lion shifter, from the Black Mountain Pride." Bohdie raised his eyebrows, then winced as it tugged at the wound on his face. "You are going to need stitches. Come through to the treatment room."

"Is my doctor supposed to be a human that can't be more than what, fourteen?" he whispered to me and I shook my head.

"She's seventeen. By the time she was fourteen, she'd completed her Doctor of Medicine and a PhD in Molecular Biology. She could probably reconstruct you from parts if you needed it."

"Holy shit," Bohdie whispered, and when Stacey pointed to a chair, he willingly obeyed.

She pulled on gloves and poked at his wound. "Blunt force trauma. Three stitches should be enough. You are a full-blooded lion shifter; your natural biology will take care of this and the stitches will just be subsumed by your epidermis. Best to stem the bleeding and aid in the healing."

She quickly prepped what she needed, gripped his skin between her fingers and applied the stitches with ease. "What hit you?" she asked, not conversationally, because Stacey didn't do small talk. More likely, she was cataloguing his injuries, so that if she ever saw it again, she'd automatically know what it was.

"Baseball bat."

She frowned. "That wouldn't have sustained a wound of this magnitude."

He gave her a lopsided grin. "It does when it has an angry Alpha on the other end of it."

Stacey's eyes slid to mine, and she lifted her own brow. Yeah, I didn't need to be a genius to know that the Alpha on the other end of the bat had been Christopher.

I shook my head, dragging my lip between my teeth and gnawing at it. "I'm so sorry."

"He's just protective," Bohdie said soothingly.

Stacey snorted. "Overly so, but I guess he is also dealing with the emotional blowback of the events of three years ago."

My breath stalled in my lungs. "Stacey..." I warned.

But I should have known that I'd have to be more direct. Stacey didn't understand tonal cues. "Enit was attacked in the women's bathroom by an Alpha," she continued as she applied the last bandage.

"Stacey, stop," I said sharply, and her gaze whipped up to mine. She frowned, as she looked at my face, judging my expression from her mental catalogue.

She tilted her head slightly. "I didn't realize it was a secret."

I wanted to run away, but before I could, the deep rumbling snarl emitting from Bohdie's chest had us both glancing his way. His eyes had gone completely golden, his lion so close to the surface that I knew a change was imminent.

"Stacey, please get behind me," I said, working hard to keep my voice even. She looked like she was about to protest, so I dragged my gaze from Bohdie. "Stacey, please," I whined.

She moved away, never taking her eyes off Bohdie, even as his body rippled with the urge to change. He was fighting it off, but his lion wanted out. I pushed Stacey gently behind me, feeling better that she was out of the way of a swipe or accidental bite. I squeezed her hand, her soft fingers twining with mine, before I let go and stepped toward the enraged lion.

Calming enraged Alphas, I could do. Besides, despite the fact he was about to turn into a big cat, I felt entirely safe with Bohdie. My wolf wanted to bust out and meet his lion face to face, but I pressed back for control. Neither of us was going to shift in the infirmary.

When I was in grabbing distance, I met his gaze. "It's okay, Alpha. I am okay. Scent me in the air." I reached forward and pressed my hands to his chest. "Feel my touch. I am okay."

I should have expected his hands to whip out and grab me, but I still yelped a little as he tugged my waist and pulled me onto his lap, nuzzling my neck and breathing in lungfuls of my calming scent.

Where I would normally seize up like a deer in the headlights, I allowed myself to relax into his aura too. I inhaled the powerful pheromones that he gave off, the ones that promised safety and virility. That promised pleasure and abundance. It was primal and intoxicating, and I shook my head to clear my mind. Because I wanted to lick him to claim him as mine, like he was a cookie and not a six-three wall of muscle.

I could feel the lion retreat, and the tension left his body.

"Never again, Enit. I swear it. Never again."

It felt like a promise he shouldn't be giving me right now. We didn't know each other; he was basically a stranger, an unknown Alpha. I should move. Run as far and fast as I could in the direction of Christopher or Mouse or someone who would keep me safe. So that nothing could touch me—not the good, the bad or the ugly.

But still, being in his arms felt right, so I didn't say anything. I just lay against his purring chest and basked in the safety he presented, just for a little while longer.

4

STACEY

I had indigestion. Although I hadn't eaten any inflammatory foods for lunch, that could be the only reason my chest burned like this.

I snorted at myself. Yeah, probably wasn't the salmon and rice I'd had. What I was feeling was jealousy. I was self-aware enough to recognize that the sight of Enit in the lion shifter's arms made me feel... off.

The lion shifter's change receded as Enit's Omega pheromones wrapped around his body, filling his senses and calming him better than any shot I could give him. She had biologically evolved to counteract the overdeveloped protection response that was prevalent in Alpha shifters.

"I'm sorry," I said to Enit, the danger now passed.

She looked up at me almost dazedly from the

Alpha's lap. If an Omega's pheromones made Alphas docile, then the Alpha pheromones pumping out that scent of safety were like a drug to an Omega. Like catnip.

I tensed my jaw. Yes, this was definitely jealousy.

Enit's gaze softened as she looked at me, and I swallowed hard. "It's okay, Stace. You're right, it isn't a secret. I just liked that there was someone who didn't know I was weak."

I frowned. "Why would anyone think you were weak? What happened was very obviously not your fault. To blame you for the biological shortcomings of an Alpha is as ridiculous as blaming the seal that gets caught by the orca."

Another low rumble from the Alpha had Enit sitting up, alert. He looked at me with those blazing gold eyes. "Anyone who attacks an Omega is not an Alpha. They are dirt."

Well, we both agreed there. Enit was looking warily between us, like she was wondering if she needed to move me from harm's way again. She had thought this Alpha—who she looked very comfortable with—would attack me, and she'd protected me.

The thought made that little spark of emotion that I'd tried to smother, flicker back to life. I wasn't in the habit of lying to myself either. That emotion was love. Three years ago, I'd loved Enit, in a way I didn't think I could love a human being.

It was different to the love I felt for my parents or my younger siblings, or even my brother Daniel, who was the only person I loved in a way that was messy and jagged. I didn't like messy and jagged, but Daniel and I had been through too much for our bond to be anything but a lifebuoy in shark-infested waters.

No, what I felt for Enit was... complicated. I was a prodigy. They all said so. But you know what they don't tell you about being a genius? That it sucks the magic from the world. Even in a world of shifters and preternatural anomalies, if I studied them, I knew I would find a biological imperative that led to their evolution into something more.

I'd never met the witch who worked the wards around the Academy, but if I did, I wondered if she'd let me study her magic, and if I could find the science behind it.

But worst of all, science was the executioner of the notion of love. Love was just a physical imperative that resulted in a chemical change in the brain. It aided in the survival of the species and therefore, the notion of love had been romanticized for time immeasurable.

I knew that. My brain knew that.

But my heart? It was so completely confused by the physiological responses I got around Enit. It beat faster when I saw her in the hall, or when she smiled at me. It had been crushed when she'd rejected me.

And the small smile she gave me just now? It began

the process of mending my heart together again. But I wasn't sure I could take rejection a second time.

I turned away, cleaning up the workstation and snapping off my latex gloves. I did the deep breathing exercises my mother Layla had taught me, the ones that allowed me to center the whirl of my thoughts. When I decided that I had my physiological responses under control, I turned back to the pair in my treatment room.

Enit had climbed off his lap, which was something. Not that I begrudged her happiness. I didn't want her all to myself. I could be a lot.

My brain never switched off. I was distracted all the time. Sometimes I forgot to eat, or call, or sleep. I was bad at expressing emotions or understanding other people's emotions outside of a psychological context.

I hated being out of control and I feared the unknown. Like I said, I was a lot.

I suddenly realized the feeling that was making my chest burn wasn't jealousy that he was touching her. No, it was regret that she wasn't touching me too.

"We best get started. You're fine, Alpha. Keep the wound clean and it should heal with the day."

He uncurled his body from the chair, giving me a smile that I'm sure made a lot of girls fall at his feet. "Bohdie." I cocked my head to the side and frowned. He frowned right back. "My name, it's Bohdie."

"I know. Enit introduced you when you walked in."

Bohdie looked at me again, his eyes considering. "I'd like it if you called me by my name, and not my designation. You don't call Enit 'Omega.'"

"I've known Enit since I was a child. Before I understood the variances in designation."

Enit clicked her tongue. "You're being deliberately obtuse, Stace, and you're better than that," she said with gentle reproval.

I shrugged at her and she shook her head at me like she used to. "Fine. You'll survive, Bohdie. You're fine to go back to class. I'd avoid Christopher's baseball bat in the future."

He looked at me and laughed. "I'll take your advice, Doc." He turned and dipped his chin at Enit, his eyes downcast respectfully. "Omega."

A pretty pink flush lit up Enit's cheeks. "Alpha."

Then he straightened, and bent down, kissing her cheek. "Oh, I nearly forgot." He reached into his pocket and pulled out a small bag of Skittles, pressing them into her hand. "I'll see you later, Enit." He loped toward the elevator. "See you later, Doc. Nice to meet you."

Then he was gone.

Enit's eyes lingered on the doors, and my eyes lingered on her. She was interested in the Alpha, past the biological draw. There'd been plenty of Alphas at Eden through the years, and she'd shied away from nearly all of them. But I could almost see the connection between her and Bohdie.

Her gaze whipped back to me, and I saw her shift from foot to foot uncomfortably. "How have you been, Stace? I feel like I haven't seen you in ages."

I shrugged. "I saw you in the cafeteria sixty-seven days ago. You were wearing pink."

She laughed, and the sound danced along my skin, making me feel happy too. "An eidetic memory is definitely handy."

She was wrong on that front. I would take writing things down over having memories of every awful damn thing that ever happened. But I didn't tell her that. Instead, I turned on my heel and walked out the back door of the treatment room, which led into the lab.

I could hear Enit moving quietly behind me as I spoke. "Miss Pea said that they are having trouble finding you an Omega teacher, and that she thinks that learning scientific healing methods would aid in your future position as Pack Omega." That chest pain was back when I thought about her marrying into some Pack and leaving me. I pushed the feeling down. "From my research, historically Omegas tended to double as Pack healers, so I agreed that learning some general medical procedures would be beneficial. Perhaps, you would let me study you in return, for my Alpha/Omega dynamics research, to see what genome defines an Alpha from an Omega or a beta. You and your littermates are an interesting case study. What is the statistical probability that there be one of each designation in the same litter? You aren't identical triplets, so there was trizygosity, but does that mean that nature balanced you and Christopher? Or perhaps Christopher and Carmen, as they share the same physical characteristics."

"Stacey—"

"But even that seems unlikely. What I need is a larger sample group from differing—"

"Stace!"

I stopped and looked over my shoulder at her.

"You lost me at tri-zi, uh, trisyo..."

"Trizygosity," I supplied and she nodded.

"Yeah, that. Science isn't one of my areas of learning. But I'm happy for you to study me. I could probably talk Carmen and Christopher into it too."

I smiled and it stretched my face uncomfortably wide. Yes! They definitely wouldn't say no to Enit.

"I'm also happy to assist you in your studies, but I don't understand any of it, okay?"

I nodded. I'd take it. "Let's go. We have rounds to do."

THE PREVAILING professional opinion was that I was asexual. Which made sense. Knowing at an early age what is actually in bodily fluids definitely aids in your sexual identity, or lack thereof. But watching Enit talk to my patients, and the other students, with her face so painfully open—well, it made my skin feel too tight on my body and my chest felt too full.

I thought back to that kiss. I'd just been a silly kid with an infatuation, but what I'd felt when my lips touched hers was still something I thought about.

"Stacey, are you listening?"

I realized I was looking at her but not listening. "I'm sorry."

She smiled at me, reaching out a hand to rest it on my forearm. That's what I liked so much about Enit. She always made me feel seen. "I said I thought I might split my spare class time between here and tending the traditional medicine garden."

Oh. I kind of liked the idea that I'd have her down here in my territory three days a week; I'd missed her. I wouldn't say that though.

I forgot that Enit could read me better than anyone. "You can always come up and help me. How long has it been since you've been out of the lab?"

I frowned. "I go home every night?"

She laughed, and it was high and sweet. Musical. Researchers in the field of Auditory Science should study the sound. "I meant during the day, when you aren't working. When was the last time you went anywhere that wasn't the lab or your house? When was the last time you left Academy grounds?"

"July fifteenth. I went and bought the kids presents."

She shook her head. "That was nearly six weeks ago, Stace. That's it—it's now part of my Omega Studies to ensure you get outside in the sunshine at least once a week."

I nodded, not even letting myself think of the wasted hours. I wanted to spend those few hours with Enit more than I wanted to run another test.

The elevator announced its arrival, its doors sliding open. She stepped toward me, wrapping me in her arms. "I enjoyed today. I've missed you."

Then she disappeared into the elevator and I was left with the feel of her arms around me and a desire in the pit of my stomach. I wasn't yet sure what the desire was, however.

No. Definitely not asexual.

5

ENIT

The biannual party in the woods outside of Eden was in full swing. Normally, I hated these things, but Christopher and Mouse thrived in scenes like this. The vibe of the place was electric, everyone wild and their potential unspent. Plus, it was only the older kids, so there was booze and always at least one couple having sex in the woods. Some people used it as an opportunity to shift forms and mingle with other shifters. Despite Eden being completely safe, there wasn't a lot of opportunity to embrace your other form.

Carmen was flirting with the new combat and weapons tutor, Sammie. Bohdie was beside him, his eyes sparkling in the firelight. I looked up at him from beneath my lashes, not game to look him completely in the eye. I was kind of embarrassed that I'd been sitting in his lap a few days ago.

"Omega," Bohdie said softly, dipping his head.

I put my hand on his bicep. "Tonight is a party, Alpha. You can relax."

Mouse saw my hand on Bohdie and before I could protest, she was dragging me away, making excuses that we had to go rescue Christopher. But when we got to my brother, he seemed to be doing just fine. There was a pretty little shapeshifter in his lap, whispering in his ear, and I resisted the urge to roll my eyes as he laughed. It wasn't his real laugh, just that haughty one he did when he was trying to pick up girls.

Mouse cleared her throat as another pretty shifter —I think she was a wolf too if my nose was right— crawled up beside him.

"If you bitches are quite done with your pawing, Christopher, I think—" Mouse cut off as something caught her attention over my shoulder. "Oh no, that bitch did not just do that," she growled and was gone.

Christopher watched her go, the alcohol easing the frown on his face. "Do you know what she wanted?"

I shrugged. "Probably just offloading her responsibility of me onto you, so she can go play tonsil hockey with the new combat teacher."

Christopher frowned, pushing the shapeshifter girl off of his lap. He missed her glare but I didn't care. "You aren't a responsibility and no one offloaded you, Enit."

I rolled my eyes, and suddenly I could hear Teesha yelling. We both looked over my shoulder and Christopher watched the scene warily, his body tense. But Sammie dragged Carmen away and Bohdie held Teesha back. Christopher's eyes still watched as the tutor dragged our sister into the trees. We knew each other well enough to be confident that if Carmen was unhappy, the whole world would know it. Still, we watched with our supernatural eyesight for any sign of unease, ready to ride to the rescue. When Carmen's angst turned to kissing, I looked away.

Which meant I looked right at Bohdie with Teesha in his arms.

My wolf surged to the surface, and a low growl rolled across my lips. Christopher's brows raised. "Did you just growl?"

I was placid. It was an Omega thing. We were peacemakers. But what I wanted to do to Teesha wasn't even a tiny bit peaceful. I was moving toward them before I consciously realized, which was usually a good indication that the wolf was riding me hard.

Christopher gripped my arm. "What are you doing, E?"

I shook my head. "Go back to getting slobbered on, Christopher. I'm safe with Bohdie."

Christopher narrowed his eyes and he muttered something under his breath. "How can you know? He could just be hiding it well."

He had a point, but really, that went for any Alpha in my life, including Carmen's best friend Bobby. But I just shook my head. My wolf just knew sometimes. It knew with Bobby, and it knew with Bohdie.

"Trust my instincts, Christopher."

My brother shook his head. "Don't you realize, Enit? We trust your instincts more than anyone else's in the whole world. I just want you to be safe."

I hugged him and then pushed him back toward the area where he'd been sitting. "Don't get chlamydia," I teased and strode over to where Bohdie was still trying to extricate himself from Teesha's hands.

I cleared my throat and Teesha whipped around. "Excuse me? Can I have a moment with Bohdie?" I asked her politely.

"Fuck off, freak."

Teesha wasn't Alpha, but like Carmen, she was a very strong beta. It was why they hated each other so much. I resisted the urge to do what she said, but unlike with Carmen, if she threw a punch at me, there'd be hell to pay. And not just with the administration.

After the... attack in the bathroom, it seemed that the Apex Alphas—Alphas so strong that you knew they were destined for future leadership, like Christopher, Kingston, Bobby and a couple of others—got together and in no uncertain terms, put me off limits.

On pain of death.

Only one shifter had tested that limit. They didn't go here anymore. So, while Teesha would be a bitch, she wouldn't put her hands on me.

Bohdie didn't know that though. His low, rumbling growl echoed around the clearing, and Christopher was by my side in an instant. Guess he didn't trust my instincts that much after all. "Fuck off, Teesha," Christopher snarled and she bared her teeth.

"Screw you, Christopher."

Christopher visibly shuddered. "Once was enough. I'd rather stick my dick in a woodchipper than go back for seconds."

Teesha flounced off, her eyes shiny and her cheeks flaming. I lowered my eyebrows. "That was a little harsh."

Christopher let out an exasperated huff. "She called you a freak, E. She doesn't deserve your empathy."

I shrugged. Everyone deserved empathy, even trash beings like Teesha. "I'm fine, Christopher. You can go back to the party."

My brother eyeballed Bohdie a little more, and whatever silent conversation they were having didn't look like it was going well. Eventually, I shoved at Christopher's chest and he strode away in a huff.

That just left me and Bohdie. "I don't think your family likes me."

A laugh burst from my lips. "Don't take it personally. They don't like anyone."

He held out a hand and I stared at it for a moment, at his wide, flat palm and long, elegant fingers. He had beautiful hands, the kind you imagined running over your body. I placed my palm in his, and breathed through the jolt of our connection.

Bohdie pulled me softly closer until there were just the two of us in that clearing. Despite the smell of the fire and the raucous laughter, all I could see were those liquid gold eyes.

"Would you like me to kiss you?" he whispered, the warmth of his breath brushing my cheeks. He was tall, much taller than me, so I knew he must have already been curling toward me, the pull of our connection affecting him too.

There was only one answer to his question. "Yes," I breathed, and his eyelids hooded as his irises darkened with desire.

He leaned closer and brushed his lips across mine, like he was tasting me, testing the waters. When I didn't pull away, his lips pressed against mine harder. He pulled me closer until our clasped hands were pressed between our chests and his other hand was on my hip. He deepened the kiss, sliding his tongue past my lips and using it to stroke mine.

I let out a squeak of surprise, or maybe it was a moan

of desire, and curled my body into his. It didn't matter that we were at a party filled with our peers, seventy percent of whom could probably scent the desire pooling low in my body. This place was awash with the smell of lust.

I slid my free hand up his strong chest, feeling his heart beat beneath my palm.

Then someone was grabbing me by my arms and moving me bodily away. No prizes for guessing who that was.

"Back the fuck up, asswipe," Christopher growled, but Bohdie just grinned at him goofily and I couldn't help but grin back. I'd put that look on his face. Me.

Christopher dragged me away, and I looked over my shoulder at Bohdie.

"Check your pockets," he mouthed, pointing to his own pockets.

Subtly slipping my hands into the pocket of my dress, I pulled out a tiny box of conversation hearts, his phone number written in Sharpie on the back. My lips curled into a smile of their own accord, and I put the box back in my pocket. I had no idea when he'd done that, but it was... desperately cute.

Christopher stomped to the car, texting Carmen as he went. But we left without her, and he gave me the silent treatment all the way home.

"I don't know why you're being such a hypocrite right now," I grumbled as we pulled into the driveway of our house in Dark River. "Girls were all over you all night, but I can't kiss a guy?"

Christopher slammed out of the car. "You can kiss whoever you want, Enit, as long as it's not an Alpha. How do you know it's what you really want? How do you know it isn't just your Alpha and Omega pheromones telling you that this is what you *should* want? It's just another way of coercing something from you that you don't want to give, but this time you're too—" He cut himself off, and I tensed my jaw.

"Stupid? Weak?"

Christopher growled. "You are neither of those things, and you know it. Too caught up in the feeling of it to think clearly."

I stomped up the steps and slammed into the house. No one was home. This was prime time in Dark River. Everyone would be out doing their jobs, living their lives.

Even the dead had more freedom than me.

I whirled around as Christopher followed me through the door. "I can assure you, I see perfectly clearly. No one—not you, not Carmen—learned the lesson about Alphas as well as me. I'm the one who still has nightmares about it. So trust me when I say that I am not caught up in the fucking Omega pheromones, brother. And I'd appreciate it if you stayed the hell out of my business."

"I am your Alpha," he grumbled.

"Dad is my Alpha. You are my brother and I love you more than anyone else in this world, other than Carmen. But I will get her to punch you in your damn face if you don't pull your head out of your ass and let me *live*."

With that I stormed into my room and slammed the door, resting my back against it. Then I pulled my phone and the box of hearts from my pocket. Putting the number in my phone, I sent a message to Bohdie before I lost my nerve.

Me: That was a pretty good kiss. Can we do it again?

The message came back almost instantly.

Bohdie: As often as you'll let me.

I did a silent squeal and fell into bed. I didn't think I'd be sleeping anytime soon though.

6

BOHDIE

"**B**eatrice, you are the very light of my life. If I was fifty years older and possibly undead, I would sweep you off your feet."

The round, grandmotherly Scottish vampire waved a hand at me. "Enough of that. I have bottles of scotch older than you." She handed me the picnic basket. "These are all Enit's favorite foods, but listen to me well, lad. If you so much as hurt her feelings, I shall feed from your corpse until you are a mere husk."

I just grinned at her. "If I hurt Enit, you may need to get in line. But I swear, I have no intention of hurting her."

And I didn't. The last few weeks had been a series of stolen kisses in dark hallways and I felt so damn alive. But I never pushed it further than kissing. I wasn't going to screw this up just because my dick ached at the sight of her.

Beatrice tapped my cheek. "You'd better make sure you don't," she said in a smiling, pleasant voice. "Now be gone with you."

Beatrice owned a diner in Dark River with her husband, but I'd recently found out that her diner supplied some of the baked goods to the cafeteria here, and I made a call. Beatrice, despite her threats of exsanguination, was a bit of a romantic, and she happily agreed to my request.

I was taking Enit on our first real date, and I wanted it to be perfect. I'd scoped out the perfect place near an ornamental pond. I bought ducks with ducklings from a local farmer and put up a very, very stern warning on the school bulletin board that anyone caught eating the damn ducks would be eaten themselves.

I basically bounded to the greenhouse where Enit's herbology class was held. It was her favorite class, so she was guaranteed to be in a good mood. Throw in the fact that it was a beautiful day, and it was perfect. She was going to be so fucking wooed.

I slowed as I got to a grassy section of the grounds, just before it turned into the woods. Standing there in the sun, doing Tai Chi, was Stacey. I chewed my lip as I watched her. She was... different. Human. So fucking smart it made me feel like a neanderthal. One hundred percent different to me in every way except one.

She desperately wanted Enit.

I was pretty sure Enit was oblivious to the longing that filled the girl's eyes when she watched her. She did a good job of locking it down whenever she thought Enit was looking, but she couldn't sneak it past me. I understood that feeling better than anyone else in the whole world.

As if she could feel my eyes, Stacey turned to look at me. I straightened my shoulders and walked over to her. We should sort this out now, just so she knew that Enit would be mine. I could almost see Stacey throwing up her walls and I could appreciate her wanting to protect herself. It would have been hard enough being a human in the Academy; but being a genius? Her intellect would have isolated her even more.

"Hey," I said, lifting my hand in greeting.

"Alpha," she replied, not slowing her movements.

"Beautiful day for Tai Chi."

Stacey just nodded at my small talk. She eyed the basket in my hands. I lifted it.

"I'm taking Enit on a surprise picnic."

Her movements faltered and I saw her swallow hard. Her heart pounded so loud I could hear it easily. "She'll like that. She enjoys being outside." She paused. "She really likes you."

I wanted to be selfish. I wanted to thank her for her compliment, walk away and go enjoy my date with the girl I wanted to be my girlfriend.

But the level of sadness that permeated from the girl in front of me made my lion whine softly. He was a softie, except when there was a threat to those he considered his Pride. Why he was so damn interested in Stacey—a girl who I definitely *wasn't* attracted to in the slightest, despite her obvious beauty—was completely beyond me.

But both the lion and the man hated that she was sad.

I sighed. "She likes you too, you know."

This time she faltered completely, her feet both planting on the ground. Her lips slipped open slightly. The look of astonished hope told me I'd made the right decision. However, she quickly shuttered her expression. "I think your hypothesis is wrong. Enit views me as a friend." She narrowed her eyes. "If you are saying all this in an effort to get some juvenile *ménage à trois*, you are sadly mistaken. I couldn't be less interested in you."

I couldn't help the laugh that bubbled from my chest. "Duly noted. I can swear to you that I'm not chasing a threeway. I only want one girl, and her class is about to finish. Just..." I paused. "I want her to be happy, you know? And I see how happy you make her. She needs softness, someone that *she* chose, who isn't influenced by the whole Alpha/Omega dynamic. And my lion likes you."

"What are you trying to say, Bohdie?"

I grinned at the fact she didn't call me Alpha. See? Baby steps. "I'm saying that if you want to pursue her too, I won't get in the way. We don't have a problem, unless you want her to yourself." I let the steel back into my face and my tone. "Then we'll have a really big problem."

Stacey considered my words. "Polyamory is a well-established social norm in supernatural society."

I chuckled again. "I know."

"I'm aware of my shortcomings. I'm cold. I overthink things, and I'm bad with emotional cues. I find it difficult to maintain relationships when I get caught up in my work. I would be a bad partner for Enit." She tilted her head and considered me. "However, adding you would satisfy her shifter nature. You cannot help but nurture and support her." She chewed her lip and it was the first sign of uncertainty that I'd seen on her face. "I'll think about it."

I grinned, glancing at my watch. "You do that. See you around, Doc."

I trotted away, arriving at the greenhouses just as the bell that announced the end of the class echoed through the clearing.

Enit was the last out of the greenhouse, holding herself apart from her classmates. She spoke softly to the teacher, who was a slight guy absolutely covered in hair. Not a shifter. Just like, a really hairy man.

As soon as she stepped out into the open, her eyes whipped to me. The teacher's eyes followed her gaze, and he smiled softly. "We will discuss interspecies grafting next week, Enit. Go and enjoy the day."

Her smile as she walked toward me was so fucking beautiful that I forgot to breathe. Then, in view of everyone, she stood on her tiptoes and kissed me.

I wrapped my arm around her waist and pulled her tightly to my chest. I kissed her softly at first, just tasting her and letting the sweetness of her body settle into my bones. As the kiss went on, the intensity ratcheted up a notch. I plunged my tongue into her mouth, catching her little moans until I had to pull away with a gasp.

She looked up at me with a small, smug grin curling her lips and hooded eyes. She looked entirely too fuckable and I almost forgot that I was trying to woo her gently.

"Omega, you are playing with fire."

"Maybe I like fire, *Alpha*," she purred and I almost wondered if I was wrong and she was a lion shifter too.

I grabbed her hand and pulled her away toward the pond before I did something stupid, like drag her back into the greenhouse and fuck her until she screamed my name. She chuckled a low sound, filled with heat, and honestly, I should have been awarded some kind of sainthood for taking things slow because she was designed to tempt me.

"So, what's in the basket?"

I wrapped my arm around her shoulders and pulled her close. I couldn't help it. "It's a surprise."

Her eyes lit up and she did a little happy dance on the spot, and I vowed to surprise her for the rest of our lives.

My steps faltered at the thought. When had I started thinking of us in the sense of forever?

That was an easy answer, if I really let myself be open to the idea. I'd started thinking of her in terms of forever in that moment between laying eyes on her for the first time and her sister punching me in the nose.

I led her around a copse of trees and over to the lake. It was pretty idyllic, but obviously man-made. They'd designed it with care, though. There were small rocky outcrops and water lilies. The water was clear enough that I could see fish swimming around in the depths. The ducks I had introduced swam happily on the water, with little fluffballs of yellow following along behind.

"Ducks! When did we get ducks?" she squealed, letting go of my hand to race to the edge of the water.

"Yesterday. They have a hutch on the other side of those reeds. I paid off one of the juniors to lock them up every night to make sure they're safe. I also made sure the same junior knew to spread around the devastating level of bodily harm that'd happen if someone ate them in their shifted form."

She gaped at me, her eyes wide. "You got the ducks?"

I nodded. "Every pond needs ducks. Really sets the mood."

She sprinted back from the edge of the pond and I only had a split second to lay down the basket before she launched herself into my arms again. She wrapped her legs around my waist as she kissed me with so much passion that it was me who was moaning. Holding her tight against me with one arm, I slowly lowered us to the grass, not breaking the kiss, until I was laying on my back and she was on top of me, her knees either side of my hips. I let her take control, and when she pulled back with a gasp, it was my turn to grin smugly.

"You are really something, Bohdie. Thank you."

I just hummed happily and captured her lips again. She didn't understand. I was only just getting started.

7

ENIT

I was lost in the feel of Bohdie beneath me. His kisses consumed me, his warmth surrounding me completely. He was everything I could ever hope for in an Alpha pairing. He was sweet and considerate. He respected my boundaries and he'd bought me actual freaking *ducks*. I know that was hardly the deciding factor in choosing a life partner, but damn, it helped.

I kissed him harder and ground my hips against him, making him groan as he buried his hands in my hair and tugged me back gently.

"Enit, fuck," he whispered, kissing me again like he couldn't help himself and I smiled against his lips. For once, I was the one with the power. His other hand slid down my side to grip my hip, and he held me firmly as he ground up against me, making me moan. I could feel the hard line of his cock pressed exactly where I wanted him so I rolled my hips, closing my eyes as I kissed him deeper. I wanted to taste him, wanted him to taste me. I'd never wanted a guy the way I wanted Bohdie. The last few weeks had been constant breathless kisses, getting more and more heated. More and more bold. I wanted the whole Academy to know that Bohdie had chosen me over anyone else.

As I felt his hard chest under my hands, my brain began to protest that he could have any girl in this school. The beautiful ones like Teesha or even his friend, Cara. But he was out here, giving me flipping ducks. If this was a complicated ruse to get into my pants, he deserved it, honestly.

His hands slid up the backs of my thighs, and he hummed happily before dragging himself away again. He grabbed my waist and lifted me off his body and onto the grass.

Panting, he curled his body back up into a sitting position. "I didn't expect that kind of response, but I'm not mad about it, that's for sure." He grinned at me, and that expression did weird things to my heart—and lower down my body. He leaned over and kissed me gently on the cheek. "I'm going to woo you, Enit Baxter. Starting with a beautiful picnic on a beautiful day, with the most beautiful woman I've ever laid eyes on."

I felt the heat in my cheeks and I chewed my lip. I

could smell the food in the basket, my nose twitching. Wait a minute... "Is that Beatrice's cherry pie?"

Bohdie's grin was back. "Yep," he said, popping the P and looking adorably smug. "As well as some kind of quiche she said you liked and Philly cheesesteak hoagies."

My eyes got even wider. He'd gotten all my favorite foods. Was this guy for real? I narrowed my eyes at him.

"What? You don't like it?"

I shook my head, lifting his arm, holding out his hand so I could search him thoroughly. "No. It's perfect. This whole thing is perfect. I'm looking for your flaws. You can't be this... perfect."

He fell back on the grass laughing, and I couldn't help but lean onto his chest again. "I'm not perfect, Enit. I'm quick to anger. I use my fists when I should use my words sometimes," he paused, looking at me intensely. "Never with you though. Never."

I gave him a lopsided grin. I remembered his face when Mouse had punched him in the nose. I knew he could have hit her then, but he'd held back, even though shifters were an equal opportunity society in that regard. We were all animals in the end, and while some were treated with reverence or gentleness, everyone one in their prime was considered equal. You threw a punch, man or woman, you could expect a fist back.

It had shown how much control Bohdie had over his beast that he hadn't put her in her place. Or it might have just been Christopher right up in his face. Who could tell?

Instead of telling him all that, I just snuggled my face into his chest. "I know." I pulled out the two foil-wrapped sandwiches and handed one to him. "You don't want to miss this."

I unwrapped mine and moaned. So damn good. I wasn't sure what Bert put in it, but it was addictive.

Bohdie rested on an elbow and took a bite of his own sandwich, giving a guttural groan that had my stomach clenching in lust. He looked at me seriously. "Is Beatrice single?"

I laughed. "She's married to Bert, who's the one that actually makes the sandwiches. Have I been turfed out so quickly?" I teased.

He leaned over, kissing me between bites. "Never. But we could always add her to your harem, right? We've already got Stacey, what's one more?"

I choked on my food, my eyes shooting to his face. His words were teasing and light, but I didn't miss the assessing look in his eyes.

"What do you mean?" I squeaked out, trying not to sound panicked and failing miserably. I'd spent a couple of hours with Stacey this week, and if I was honest with myself, I kept finding reasons to stay back with her after my assigned time was done. I would start tasks with ten minutes until my study period. I would purposefully distract her so she didn't know the time.

I knew why I was doing those things, and I felt guilty as hell as I sat here with Bohdie now. He'd been the perfect gentleman and when I was with him, I felt alive.

But I was still being dragged back to Stacey over and over again, like I couldn't help myself. We'd so easily fallen back into our old roles, me gently teasing her, Stacey being intense and passionate about the strangest things.

I loved watching her face when she talked to me about a project, or even something like geophysics. She was so beautiful in those moments. Her warm skin flushed, her beautiful caramel eyes alight. She stole my breath away.

I'd never told anyone about our kiss that day. Or about her declarations of love. Definitely not about my own confusion. Now Bohdie was here, laying it all out like it was no big deal and I was pretty sure my heart was going to beat right out of my chest.

Bohdie put down his sandwich wrapper—somehow he'd managed to inhale the whole thing in three bites—and reached out to drag me onto his lap. "Princess, relax. It's no big deal. Me and Stacey are cool. We talked it out earlier, and I told her that I was okay with whatever you wanted. You deserve all the happiness I can give you." He snorted softly. "She's a little weird, but I kind of like it."

The idea of Bohdie liking Stacey like that twisted me all up inside even more. She was absolutely beautiful, why wouldn't he be attracted to her? Jealousy pounded through my veins, but I didn't know exactly who I was jealous over. I didn't like the idea of them being together at all, which was selfish of me. Why was I allowed to want them both, but they couldn't want each other? How spoiled could I be?

"Enit, I don't know what the hell you're thinking, but stop it. I'm not even remotely interested in Stacey like that. Not even a little. I'm a one girl kind of lion." He leaned forward and kissed me quickly on the lips. "In case you've missed all this"—he waved a hand to the basket and the pond—"you're that one girl." He laughed. "Plus, the only way Stacey would be interested in my body is if I was a cadaver."

I choked on a laugh because he was probably right. I buried my face in his neck, not ready to meet his soft golden eyes. He saw too much already, and I wasn't ready to bare my soul like that. "I can't help wanting her. I tried so hard not to, Bohdie. She's human. She's a woman. I'm an Omega. She's so damn smart that she talks circles around me and I couldn't possibly be enough to satisfy her mind, you know? I have so many reasons and excuses."

Bohdie stroked my back. "If it makes you feel

better, I don't think there's a person alive who could keep up with her brain." He turned his head to the side and kissed my temple. "So what happened?"

"She told me she loved me. Then I was attacked. In my brain, I bunched them together and I hid away from my feelings, wrapped myself in fear. I ran away because facing everything was just too hard." I shook my head. "Then my Omega Studies teacher fell through, and Miss Pea decided I'd be better off being down in the infirmary with Stace while they found a replacement, and all those feelings came rushing back, despite how into you I was. How into you I *am*. I really like you, Bohdie." My words were soft but I pulled back to look at his face. He was smiling at me, the look in his eyes filled with unsaid promises.

"I really like you too, Enit." He kissed me softly again. His kisses were like a drug; I couldn't get enough. "Though I know an Omega. A wolf one too. I can introduce you if you want? Dawn is the sweetest." He frowned. "Actually, she looks a bit like you. Is the white hair an Omega thing?"

I shrugged. I had no idea. Madame Turia certainly didn't have it. "The Omega teacher didn't, but it might be a species thing. I've never met another Omega wolf."

He frowned and nodded. "I'll set something up."

Shifting back onto the grass, I lay down on his chest and listened to his heartbeat while we talked.

About his Pride, and how I ended up living in a town filled with vampires. The steady rumble of his voice was soothing, and when we fell silent, his low purr vibrated through me. My whole body went lax. It was like a drug. Like meditating while high. I was filled with good food, lying along the body of the hottest guy I'd ever seen, watching fluffy ducklings swim around.

I never wanted to leave this moment.

I broke the silence hesitantly. "So, you're cool with Stacey?"

He wrapped his arms tighter around my body. "Whatever you need, Princess. Whatever will make you happy." He paused. "Except another Alpha. I'm not sure my Lion would like that very much. Both me and the lion like Stace though. I think it might take her a little longer to warm up to us but we'll win her over eventually. Maybe we'll offer to be test subjects or something. She doesn't seem like the kind of girl to be swayed by candy."

I laughed. Yeah, I was pretty sure I didn't deserve Bohdie, but I was certainly glad he was mine.

8

———————

STACEY

I couldn't concentrate and that was perplexing. Aggravating, even. The words of the Alpha kept going around and around in my head. Logically, what he proposed made a lot of sense. After all, it was illogical, or at least unusual, to assume that one person could be everything another person could ever need. As he proposed, two people would satisfy the majority of the needs she had, both physical and emotional.

What I was stuck on was what I actually brought to the equation. I wasn't a particularly physically affectionate person. I wasn't emotionally aware either. The only thing I provided was aid in any cryptic crossword puzzles she had, or perhaps a burden she needed to care for. Enit was a nurturer—it's what I loved about her, what drew me to her to start with. As a small, awkward child who'd grown up in the sterile walls of a research facility, who didn't know how to run and play with anyone but Daniel, I'd been so lost and confused. Despite being a year or so older than me, Enit had seen me, taken me under her wing and that was the end of it really. I'd found my place, way back then, and I never wanted to leave it. But I was just a bird with broken wings to Enit; would that be enough for her? For the both of us?

As if summoned by my thoughts, the door to my lab swung open and Daniel walked in. Attached to his back was one of my other siblings, Hannah. She launched herself from his back toward me, her body strong and agile from her Lycan nature.

"Staceeeyyyyyyy," she squealed as if I hadn't seen her less than a day ago for dinner. I barely caught her in my arms with an *oof*.

She snuggled into the hug, inhaling me deeply. Watching the development of my siblings had been an interesting academic study, but I loved each of them. "Hello, Hannah. Are you spending the day with Daniel?"

She nodded furiously. "Mamma is going to have the baby soon and Dadda said that I was too crazy for Mamma to handle while she's as big as a whale."

Daniel laughed. "Hopefully he didn't say that while Mamma was in the room if he wanted to retain his life," he said, winking at Hannah but raising an eyebrow at me.

"Not if Hannah wants any more siblings," I added, sliding my littlest sister to the ground. "I'll go over and check her condition when I finish work."

Daniel waved me away. "Alistair is all over it." He used his telekinesis to pick up Hannah and move her away from my experiment, holding her in the air while she giggled and thrashed around. Hannah was three, so she was at the age where she touched absolutely everything.

"I thought you might want to come for lunch and help me to keep her entertained for five minutes."

I frowned. I was meant to head to the gardens to see Enit, but I didn't think she'd mind me bringing Daniel and Hannah. She was always good with the children. Part of her Omega nature, I theorized.

I nodded, packing up my equipment quietly. "That would be fine, but I am meant to spend it in the sun with Enit in the gardens."

Daniel's eyes opened wide. "Enit? I didn't think you were friends anymore." He said it softly, but I still winced.

Shrugging, I slipped off my lab coat and hung it on the back of the lab door. "Miss Pea put her down here with me while they find her a suitable Omega Studies tutor."

If anyone knew about my feelings for Enit, it was

Daniel. Daniel knew me better than anyone in the whole world.

Using his ability, he floated Hannah back down into his arms. "And how do you feel about it?"

he asked, like quantifying my emotions was easy, but it wasn't really. So I just shrugged.

"Fine. I'm not sure what I can teach her other than general medicinal treatments, but she seems to enjoy it."

Daniel tilted his head at me. "That's not what I meant, Stace, and you know it."

The elevator doors opened and we stepped inside. Hannah promptly began to stare at herself in the mirrored walls like a parakeet, fully immersed at staring at her own face.

Daniel cleared his throat, and I knew what he said next was going to be serious. "Stacey, you've been in love with her most of your life. It would be difficult to be in a room with the person you loved who..."

He trailed off, but I could take an educated guess at his next words. "Rejected me?"

Daniel sighed. "Yes. But no. We both know there was more to the whole thing than that."

I was silent as we stepped from the elevator, walking through the long glass and concrete halls of the Academy.

When we stepped out into the fresh air, I sucked in a deep lungful. Enit had been right about me needing to get out of my lab more. I turned to look at my brother, his face so like mine. His eyes were the same color as mine. We could almost have been twins, except there were several years between us.

"It isn't hard at all. It's the most natural thing in the world and it scares the hell out of me."

Daniel gave me a soft look, stepping in to hug me, squishing Hannah between us. The tiny Lycan didn't care though, she just wrapped her arms around my ribs and screamed, "GWOUP HUG!"

I laughed softly, taking a moment to hug them back. Then I stepped away, leading them to the back half of the Academy where the gardens and farms were. We created a lot of our own produce here. We were big on self-sufficiency, though we were a large school with hundreds of students, so a lot of stuff was still shipped up here.

"She's fallen in love with a big lion Alpha. Neither one of them will admit to it yet, but all the evidence points to them being perfect for each other."

Daniel wrapped an arm around my shoulders, pulling me into his side. "I'm sorry."

I shook my head. "Don't be. He insinuated that he would be okay with Enit pursuing a relationship with me too, if that's what she desires."

Daniel narrowed his eyes. "Really?"

I nodded and watched Hannah race ahead of us, students dodging her like she was a missile. Which she kind of was. Injuring Hannah, even accidentally, would bring the ire of Micah down on your head, and everyone was scared as hell of our Lycanthrope father. Unnecessarily, of course. The man was as soft-hearted as they came. He hadn't even blinked when Layla had insisted they adopt two science experiments into their family. Instead, Micah, Alistair and Locke had loved us unconditionally.

I didn't try and analyse why they loved us when we were a visual representation of the worst time in their lives, I just soaked in their love. Especially that of Layla, our mother.

Daniel didn't say much else and Hannah zoomed around on slightly unsteady legs as we walked along the uneven paths. In order to minimize detection, they kept the area around the Academy as natural as possible. No concrete paths and only one real cleared field. Even the livestock wandered among the treed fields.

We stepped through the gated fence to the medicinal garden, and my eyes went straight to Enit. She was on her hands and knees, muttering under her breath about weeds.

I cleared my throat and her head popped up like she was a meerkat shifter.

"Stace! You're early!" She climbed to her feet and spotted Daniel. "Daniel!"

She raced over to see my older brother. They'd gotten along well when we were kids, Daniel being one of the few people that Enit's brother didn't growl at. Maybe it was because Daniel was human, maybe because Christopher and Daniel could relate on a deeper, more dysfunctional level—I wasn't sure. Men were a mystery even to me.

Enit threw herself into his arms and he hugged her back. "It's good to see you, E. We've missed you."

Her eyes darted between me and my brother, not missing the *we* in his words. He could have meant the family, but we all knew he was referring to me. I chose to ignore the bluntness of his words.

She bit her lip and gave a tight nod. "I missed you guys too." Hannah peeked out between mine and Daniel's legs. "Who's this?" Her smile was bright and warm, and I could spot the exact moment Hannah became enamoured with the Omega wolf. Although technically not the same genus as wolf shifters, there was still that draw. Hannah would be as susceptible to Enit's Omega traits as the rest of the shifter population, even if it wouldn't produce the same visceral response as it did in wolf shifters.

"This is Hannah."

"No way? Baby Hannah? How'd you get so big?" she cooed at my sibling, who was now pushing past our legs and climbing Enit like a tree. She'd been a few months old when Enit and I had drifted apart.

Hannah looked at her very seriously. "Broccoli."

Enit snorted, but gave her an equally serious nod.

"Ah. Makes sense. Want to go pick some flowers for me? See those white ones on that bush there? You can pick them all and put them in this jar. What do you think?" She held out a glass jar and Hannah whooped with joy as she took off running, the jar tucked under her arm. The flowers were chamomile, completely harmless, and this was grown-up approved destruction. Right in Hannah's wheelhouse.

Daniel's phone chimed and he grinned. "Can you guys watch Hannah for a little bit? I'll be back in like, an hour, I promise."

I frowned but nodded. Enit raised an eyebrow. "I know that grin. It's an 'I got a girl' grin. Who's the lucky woman?"

Daniel mock-zipped his lips and then in the next moment, he was gone. Enit sat down on the corner of a raised garden, and patted the spot beside her. I sat down close enough that I could feel the heat of her body against mine.

"How was your date the other day?" I asked softly, keeping my voice completely neutral like I had no vested interest in her answer.

"He bought me ducks."

I frowned. I'd seen the picnic basket. There were no ducks in it. "Like, on a sandwich?"

Enit threw back her head and laughed, the sound so pure that my heart constricted in my chest and I had to remind my body that it physically needed to breathe.

She nudged me with her shoulder. "No. Not on a sandwich. He'd put them in the pond. There are ducklings too—you should take the kids down to see them sometime."

I raised my eyebrows, reassessing the Alpha. No, Bohdie. I was to call him Bohdie. That was a smart move. Enit's Omega nature was naturally drawn to vulnerable things, to nurturing and nature. Not saying she was designed to love baby things, but she'd evolved to temper the harsher nature of an Alpha, and that meant caring for the weak and vulnerable, not just protecting them. To do that, it meant you had to *care*. And that was the real danger to Enit. She was incapable of harming another living being. "That sounds... nice."

"It was." She looked at me out of the corner of her eye, though her focus was on Hannah to ensure she didn't hurt herself. "He told me he spoke to you."

I froze. I didn't breathe. Didn't blink. I couldn't even make my mouth form an O.

She turned, her eyes traveling over every inch of my face. Then she leaned forward and kissed me.

I sat like a statue, my body completely locked up as her lips brushed mine, sipping at them with the barest of touches. Then her tongue flicked out, running over my bottom lip, and a small, shuddering sound escaped my throat. I closed my eyes and deepened the kiss slightly, tasting her on my tongue.

Oh no.

I broke the kiss, stood so fast my head spun, scooped up Hannah and the jar of chamomile flowers, and ran out of there as fast as I could go.

I didn't look back at Enit's stunned face.

9

———————

ENIT

Mouse had managed to get herself tangled up in something bad.

I was mad at Mouse for keeping secrets, but I really couldn't talk. I'd been keeping secrets too. But Mouse was all caught up in some messed up shit, and in true Mouse fashion, had managed to rescue an enslaved fire Djinn and enrage a murderous slave owner. The whole thing had thrown our family, and the Academy, into a total freakout, not that you would tell from Mouse's reaction. She was happy as a pig in mud, especially now that her and Bobby had worked out their shit.

It was rough there for a moment, and Mouse had been so damn angry at me. But when there was a threat to our little Pack, we did what we always did. We pulled together.

We still got shipped off to the Academy to live on campus for a little while though. It was tumultuous and worrying and it made my wolf whine in anxiety.

With everything that was going on, I'd managed to avoid Stacey for the last few weeks. I'd kissed her and she'd run away like I'd attacked her. Bohdie, however, had become even more protective, growling at anyone who so much as looked at me funny, like the threat had come from within the Academy. It hadn't—it was some psycho on the outside who thought of people as property—but he still felt useless. So I let him snarl and growl, calming him however I could.

My Omega abilities were getting a crazy workout if I threw in the anger that Christopher was feeling too. My brother was frustrated that there was a threat to Mouse that he was helpless to fight against. The memories that Flint, the fire Djinn, had caused to resurface had shortened his temper as well.

How did he channel that rage? Well, it wasn't into therapy, that was for sure. No, he channeled it into doing dumb shit to Cara, Bohdie's friend from Black Mountain and Christopher's current nemesis. And if she wasn't around, he took it out on Bohdie.

Christopher's protectiveness of me doubled, and more than once in the last couple of weeks I'd found him beating the crap out of a high school senior who'd said god knows what. I'd broken up even more fights between him and Bohdie.

They were so volatile on the topic of me that people were scared to even look me in the eye. To appease my brother, because I knew—through my Omega abilities and just good old-fashioned intuition —that this whole situation was because of our fucked up beginnings, I stopped seeing Bohdie during the day.

But at night, when the Academy had gone to bed, I'd sneak out of my dorm room and down the hall on silent feet. I'd meet him in the library, or if the night was warm, down by our pond.

Now, dressed in Bohdie's oversized hoodie and some tight yoga pants that belonged to Mouse, I crept out of the rear fire escape and Bohdie was there. Waiting for me with his arms open.

I raced into them and he kissed me like I hadn't seen him in months, rather than hours.

His hands slid over the smooth fabric of my yoga pants and up to my ass. He groaned as he squeezed lightly. "Missed you, Princess."

I snorted. "Are you talking to me or my ass?"

He kissed me softly. "A little of both?"

I slapped his chest and he chuckled as he stepped away, his hand coming up to grab mine. As we got to the path that would lead to the pond, I tugged on his hand to stop him.

"Bohdie?"

He looked down at me, his brows drawn. "Yeah?"

"Do you think we could go to your place tonight?"

I felt his whole body still. "Everyone's probably asleep, if you wanted to visit them."

I almost snorted at his roundabout way of asking why. "I don't want to visit with anyone else."

He drew me in, protecting me from the cool night breeze. He dipped his head closer to my face, until his lips nearly brushed mine. "What do you want?"

I chewed my lip. I could do this. Be brave. Say what I wanted. I sucked in a deep breath. "Iwanty-outomakelovetome." It came out in one long word.

He raised a brow, a grin starting to curl his lips so a dimple appeared on his cheek. "What was that?"

I met his golden eyes. "I want you to make love to me. You, uh, should know that I've never, you know, never..."

He took pity on me. "Made love before?" He held me so close, like he was shoring up my strength with his.

"Yeah. That."

He grabbed me up in his arms, banding them around my back as he kissed me with so much heat I gasped. I wrapped my legs around his waist and he held me easily. He walked like he knew where he was going, sure-footed as he kissed me deeper. I got lost in the feel of his body curled around mine. Or was mine curled around his? Didn't matter because I was being consumed and I loved it. Somehow, we were walking through his front door, and Bohdie was silent on his feet despite the extra weight of me. I envied his agility.

I gave into my instincts and thrust my tongue into his mouth, rolling my body against the brush of his hard cock.

He groaned, and accidentally banged my elbow into the door frame. I hissed out a pained noise, but laughed. I was giddy on the pheromones.

"Shit, fuck, sorry," Bohdie whispered, holding me impossibly tighter to his chest. "If you want to make it to my room in one piece, you should probably resist grinding on my dick."

Just to show I had no self-preservation skills, I ground my core against the hard line of his cock again and he moaned.

We made it through another door and he visibly sighed in relief as he dropped me on the bed from a height, making me bounce and the breath rush from my lungs.

He crawled up the bed after me, his hard body between my thighs and his nose inches from mine. "Thank god. Enit Baxter, I am going to fuck you until you can't remember your own name," he purred, like literally purred. It rumbled through his whole body, and through mine, and I made a surprised squeak.

"Like the purr, hmm?" His lips were pulled into a sinful smile that made my core clench. "Let me show you what it can really do."

He peeled off my yoga pants slowly, and I lifted my butt to help. Once he got them to my feet, he pulled off my sneakers and pants in a few hard tugs. From where he was at the end of the bed, he looked up at me with absolute adoration. The kind that made my heart beat faster.

His face turned serious. "If at any point you want to stop, you have to tell me, okay?" I nodded but he frowned. "I mean it, Princess. I know your designation means you're more likely to give me what I need, even to the detriment of yourself, so I need to know if anything makes you feel uncomfortable or if you've just had enough. You can tell me—I won't be angry or frustrated. But if I did something you didn't one hundred percent enjoy, I would hate myself. Pinky swear."

I let out a laugh that could have been a whimper of relief; I couldn't tell over the roaring of my blood in my ears. I was doing the right thing, chosen the right man. I'd never been more sure of anything in my life.

I reached out and grabbed his pinky, hooking it with mine. "Pinky swears are the weirdest foreplay ever, but I promise."

He puffed out a breath, and it dislodged some of the golden hair from his forehead. "Good." He moved back down my body to my knee, then ran his tongue up the inside of my thigh, until he was at its apex. He scraped his teeth over the crotch of my panties, making me gasp. He bumped my clit with his nose, and I lifted my hips up to meet him.

He pulled back and by the grin on his face, I knew this wasn't going to be a quick wham, bam, thank you ma'am, kind of fuck.

He was going to tease me until I begged. Damn Alphas. Even as I thought about it, I was smiling. I didn't even know why. I felt giddy with happiness.

He blew against the dampness of my panties, cooling the hot flesh beneath the thin strip of fabric. My smile turned into an O as I gasped again. He tugged my underwear off, his fingers almost as eager as I was. Although I felt a little shy about having his face so freaking close to my naked vagina, I was embracing it. Taking a leap of faith.

And when his tongue swirled around my clit, I wasn't just taking a leap of faith, I was freediving into pleasure. "Holy shi..." I moaned, my body curling beneath his mouth as he pressed his tongue flat against my clit and then *purred*. The vibration shot straight through my body and my legs shot straight out like I was a scared goat.

"Oh my god!"

His chuckle broke up the purring, and then he was slowly lapping at me in the most torturously sensual way ever. I twisted my hands in his hair, clutching him close. My body moved against his face of its own accord, seeking more and more pleasure.

My very first non-solo orgasm came out of nowhere and hit me like a freight train. My thighs clenched around his ears, but he didn't stop, lapping and sucking at my body and then plunging his tongue inside me.

He growled his approval at the feel of my body fluttering around his tongue, which just made me come harder.

"Bohdie," I gasped, and he pulled back, his face shiny and his teeth flashing in a smug grin.

"Mmm Princess, you taste divine. I could die happily between your thighs."

He moved his way up my body and when I was bracketed between his arms, my heart started to race.

But not in a good way.

He leaned down and kissed me, nipping at my neck, and sweat broke out across my skin. When he slid his hand down my stomach, I froze. Suddenly it was a different time, a different place, a different Alpha's hands.

Bohdie noticed immediately. He reared back, his eyes searching my face. "Enit? Princess? Are you okay?"

I wanted to cry. Dammit. No. Why the fuck couldn't the past stay in the past? Why was I always so fucking defective?

Tears of self-pity tracked down my cheeks, and Bohdie sprung away like he was on fire. He stared at me for a split second, before coming to kneel down beside the bed. "Baby, talk to me. What's wrong?"

"I'm broken," I sobbed. "I just want to make love to my boyfriend without all my"—I let out a choked hiccup—"baggage."

He stared at me for a moment. "This is about what Stacey mentioned? About your assault?" I winced at the word "assault" but nodded. He reached up and grabbed my hand. "We can work up to it, Princess. We don't have to do it all at once."

I let out a frustrated yell. "No. I want to do it tonight. I don't want to be broken anymore."

He leaned forward a little, keeping his body from crowding me. "Okay, baby. I've got an idea. Do you trust me?"

I nodded. I did. Despite my freakout, I trusted Bohdie. I wouldn't be here if I didn't.

He nodded and stood. "Okay. Give me a minute. Don't go anywhere." He disappeared into his closet, and I was left half-naked on his bed, my self-loathing rolling around in my brain.

He came back holding a tan leather belt. He did a complicated loop, and then I swear, he origami-ed it into a set of cuffs.

"Were you a boy scout by any chance?" I said in a husky voice.

He shook his head as he slowly stripped off his clothes, and I totally forgot what I was saying. Because he was unleashing inch after torturously slow inch of that perfect golden flesh and my brain just melted into goo. He reached into the drawer, pulled out a condom and put it on with practiced ease.

When he was naked and protected, he kind of unceremoniously flopped onto the bed beside me. He turned his head, capturing my lips in a kiss that felt more like a promise. I deepened the kiss, my body taking over from my whirring brain.

He pulled back with a groan. "Pull the belt end," he murmured, his voice rough with lust. I looked above our heads, and realized he'd shackled himself to the headboard. Made himself vulnerable for me. That had to go against all his Alpha instincts.

"Bohdie," I whispered, but he was shaking his head.

"Tighten the belt, Princess, and then press that beautiful fucking body against mine. I'm dying for you right now."

I tugged at the end of the belt. "Harder, baby." I tugged it until it sat snuggly around his wrists, but there were arteries and all sorts of things in the wrists that I didn't want to damage. Besides, he was a damn Alpha lion. He could snap those cuffs in an instant.

But the illusion of control? It was calming the raging tumult in my brain.

When I was sure they were tight but not too tight, I straddled his lower abs, curling my body so I could kiss him. He pressed up like he couldn't help himself, and I felt the slide of his cock against my ass as he plunged his tongue into my mouth. I broke the kiss and pulled my shirt over my head, quickly followed by my lacy bra. Bohdie's eyes ate me alive.

"What do I do now?" I whispered, and he gave me that sexy, crooked grin.

"Whatever you want, Princess. You're setting the pace. You're in control."

Me. In control. I wanted to laugh, but he was kind of right. I had an Alpha lion beneath me, his throat bared. Vulnerable. I was doing this on my terms, and Bohdie was letting me. I knew what I wanted, what Bohdie wanted, and now was the time to take it.

I lifted myself off his hips, scooting down, my core running over Bohdie's cock, making us both whimper. My hand stroked the hard length of his cock, lining him up with my entrance. Bohdie looked flushed, his muscles taut like he was straining. Deep down, I knew he was straining to keep himself still.

"Go slow, Princess. Easy."

He cooed sweet things, little words of encouragement, as I sank onto his dick. As the head breached my entrance, he started to swear softly. His body glistened and I could tell he was fighting himself.

"Jesus, Enit. You feel so fucking good. Oh, fucking Moon Goddess," he groaned as the slight sting passed and I continued my slow descent to take him all. An inch or two from bottoming out, I let myself drop, making us both shout.

I rested there for a second, my body acclimating to the fullness of Bohdie. It felt delicious and wicked and so damn right.

"You okay, Princess?" I dragged my gaze from where I was staring at our joined bodies to meet Bohdie's eyes. There was real concern there, and I couldn't—no, didn't want to—contain the smile that broke across my face.

"I don't think I've ever been more perfect."

He curled his body up as far as he could and I leaned forward, my hands on his shoulders, to kiss him. His kiss was soft and beautiful, the kind of kiss you remembered forever. He pulled back, his golden eyes sparkling. "You are perfect."

I grinned against his lips, pushing his chest until he was flat on his back again. Then I dragged myself back up his dick, and my eyes crossed. Holy shit. That was good.

Eventually, after a few more experimental slides, I hit a rhythm that promised to destroy us both. Bohdie was groaning, his hips rising to meet mine, by no means a passive participant in our lovemaking, despite the fact he was still tied to his headboard.

The orgasm came from nowhere. It was a steady hum deep in my belly in one moment, and then it was a baseball bat hitting me up the side of the head the next.

I flopped down as my muscles turned to jelly, and Bohdie caught my lips, his hips rolling as he thrust his way through my orgasm, and then the next.

Finally, he buried his face in my neck and came with a shuddering gasp.

I collapsed down onto his chest, my lungs burning, my body on fire. I used my shaky arms to release the belt, and his arms came straight up to wrap around my waist, holding me to his chest.

"I don't know what I did to get so lucky," he whispered into my hair.

Me either, but I would do it a thousand times over if it meant I got to keep Bohdie forever.

ear Enit, Unfortunately, the other day I had an involuntary muscle spasm that resulted in me sprinting away from you. Apologies.

No. We both knew that was bullshit.

Dear Enit, I am sorry I am such an emotionally stunted failure of a human being.

Well, that was the truth at least.

Layla walked into my kitchen without knocking. It didn't ever occur to Layla to knock. She was days away from her due date and she looked exhausted.

"Sit. I'll take your blood pressure."

Layla huffed out a laugh. "Immortal, remember?"

"Fine, I'll listen to the baby." I grabbed my stethoscope and made her sit so I could listen.

Everything sounded wonderful, but I was never not worried. I owed Layla so much. Not just Layla though.

"Do you ever wonder what Porter would have made of this place?" I asked softly, and Layla froze.

We didn't speak of the time before Eden Academy very often. It was like a fairytale, but one of the gruesome ones that warned you away from things. Once upon a time, two children were stolen from their family, kept in cages, and studied by scientists who wanted to replicate their abilities, under the watchful eye of a secret, evil organization named The Hounds. A kindly doctor kept them safe, but couldn't rescue them. Then one day, a beautiful heroine arrived, and promised she'd free the children. White knights arrived, twisted monsters who were really good instead of evil, and fought the children's captors until they were freed. Unfortunately, the kindly doctor died in the end. The rescuers took the children to a forest far, far away and they all lived happily ever after.

Except for all the PTSD.

It was the past, and it was best left there. But my brain could never just forget things. It remembered everything. I remembered the day Daniel and I were kidnapped. I'd been a toddler, but I still remember my father being shot right in front of me, and being herded into the back of a van, clinging to Daniel.

I remembered Porter, his soft, gentle face promising us we would be fine, as we were put into observation rooms that would be our home for years afterwards.

I remembered the day Layla arrived, heralding the start of a new beginning.

The carnage of the battle between Eden and The Hounds, when Layla's mates came to her rescue.

Porter being shot. The blood.

"I think Porter would have loved it here. He'd be really proud of what you've accomplished and who you've become, Stace," Layla said softly.

I wasn't so sure, but I didn't say anything. "Everything sounds fine," I said, curling away. Medicine I could do. Research, science, mathematics, these all made sense.

Feelings... not so much.

Layla grabbed my arm and pulled me against her chest. Which was a bit uncomfortable considering how much baby there was. She wrapped her arms around my shoulders and squeezed me until I was forced to hug her back. I relaxed in her hold, and just let her strength and sweetness supplant my worries.

"Do you want to tell me what's wrong? Why are you bringing up Porter?"

I chewed my lip, glad she couldn't see the tell. "I think that time in the labs, it broke something in me." She squeezed me tighter. "Layla, breathing is necessary for survival for most of us," I gasped out.

She drew back so she could look at me, her usually soft face stern. "You are perfect. Strong. Smart. Beautiful. A survivor. I wouldn't change you for the world."

An overwhelming surge of love and gratitude swept over me for this woman who was my mother. "Thanks, Layla."

She released me and I sat back in my seat. "Is this about Enit Baxter kissing you the other day? It made quite an impression on Hannah."

My face flushed such a bright red that I wondered if it would burst the capillaries in my cheeks. "Perhaps."

Layla raised an eyebrow. "Hannah said you ran away like she had cooties."

I snorted out a laugh. "I guess it may have looked that way."

"Do you want to talk about it?"

There were a lot of studies that theorized that talking with a trusted person eased stress and anxiety, and there was no one I trusted more than Layla, except perhaps Daniel. "I'm not sure if you are aware, but romance has never been a big motivator for me. I'm fairly sure that I've never grown out of the stage where boys have cooties. I just don't feel sexual attraction to anyone. Anyone except..." I swallowed the lump in my throat.

"Enit," Layla supplied.

"Yes. She makes me feel things that I don't understand, and I hate not understanding things." I sucked in a deep breath. "Why does she make me feel like this, and no one else does? Is it a physiological response to her Omega designation? Are my feelings not really mine but an evolutionary biological response?"

Layla frowned, considering my words. "Hmmm. Let's talk about Christopher, her brother. When you're in his presence, do you feel the urge to submit to his dominance? Or fight him?"

I snorted. "Highly unlikely." I liked Enit's siblings. They loved each other with such overwhelming protectiveness, and it reminded me of my relationship with Daniel. When you go through something traumatic as children, the bond is stronger than that of normal siblings.

But I had no urge to bare my throat to Christopher.

Oh.

"Oh, I see what you are saying."

Layla gave me a small smile. "If your response to Enit was due to her Omega designation, then logic would say that you are susceptible to all pheromonal stimuli. But you aren't." She rubbed my arm soothingly. "You're a scientist, Stacey. You know that there is fluidity to everything. You can't always predict the exact same results in every experiment—there are all sorts of environmental factors that can alter the outcome. Sexuality and attraction are the same. You're asexual, or maybe demisexual, or maybe none of those things. But none of those labels mean that you can't be physically or romantically attracted to a pretty little Omega wolf who looks at you like you're the most wondrous being in the world. You have to stop looking at yourself like a failed experiment, searching for environmental stumbling blocks about why you aren't like the 'control group,' and instead let yourself feel. Let yourself live. Some things defy explanation and love is definitely one of those things. Give yourself permission to just experience it, without having to find out the why."

I bit my lower lip, the lump in my throat too big, until I was forced to clear it. "You've been spending too much time with Alistair this pregnancy," I teased softly.

She waved me away with a grin. "Both you and Alistair are scientists. I picked up a bit along the way." She pushed herself out of the chair, and waved me in for another hug. "I love you so much, Stace. You are the most amazing daughter any mother could ask for. We are so damn proud of you." She stepped away. "Now, stop hiding away, and go find Enit and tell her how you feel. Then bring her and her pretty lion Alpha around for dinner one night."

I let out an undignified squeak. "You know about that? That she's dating Bohdie too?"

She nodded. "Yep. Not much happens in this Academy I don't know about. And if you wanted to be with the lion Alpha too, your dads and I would be happy for you."

I gagged a little and Layla put her head back and

laughed so hard she had to hold her stomach. "Or not," she wheezed. "Stop before I give birth on your kitchen floor." She shooed me out my own front door before bustling away.

Damn, I loved her too.

Locking my door, I strode toward the dorm buildings. Layla was right. I didn't have to freak out about this. My dream was just there, waiting for me to take what she was offering. I just had to have the bravery to do it.

I marched with single-minded focus toward the dorm rooms. When they'd been moved in here, I'd subtly made enquiries about which dorm room she was put in. It wasn't weird. We were friends, even if I had run away like she had cooties when she'd kissed me. Hannah had that right at least.

I stopped outside of her door, raising my hand to knock.

Then I stilled. This was stupid. She definitely deserved better, and the more I thought about it, the more likely it was her Omega designation causing these feelings. The pheromones were different between Alpha and Omega, maybe that's why Christopher didn't affect me at all.

I should go and study myself.

I walked away, striding back down the hall. This was stupid. I should be in the lab anyway. My samples should just about be ready.

The elevator door slid open and I stared at myself in the wall mirror at the back of the enclosed cube. My hair was a wild riot of curls. I looked like a scared kitten. Scared of the softest, sweetest person on the earth. I at least owed her an apology.

I stepped back into the hall and let the doors slide closed behind me. I strode back to her door, lifting my hand once more to knock, then pausing.

I was scared. Terrified.

The door swung open and then Enit was standing there, her blue eyes looking like deep pools in her face. "I could smell your anxiety."

Layla's voice telling me to let myself live played in my head, so I launched myself at Enit awkwardly, grabbing her face and kissing her. She let out a shocked squeak, kissing me back as I pressed her further into her room.

Her hands clung to my arms as she tripped backwards, falling. And I fell with her. At least, I did until hands reached out and grabbed me, pulling me back up straight.

I looked up into the face of a smiling Bohdie. "What's up, Doc? Glad you came to your senses."

He kissed the top of Enit's head and left, shutting the door behind him. I could hear him whistling happily in the hall.

Enit grabbed my hand and pulled me toward the bed, the only real piece of furniture in the room.

The tinkling sound of Enit's laughter had me turning toward her. "Don't look at the bed like it's about to eat you, or like I'm about to eat you. I just thought we should talk."

Oh yeah. Talk. That was probably a good idea. She sat down and patted the bed beside her, her face shining and beautiful.

Yeah, I loved her too, whether it was the right thing or not. I wouldn't tell her that—it was way too soon—but I knew in my soul that I loved her. Had always loved her.

Now I just needed to make her love me too.

11

———

ENIT

My lips still tingled from Stace's surprise kiss. Not what I thought was going to happen when I opened the door, her anxiety from the other side making my Omega wolf whine. I was just going to console her, tell her I understood that she didn't want to start anything between us, and send her on her way.

That wasn't how it happened, obviously. Instead, she was now sitting ramrod straight beside me, smelling of anxiety and that slightly chemical smell that clung to her from being in the lab. I was silent, knowing that Stace liked to work her way through her own thoughts before she voiced them. It was part of the reason she was teased so much when we were kids. People thought she was snooty because she wouldn't answer them when they asked her questions. They thought she was stuck-up, but really, she was just processing, going through all the variables before coming up with the answer needed. If they'd spent just a few more minutes with her, they would have known too how amazing she was. Brilliant beyond anyone's understanding. Sweet in her own way.

I could still taste her on my lips. I wanted to do it again, but I held back. She chewed on her lip, and then looked at me, her big dark eyes staring at me like I was a bug under a slide. Like she couldn't quite work me out.

I liked being Stacey's enigma.

She cleared her throat and looked at the opposite wall. "When you were thirteen, and I was twelve, Christopher got into a fight with Kingston. We'd been on the other side of the campus, and you cocked your head to the side and started running. I followed along behind you, running as fast as I could but still much slower than you. I tripped, scraped up my knees real bad. Do you remember?"

I nodded. It had been one of many fights between King and Christopher, until they came to an uneasy truce in junior year. They were both strong Alphas, both incredibly stubborn. Way too alike to ever get along.

"Well, when I got there, you were standing between

these two pubescent Alphas. I mean, they may have been thirteen but they were still nearly six feet tall and twice your body mass. You had a single hand on each of their chests and were murmuring something to them. In that moment, I realized how powerful you were. You could stop wars."

I snorted a laugh. "I promise you it wasn't that dramatic."

She waved me away. "Anyway, you looked over, and saw me standing there with two bleeding knees. You just dropped your hands, running straight over to me and making a big deal about the fact I was bleeding. You went against your Omega instincts to tend to me." She turned, meeting my eyes briefly. "It was that moment that I realized I might love you one day. It took a few more years before I could actually categorize the feeling."

My heart stuttered to a stop. I knew what she was saying, but I was frozen. I couldn't even think about it; I wasn't ready to think about it. Stacey just looked at me with her appraising eyes, and then turned away again.

"I don't want you to pretend you feel the same way. I know you probably don't. But I would very much appreciate the chance to show you. And maybe, one day in the future, you might love me back. I can't, uh, promise you wild sexual relations, or even good emotional support. But I promise, I will never feel about another living being the way I feel about you."

I had no words. No "me too" that would make this a Hallmark moment. Not because I didn't think I could love Stacey like that, I definitely could, but I was cautious. If I gave away too much of my heart, would I survive if it broke?

So instead, I leaned forward, kissing her softly. "I'd be honored if you'd be my girlfriend."

She smiled at me then, a smile that consumed her entire face, and it was so rare that I didn't even blink so I wouldn't miss a second. I smiled back, and pulled her into my arms, wrapping her up against my body. Mainly so I didn't have to see that smile fade when I brought up our very first relationship hurdle—in the first ten seconds. That had to be a record, right?

"About Bohdie..." I started.

She pulled back, taking my cheeks in her hands. "I like the Alpha. He is kind and you smile more when he's around. What he can give you is visceral and emotional. He can give you what I can't, and I don't just mean a penis."

"Stacey!" I gasped, and she smiled at me smugly. But that smile slowly faded.

"I don't offer you anything really, but I hope you'll still have me."

I frowned. "What do you mean? You have a lot to offer, Stace. You're as nurturing as you are challenging." She snorted. "I mean it. You are so sweet with your siblings. You are compassionate, clear-headed, and so soft. Except your brain. That is a weapon. You're brilliant. Devoted. And so very, very beautiful."

A flush climbed up her cheeks and I felt the urge to kiss her one more time, but I resisted. If I kept kissing her, we'd never get anything sorted. I stood and held out a hand. "We better go and find Bohdie and tell him the good news."

THE NEXT FEW weeks felt almost blissful. Bohdie and Stacey fell into something like camaraderie, though usually it was just Bohdie being playful and Stacey making quips. But he'd started inviting her on our picnics, or he'd laze on the grass as I'd take her through the medicinal gardens, pointing out plants used in traditional medicine. It was idyllic. Perfect.

We spent time separately too, me sneaking into Bohdie's room late at night and making love until I gasped his name. Then we'd watch movies and cuddle. I spent whole days with Stacey down in her lab, helping with patients. Bohdie had come through with another Omega tutor for me: Dawn from the bear Sleuth near his home. Unfortunately, she couldn't start until next semester, as she was down in Las Vegas for something. Bohdie wouldn't say what, though I suspected he knew. There was something strange about the inhabitants of Black Mountain, Bohdie's home territory. I just didn't know what it was.

Thankfully, both my siblings were distracted, Carmen with her new beaus and Christopher with... whatever the fuck Christopher did. Though he still escorted me from our dorms to my first class every day. Then he was gone until the last class of the day, where he'd collect me from

outside my classroom. But that time in between? It was all mine.

Stacey, Bohdie and I ate our lunch at the pond, which was definitely our spot now. I even managed to lure the ducks over, along with the ducklings which were now in the tall gangly stage. Stacey sat on a rug beside me, our shoulders touching. I was introducing her to the idea of public displays of affection, or affection at all really. As much as her eyes mapped me every moment, she wasn't huge on touch, and that was okay. But my wolf craved it sometimes, so we started small.

I threw pieces of chicken from my sandwich to the ducks, because I'd read bread was bad, but then I felt guilty feeding them their land-dwelling cousins. I made a note to buy some proper pellets so I could feed them and not feel guilty.

"One of the kids in my Alpha class said it was fight night," Bohdie said, his eyes sparkling up at me from where his head rested in my lap. I stroked my fingers through his golden hair and he purred.

I rolled my eyes. "I hate fight night."

Stacey snorted from beside me. "It keeps me busy. It's been too quiet down in the infirmary."

Bohdie laughed. "Well, aren't you the bloodthirsty one, Doc." His amused eyes slid back to me. "I'd like to check it out, but you don't have to come if you don't want to."

I folded in half to kiss his lips. "I usually go. It's kind of an unwritten safeguard that if any of the Alphas go too far, I'm there to calm them." I slid my eyes to Stacey. "Not that Micah ever suggested it."

Micah was her father, in every way that mattered. We'd all bonded over our slightly shitty childhoods, but in my opinion, Stacey's was the worst, though she wouldn't think so. But to be kept in a cage for so long as an experiment? That shit was fucked up.

Actually, the fact we all had such shitty beginnings was proof that even though the world was an awful place, we didn't have to be shaped in its image. We could be better people than my original Pack Alpha, or Bohdie's grandfather, or the fucked up organization that had kidnapped Stacey.

"So we can go?" Bohdie said hopefully. I was getting the impression that being trapped here was grating on his Alpha instincts. If watching people thump each other made him happy, so be it.

Stacey stretched out in the sun. "I'm out. I'll have to patch up the idiots."

I smiled down at Bohdie. "We can go." He whooped

and I gripped his chin. "No fighting on my behalf. Got it?" There'd been enough violence in my name over the last few weeks.

Bohdie grinned. "Got it. I won't even challenge anyone. Going purely for entertainment."

I trusted Bohdie. But that grin? It was nothing but trouble, and not just on my ovaries.

12

The atmosphere at fight night was a beast of its own. I wouldn't be surprised if people bayed for blood and howled at the moon. One of the Lycans who ran the school stood in the shadows, talking to a human. At least, I thought he was a human. He was huge and tattooed, and had eyes that told me he'd done some seriously bad shit.

I walked into the ring of firelight, hovering close to Enit. I saw her sister with her boyfriends, and directed Enit toward them. I could protect my Omega, but the atmosphere was so violent, I could almost taste the desire on the air to spill blood. I wouldn't turn down a few extra protective eyes and fists in this situation, despite the fact that Enit seemed surprisingly comfortable right now.

Before we could make it there though, a hand

snaked out from the crowd and grabbed her, drawing her away. I bared my teeth but was unsurprised to see it was Christopher. Ugh. I needed to sort shit out with that asshole, because if I had my way, one day we were going to be family. It wasn't good if you wanted to beat the absolute fuck out of your family.

In a small gesture of peace, I didn't reach out and tug her back into my arms. Instead, I threw her a meaningful look and she nodded slightly. I went over and stood next to Cara, kissing the top of her head in a gesture that was purely brotherly.

She was burning holes in the back of Christopher's head, and that was a pastime I could get behind.

"You look completely smitten, Dee," she said, bumping her shoulder against my ribs. "When are you bringing her around to meet the family?"

I rolled my eyes at her. "You guys have already met. Besides, you'll just tell her lies about me."

Cara slapped a hand over her chest, mock outrage on her face. "I would never!" She scoffed, even as she said it.

"How did that lie taste?"

She just grinned up at me. "Like the finest chocolate. But seriously, bring her around. If you guys are going to date in the same family like some hillbilly commune, may as well indoctrinate them into the craziness before they drop your useless asses."

I wrapped an arm around her shoulders and

squeezed her. I leaned down so I was sure only her ears would hear my next words. "I see how you look at the wolf Alpha. If we're starting a hillbilly commune, you'll be joining us." She pulled away and death glared me. I just mouthed, "One of us, one of us," until she jabbed her fingers beneath my sternum and I wheezed out a breath, pain spasming through my gut. Fucking MC Princess. They'd taught her to kill before they even taught her to drive.

"You're lucky you're pretty, Dee, otherwise your Omega would dump you for someone who isn't blind and actually has a sense of humor."

I gave her a mock pout, but then Micah was listing the rules. You had to wear protective gear. You went until someone tapped out. If you didn't stop, Micah would shift to Lycan and make you stop permanently. Whether he would or not, wasn't a theory I wanted to test.

"Okay, first contenders, step up," Micah barked and Christopher stepped forward.

Great.

"Well, here's a goddamn surprise," Micah said drolly. "Ok, who are you challenging today?"

My whole body tensed, though I didn't expect anything else but the next words that came out of Christopher's mouth.

"Bohdie, the lion Alpha."

Micah rolled his eyes. "Shocker. Do you accept?"

There was no way I couldn't accept. I would lose face, lose my standing among the shifters of the Academy. Plus I really wanted to pummel the shit out of his smug fucking face.

"Yes," I said, purposefully not looking at Enit. She'd be disappointed, but this was Alpha stuff. I could be a placid kitten for her, but out here, I needed everyone to know their place—including her dick of a brother.

Micah was saying something but I was just holding Christopher's eyes. I knew the rules. I stripped off my shirt and stepped into the ring, putting on the headgear and gloves that would barely soften our blows.

"Alright. Fight," Micah called, and I stepped into Christopher's guard. I took the blow to the ribs, but I was close enough to deliver a punishing headbutt. I'd spent my teenage years brawling with bears. They taught me that it was better to go hard, then go home for a nap.

Christopher was fast. He danced out of my way, and my headbutt only crunched his nose a bit. What a pity.

I might fight like a bear, but I wasn't one. I was a goddamn lion, so he wasn't the only agile one. I dodged his blow, but it still glanced across my ribs.

"I know you're fucking her, you fucking asshole," Christopher growled, spitting on the dirt.

I snarled, curling my lip up over my teeth. I wished I was in my shifter form. I would crush this annoying chihuahua in a second. "It's none of your goddamn business." I caught him in the gut again, and he oofed out a grunt.

"She is mine to protect. You are just another in a long line of fucking Alphas who think you own her because she's an Omega. She won't be owned."

He danced out of reach of my fists, and I shook out my hand. "Except by you? Fuck off, you sanctimonious douche. She doesn't need you."

He roared, moving so fucking fast I could barely follow him with my eyes, but I felt the damn uppercut to my jaw. I skidded across the dirt, my vision spotty. He was on me in an instant, pummelling my face.

"She'll never be used by another fucking Alpha. I will beat you every fucking day until you leave."

I growled then, pushing him off me and scrambling to my feet. "She's worth it, fucker." Then I tackled his middle and brought him back down to the ground again, getting another shot to his nose and hearing it crack properly this time.

He was a wily bastard, and was soon back on top of me, pounding into my guard. I bucked my hips, throwing him off and grappling back on top of him. I laid my fist into his face a few times, the roar of the crowd burning my ears. Until Micah was there, shouting "I said enough" in our faces and yanking me off by my hair.

"Fists won't work, so I suggest you try words,"

Micah yelled, standing between us. "Or you will both lose her and you'll have nothing but your stupid machismo to blame," he said, a little more quietly. I looked over and saw Enit in the arms of the new Ifrit kid. He grinned at me, holding her tightly to his chest, his eyes challenging. I prowled toward him, and Christopher growled, close on my heels. I was limping a bit from a kick that Christopher got to my knee, so he overtook me easily.

He was before Enit, reaching for her, when she slapped him. Hard. My beautiful, peace-loving Enit just whacked him one. I couldn't help but grin smugly at him. It was his fault, after all.

Then she whirled on me and my breath caught in my throat at the look in her eyes. It was like she was looking at a stranger.

"Baby..."

She held up a hand. "I am not a bone to be fought over. Get the hell over yourselves."

She stormed away, and I moved to follow her, but Cara was there, giving me an equally disappointed look. She stared pure venom at Christopher, following my girl—my princess—into the darkness.

I was left standing beside my opponent, under the chastising glare of Enit's sister Carmen. She looked between us, and I had a vivid recollection of her climbing into my shower the other day, holding a knife to my dick and telling me not to hurt her sister. I couldn't even resist the gulp. "Fix. It," she growled, striding away.

The fire Djinn grinned at us. "Good fight, assholes," he said, and the adrenaline that was still pulsing in my veins reared up. I was going to punch the smug look off his face, then break off the hands that had touched my girl. Mine. I lunged toward him but other hands grabbed at me.

Sammie whirled me around. "Go to the infirmary. You are pissing blood and I'm pretty sure you've cracked a rib. Go."

He looked kind of disappointed in me too, so I gave him the finger. I hobbled out of the ring of light and into the darkness. Christopher slunk into the shadows in the other direction, but I would keep my senses open anyway. My knee ached something fierce by the time I got to the elevator that went to the infirmary.

I took the elevator down to the lower levels, and limped into the foyer. Stacey poked her head through the door, her eyebrows raising when she realized it was me.

"Guess I'll be the favorite for a while if this is what I think it is," she snarked, moving forward to help me into the exam room.

I just grunted my agreement. She was definitely the favorite for the foreseeable future. "She slapped Christopher, and the way she looked at me, Stace..."

She shook her head but didn't tell me that it would

be alright. I was learning that was Stacey's way. She wouldn't give you false platitudes. Wouldn't say things to make you feel better. She was all facts and logic. I liked that about her. I knew where I stood with the Doc. "Okay, Alpha, tell me what hurts?"

Her frown got more and more disapproving as I listed my injuries. Definitely a cracked rib. Maybe I'd blown my knee a bit. I'd have to tape it for a while. The cut on my eyebrow was bleeding so bad it would probably need a stitch.

"Silly Alphas. You can't see that the two Alphas she loves the most physically hurting each other would have caused her so much pain. All Alpha pheromones and not two brain cells between you," she muttered under her breath.

I winced at her words. I knew she was right. I'd seen Enit's face before she slapped the shit out of Christopher. I had some serious grovelling to do. "I think I might have fucked up, Doc."

Stacey looked me dead in the eye and snorted. "You have definitely fucked up." She pulled out a suture kit and snapped on some blue gloves. "Now sit still while I stab you repeatedly."

I raised my eyebrow and then winced. "Did you just crack a joke, Doc?"

She slid the stitch through my skin and smiled at my grimace. "I find your pain amusing, yes. Especially when you are being dumb. Especially when you hurt our girlfriend's feelings."

Our girlfriend. If someone had asked what I thought would happen when I came to this Academy in Canada, the fact I'd meet an Omega and actually *share* her with another person, let alone a human, never would have crossed my mind. I would have laughed my ass off. Like hysterical laughter.

"I know we've talked about this, Stace, but I'm really glad she chose you."

She paused her stitching. "I'm glad she did too."

13

ENIT

I was so freaking mad. Stupid, arrogant assholes. Bohdie had been blowing up my phone, but I was ignoring it. He could deal with it for a day, because as my Mom always said, sometimes men were dumb and you had to rub their noses in their own stupidity. Plus, it was Family Day, so I had a legitimate reason to ignore his calls.

I muted my phone once more, my focus back on my gifts. Mom had bought me a cute purple dress that swirled around my thighs, and Nico got me a pair of heart-shaped sunglasses, the tiny signature in the corner telling me they'd cost an absolutely insane amount. Lucius had given me a pendant necklace that was shaped like a leaf, but if you flicked the button, half the leaf fell away and it became a knife. I chuckled low under my breath, and looked at my most damaged father.

"I love it. It's beautiful."

"Yes. Though you will never need it, as I will gut anyone who even hurts your feelings," he said as he nuzzled Mom's neck. We got used to PDA really young, because not all affection was sexual. The Pack used touch like a form of comfort and communication. Lucius used it as a way to keep his demons at bay.

I opened the rest of my presents. A beautiful leather-bound journal from Walker complemented a fountain pen with an inkwell from Tex. Judge gave me an antique text on herbalism which must have taken him ages to track down, and Brody gave me a new phone, as well as a beautiful resin cover that had fresh flowers pressed into it. X bought me a set of hand-crafted knives with my name engraved in the side. I gasped when I held one and X grinned. "Ergonomic handles, perfect for stabbing or slicing."

I laughed, stepping over to hug him, and then hugging the rest of my parents. "I love my presents. Thank you." Then it was Mouse's turn, and she tore into her presents like a savage.

Christopher leaned over, handing me a small, wrapped box. I took it and sat it in my lap, but didn't look at him. "Thank you."

"Come on, Enit. At least open it."

I huffed, peeling open the wrapping. It was a

jewellery box, and I flipped open the lid. Inside, there was a small crystal wolf carved out of rose quartz. It was beautiful, and would match my collection beautifully, which he knew. Because Christopher knew me better than any other person on the planet, which meant he *knew* that fighting Bohdie would hurt my feelings. Would make me angry. But he did it anyway because I was an Omega and he was an Alpha.

I narrowed my eyes at him and bared my teeth. "Thank you. You aren't forgiven," I hissed. I would forgive him, eventually, because I loved him too. But he could enjoy wallowing in his own stupidity for a while.

I realized the parentals had stopped talking, their eyes taking in me and Christopher like they could scent the unrest in the air. They'd want to know why, and then Christopher would tell them about Bohdie, and then they'd all freak out because I was me. Scared, naive Enit.

Carmen rolled her eyes, leaning close. "You totally owe me." She turned back to our parents. "Guys, I need to tell you something."

Walker groaned about her being pregnant, and Judge elbowed him. She frowned at them both. "No, I'm not pregnant. Jesus, give me some credit. No, apparently, I have two fated mates, and the other one is a Wendigo."

Holy shit.

Christopher's eyes whipped to our beta sister. You

could have heard a pin drop. They all started talking at once, but I was watching Carmen. Her chin was raised, her eyes defiant. She'd settled on this, and no matter what our parents or Christopher said, nothing would change her mind. I envied her certainty, her willingness to make a decision and stand by it.

No one would try and change her mind. No one would ever assume Carmen was too gentle to make up her own mind. No one would ever think that anyone, mate or not, was taking advantage of Carmen, mostly because she would be the first to castrate them.

I half-listened to them argue back and forth, but my mind was with Bohdie. I didn't think I was Bohdie's fated mate. I wasn't sure Omegas got fated mates, really. We were too rare, and too necessary to Pack harmony, for us to be fated to just one Alpha. Alpha males tended to be territorial, especially wolf Alphas. Fated mates were even worse.

What would I do if Bohdie met his fated mate?

I shook my head, chasing away the thought. There was no point borrowing this kind of trouble until it happened, but it slipped into the back of my brain to niggle at me. Despite the fact that Carmen had freaking two, plus my mom and Brody, fated mates were really, really rare. Maybe there was something in the water up here.

"I promise you, Dad, that he's a good guy. I would

slit his throat myself if I thought he was any danger to me or the Pack," Carmen said.

Brody huffed. "I don't know if I find that statement more reassuring or concerning."

"Makes me so fucking proud," X crowed. "Now let's have some damn cake!"

I stood, walking into the kitchen to get plates and spoons while X started talking about stabbing cakes. Judge walked in after me, grabbing out the milk and a few glasses. He watched me with his deep blue eyes. "You okay, kid? You're very quiet."

I looked up at my dad, his brows scrunched together in concern. Eventually, we would all look the same age. Maybe one day, we would look like their parents. Judge wasn't the most affectionate of my parents, nor was he the most responsible. But Judge was the one we called when Christopher crashed his motorbike when we were fourteen, because we knew he'd fix it without giving us a lecture. Well, he still gave us a look of disappointment, and that was worse than any lecture. He was the one who watched old black and white films with me, and gave me my first beer. He was the one who didn't treat me like I was some special and fragile Omega, made of glass. He was quiet, steady protection, and I needed that more than anything some days.

I chewed on my lip, but I nodded. "Just mad at Christopher."

He raised an eyebrow. "What for?"

"Being an overbearing asshole."

He let out a bark of laughter. "He gets that from X." He wrapped an arm around my shoulders and pulled me against him. "You sure that's all?"

I hesitated. If I told Judge about Bohdie and Stacey, there was a chance he'd tell everyone else. I wasn't ready for that shitstorm. "You promise you won't tell anyone?"

Judge frowned. "Hmm, depends. Does it affect your safety?"

I shook my head.

"Will you tell everyone else eventually?" This time I nodded. "Okay, I'll keep your secret."

I took a deep breath. "I'm dating someone. Well, two someones actually."

Judge raised both eyebrows. "Ah. So this is why Christopher has his tail in a knot. You're an adult, E. It was bound to happen. Do we know them?"

I shook my head, and then stopped. "Kind of. Bohdie is a lion Alpha from Stateside. And the other one is... uh, Stacey."

Judge whistled low. "The human girl that belongs to the Lycanthropes?" I nodded again, trying to swallow the lump in my throat. "Ah, now I see. She always had a crush on you, it was easy to see. Do you not want to tell the family? Because after the Wendigo conversation, I'm pretty sure they'd be relieved you're dating a girl."

I laughed, because he was probably right. But I wasn't ready for it to become a whole thing. I was enjoying it just being the three of us without any external pressures right now. "I know. Maybe when Carmen gets accidentally knocked up."

Judge laughed. "Hush your mouth, Sugar. I'm too young to be a granddaddy." He squeezed my shoulders. "You deserve to be happy. You take as long as you need. But if you accidentally get knocked up, I'm making a lion skin rug for your mama, okay?"

I smiled at Judge. "Thanks, Dad."

I wandered into the dining room, where everyone was talking loudly among themselves. I loved Family Day, and despite the fact I was mad as hell at Christopher, I wouldn't change my family for the world.

I sat down beside Tex, and rubbed my cheek on his shoulder. He kissed the top of my head and took the plates from me. "You okay, Sweetheart?"

I squeezed his hand. "I'm great."

He tilted his head, his unseeing eyes somehow always seeing too much. Finally, he nodded. "That's good. Give the knife to X before he massacres the cake with his bare hands."

We talked and laughed for a couple of hours, and then we had to head back to the Academy. Christopher held open the back door of the SUV and I paused. "I'm still mad at you, but I understand." He gave me a hopeful smile, but I shook my head. "You're going to have to work harder for my forgiveness than that, Christopher."

He huffed and closed the door, and I settled into the back.

I waited until we pulled out of Dark River before I let forth the floodgate of questions I had. I'd kept it contained because I wanted to provide a united front with Carmen, but now I needed to know.

"A Wendigo?" I asked casually.

"Yep," she said softly, looking at me in the rearview mirror.

"They sold their souls, you know."

"Yep."

"What shifter was he before that?"

"Wolf."

"Do you think if he'd been a normal shifter, and not a Wendigo, he would have been your wolf fated mate?"

"Maybe."

"Does that mean your fated mate would have been an old guy?"

"Probably?"

"Is there like, an exorcism or something we can conduct?"

She turned to look at me. "Are you serious?"

I shrugged. I wanted to know. Blame Stacey's curiosity rubbing off on me.

"Uh, I'll ask."

I smiled at her. "I'm happy for you though, Mouse. You deserve happiness, and a whole harem of hotties who light your fire."

She snorted. "I see what you did there."

Christopher huffed, and Mouse rolled her eyes. They started to argue, and I tuned them out.

I pulled out my phone, texting Bohdie.

Me: I'm still mad at you.
Bohdie: Baby, I am so sorry. I thought with my ego instead of my brain. Stacey has chewed me out already.
Bohdie: You've never been yelled at until you're yelled at by a genius. Feel like I'm 10 again.

I laughed softly. I knew that feeling.

Me: I hate being mad.
Bohdie: I hate you being mad. I'm going to make it up to you. Just wait til you get back to the Academy.
Me: I can't wai—

The phone flew out of my hand as Mouse screamed, or maybe it was me, and I saw the grill of a black truck ram the side of my door, crumpling it like tissue paper. The SUV flipped, and I saw my phone float past my eyes, before we crashed back to the earth and my head slammed into the window.

Then darkness reigned.

A VOICE WAS ROARING in my head. "Enit Baxter, open your feckin' eyes before I ground you for life."

Dad.

My eyelids fluttered and I saw X's face, blurred but I could feel his relief. And then the pain crushed my consciousness and I fell into the darkness again on a scream.

14

The lab door slammed open, making me jump. I looked up to chastise the intruder, but it was only Daniel. His eyes were wild and my heart started to thump in my chest. Something was wrong.

"Layla? The baby?"

He shook his head. "No, Stace, it's Enit. There's been an accident."

My vision shrunk to a pinpoint of light, and I swayed. "Is she dead?"

Daniel stepped up to me, dragging me into his arms. "No. Alistair and Micah are on their way to the crash now, but they're bringing her here, Stace. She's hurt real bad. Dad doesn't know that you and Enit are a couple. He wants you to prep for surgery."

My knees turned to jello.

Fuck. *Fuck.* I couldn't lose her now. I couldn't. What if she died on the table? What if I made a mistake? What if I killed her?

Daniel shook me lightly. "Stace, you are a brilliant surgeon. The best damn brain in the Northern Hemisphere. She is your patient. That is it—there's no room for doubt right now. Get it together, because your patient needs you."

I sucked in a deep breath, staring down at my shaking hands. I could do this. She needed me. My mate needed me right now.

I straightened my shoulders.

"Call Bohdie, tell him what's happening. Then get in here and help me set up the infirmary as an OR."

I tried to remember what my lecturers at medical school had said about vehicular injuries. Head injuries were likely. She'd need a CT scan. Broken bones definitely, so she'd need emergency X-rays. Alistair would stabilize her at the site, but she'd probably need to be anesthetized.

My mind whirled with all the things that needed to be done in a short space of time.

This would be field medicine at best, and even though the treatment room was well stocked, it was still going to be frontier medicine. I didn't have the instruments needed for brain surgery.

Panic began to burst through my calm again, at

least until there was a vampire in my infirmary, appearing out of nowhere.

Enit's father, Judge. He was a tall, scary guy with eyes that seemed almost like an abyss, and he scared the hell out of me. All of Enit's parents did, probably some kind of residual hindbrain fear of a prey animal. He stared at me with those eyes. "She's on her way here. What do you need? Anything. Alistair says you are the most capable of doing brain surgery, and I trust his judgement."

I almost shuddered with relief at the offer of equipment. I rattled off a list of things and he nodded. He paused, his eyes searching my face. "Can you do this? Enit told me about you two. It would be hard. No one will think badly of you if this is too much. I can find someone else, even if I have to do it by force."

I was frozen in shock. Enit had told her father about me? I swallowed hard and looked him in the eye. "I've got this. Get me the equipment and I will make sure she lives to smile at us both again."

Judge nodded, not second-guessing me. Then he was just gone.

I was primarily equipped for research, but I had all the appropriate imaging equipment, which was fortunate. I fired it up to have it ready.

I gathered everything I'd need, or thought I'd need, but my brain was fuzzing. I didn't really know what would be required or how I would react to a broken Enit.

The doors to the surgery flung open and a wild-eyed Bohdie was there. "Doc, where is she?"

"Stop, don't touch anything!" I grabbed a set of gloves and threw them to him. "She's on her way here. Help me sterilize everything. I know she's a supernatural, but infection could still be an issue when it comes to br-brain surgery." I stuttered on the word and I wanted to smack myself. There was no place for doubt now.

Do the surgery on the patient, not the person, Stacey, I chastised, still gathering things. Bohdie pulled the gloves on, even though he looked like he wanted to shake me for answers. But I had no answers. I had only questions and more doubt.

Would I still have a girlfriend tomorrow?

Was I as good as I thought I was?

"Tell me what happened," he growled, and I recited the little I knew. She'd been in an accident. She was critically injured. I scrubbed everything I could, wiping down the surfaces, anything that I thought could be contaminated. As I told him the little I knew, Bohdie's chest rumbled louder and louder.

Before he could fully shift into a lion, Judge was back with equipment that should have been impossible to get on such short notice, which probably meant he'd probably stolen it from a hospital somewhere. It was wrapped in a blue sterilized bundle and I breathed a sigh of relief. "Thank you," I muttered, unwrapping it and setting everything up on the side bench. To calm myself, I listed the name of every instrument and its purpose, then ran through the procedure for a craniotomy in my mind.

"They're here!" Daniel yelled from the elevator, and immediately I was running. I looked at Bohdie. "I need you to control your instincts, Alpha, and keep the fuck out of the way. I promise, as soon as I know anything I will tell you." I skidded to a stop in front of him, grabbing his arm so he looked at me. His eyes were glowing, telling me he was close to shifting. "I've got this. I will let you know as soon as I know anything, good or bad. But a lion in my surgery will guarantee her death. Go."

He snarled, kissed my forehead, and then strode to the wall. His eyes were burning holes in the elevator doors as we waited for them to open. The silence was overwhelming, a demon of its own.

Then they burst open and there were people everywhere. Alistair strode out first, a broken Enit strapped to a gurney, her neck in a brace. She wasn't moving, like she was already dead. My heart stuttered in my chest at the sight of her. She was banged up, like she'd been in a blender. She was bleeding in several places, and her leg was at an odd angle. I couldn't breathe.

After him came Micah, carrying Christopher in his

arms, whose tibia I could see poking out from his shin. Behind him was X, the big, scary, scarred vampire who struck fear in everyone except his kids. In X's arms was Carmen. She was slipping in and out of consciousness.

"Stacey," Alistair's voice snapped, and I jumped. I pushed the image of Enit's normal, uninjured face from my mind. I looked down at her like I would a stranger. I checked her pupils, flashing a light into her eyes and noticed their slow response.

"Any seizures?"

Alistair shook his head.

I grabbed the side of the gurney and strode down the hall. "I need CT scans and a full body X-ray now."

I had a patient to save. I caught Bohdie's agonized expression as I walked past. I had to save us all.

My hands were cramping. I'd been patching Enit up for hours. Layla was assisting me; she'd studied to be a nurse in her younger years. X was also assisting, looming over me like a malevolent presence, even though I knew he wasn't being threatening to me. It was just his generally concerned demeanor. As it turned out, he was a pretty decent surgeon. He didn't try and take over, despite the fact he looked at me like I was a child playing Operation. I found he was less... growly, if I talked through what I was doing. Like this was my final exam, except it wasn't my medical degree on the line.

No.

Couldn't think like that.

I'd cut out a bone flap from her head over the impact site, allowing her brain room to swell while the medication I'd had Judge steal from a hospital had a chance to work. I was glad she was a supe. In a human, I was pretty sure her injuries would have been fatal. She'd be dead. As it was, her body was repairing itself slowly.

I worked on her shattered pelvis, putting it back together the best I could. I should have paid better attention during my orthopedics rotation. I looked up at the screen that showed me her vitals and breathed a sigh. Finally, her intracranial pressure was lowering, and I judged it safe to replace the bone flap on her skull.

"Up you go now, kid. I can finish this part. Broken bones is something I can fix. You go fix her brain."

I began the careful process of replacing the section of bone I'd removed with Layla's help. I placed bolts on it to hold it into place and then stitched Enit's scalp over the top. I was happy with her vitals but I wouldn't be completely happy until she woke up.

In comparison to the brain, her other injuries were run-of-the-mill. A small incision, a pin here and there. Whatever X's medical skills were, he'd stayed up to date with the most recent techniques. He didn't want to get out the bone saw and chop anything off anyway, which I was relieved about.

I put on a soft helmet that would protect her head from impact, and finally, I was ready for her to come out. I'd fixed her as well as I could. I looked at the clock on the wall—it had taken eight hours. My whole body ached, but she was alive.

She was on a ventilator to clear the fluid from her lungs. She'd stay in a medically induced coma for a couple of days, and then we would really know the extent of any permanent damage caused today.

I collapsed to my knees and the big vampire was there to scoop me up. "Come on, kid. You did good. No one could have done it better. You need to rest."

I nodded, my hands shaking wildly. "You can put me down. My knees just locked."

Both X and Layla looked skeptical but I stood on thighs that trembled. I walked out the door and straight into Bohdie.

"Doc..."

"She's okay. She'll be alright."

He shuddered with relief, then picked me up in his arms and hugged me tight. "Come on, Doc. We'll go sleep in her dorm room for a bit. It'll be good to be surrounded by the scent of our mate."

He carried me like a child, past X informing her mom about her condition, past Carmen's mates. I wanted to tell Bohdie that humans weren't scent-based creatures, but as he slid me into her bed, her pillows smelling like the floral shampoo she loved, I hypothesized I might be wrong. I drifted off to sleep in the comfort of that scent.

15

———————

BOHDIE

A week had passed. Days where she lay there like she was dead, only the small line on her monitors telling me she wasn't gone. I sat by her bedside, ignoring school and my friends and phone calls from my family.

Cara would come in and bring me a sandwich, kissing my head, but that was it. The only times I cleared out and slept were when her parents arrived to sit by her. They all watched me closely, but didn't ask questions about why I was there all the time.

Stace worked herself to the bone, and I'm pretty sure she was doing it to avoid thinking about the great love of her life lying in a hospital bed, so close to death. I'd collect her late at night to take her up to Enit's room so we could sleep. Enit would want me to take care of her. I made sure Doc ate, slept, did all those things because if our situations were reversed, Enit would do the same thing.

How I fucking wished our situations were reversed.

Finally, they were ready to wake her up, or at least lower the medication keeping her in her coma. Everyone was here, and I hovered in the back corner, unable to leave. I looked at my hands, unable to watch. What if she didn't wake up?

I breathed in and out slowly, and an arm brushing mine had me looking over. I didn't know any of Enit's parents, and they didn't know me. But this one was young, tall and covered in tattoos, looking at the bed but *not* looking. This must be Tex, Enit's dad who was a blind python shifter.

"You're the boyfriend?" he asked softly.

I nodded, and then mentally slapped my forehead. "Yes," I murmured softly.

"We appreciate you making sure she isn't alone. Enit would hate being alone."

I swallowed the huge lump in my throat. "I couldn't be anywhere else."

Tex nodded, reaching down to grab my hand. He held it firmly, giving me an anchor. I swallowed hard, squeezing it as we both waited.

There was a relieved whoosh of exhaled breaths, and I let my own escape.

"Hey Enit," came Stacey's soft voice. I was glad

she'd be the first face she'd see. "I'm just going to check your eyes."

There was more shifting around in the bed, and I caught a glimpse of her. Her body had healed well, supernatural abilities aiding her recovery. She'd be even better after she shifted to her wolf a couple of times. But they were waiting until her brain recovered. Her head was shaved, and she looked even more elfin than normal. Her eyes searched the crowd of faces, her body tense and her anxiety ratcheted high until she spotted Mouse and Christopher, and she let out a little whimper. My heart cracked. I wanted to push through all these people, gather her in my arms and promise no one would ever hurt her again.

Her eyes met mine, and the look she gave me nearly broke my heart. My knees went weak, and Tex stepped closer, letting me hold myself up and not lose any face.

I walked through the crowd around her bed. I leaned down and put my head on the pillow beside her face. "Omega," I whispered in her ear reverently. "I can't tell you how happy I am to see your baby blues again." I nuzzled her cheek, and Stacey tutted softly so I didn't nuzzle too hard. "God, I love you. You scared the hell out of me."

She didn't smile, just blinking at me slowly. I pulled back and frowned down at her.

"Boh—" She grimaced and shook her head. "Boh—" Her eyes went wide with panic.

Stacey crowded beside me. "Hey, shh. It's okay. You suffered some damage to your brain in the accident."

Enit blinked wildly, her eyes looking at her parents, tears welling up.

"M—" she growled in her throat. "Mo—" She let out a soul-wrenching wail as her mom jumped forward on her other side.

"Baby, I'm here."

Stacey grabbed Enit's chin, holding her face so she had to concentrate. "Enit, given the location of swelling on your brain, I was concerned this might happen. I'll have to run some tests, but I think you have Broca's aphasia. The part of your brain that processes speech, and tells your brain to move your mouth to speak, was damaged. Do you understand? Squeeze my fingers once for yes and twice for no."

Stacey smiled when Enit squeezed her fingers. "That's good. This will get better, I promise. It isn't permanent. I refuse to let it be." She stood. "I'm just going to do a few more tests, okay? Simple yes or no questions. Let's change it up—if something is yes, give me a thumbs up. If no, shake your fist. Do you understand?"

Enit gave her the thumbs up.

Stacey went through a bunch of physiological tests, and apart from her speech, she was happy with how

Enit was progressing. I needed to process everything, but didn't want her to think I was running away. When her family crowded around her bed, I snuck out of the room after Stace.

Stacey leaned back against the wall outside her room and huffed out a relieved sigh. I hugged her close, even though I knew she wasn't a huge fan of touch. When she hugged me back, I knew she needed it.

We all needed touch sometimes.

"Tell it to me straight, Doc. Will she speak again?"

She drew back and looked at me. "Will it affect how you feel about her?"

I reared back, stepping away. "No! Jesus, Stacey. I love her. I'm not going to run away because things are hard."

Stacey eyeballed me. "Good. The Broca's aphasia could last for a short time as her brain heals itself, or it could be forever. We just don't know. The brain is a hard organ to predict."

I swallowed hard but nodded. "How do we help her?"

Stacey chewed her lip. "Speech therapy is best. She's the same intelligent person inside her head, she's just struggling to communicate. Encouraging her to speak will help, but with easy simple sentences." She sighed. "I'll have to research it a bit more. But she's going to be frustrated and angry, Bohdie. With brain damage, people can have changes in their temperament. You have to be prepared that she might not be the same Enit as before the accident."

I was devastated. But I just nodded and slipped back into Enit's room. Her eyes met mine, like she knew I left. I gave her a soft smile, but she didn't smile back. She frowned at me, then dragged her eyes back to her family, before they blinked heavily as she drifted back to sleep. Once her eyes closed, I let myself actually feel the devastation inside my soul. Stacey's words kept going around and around inside my head, but I wasn't going to worry yet. Time would tell what hurdles we'd have to overcome, and no matter who Enit was at the end of this, she'd always be mine.

Two weeks later, Enit threw the pen across the room. "No!" she growled, and Stacey frowned at her. She put the pen back on the table.

"Yes."

Enit snarled, and I pulled her out of her chair and into my lap. I snuggled her neck, breathing in her scent. Stacey and I had a good cop, bad cop thing going for Enit's recovery, and today was my turn to be the good cop.

"I know you're frustrated, but don't snarl at your girlfriend," I chastised softly. "Pick it up and we can try one more time. For every letter you write, I'll kiss you."

She looked over her shoulder and smirked. "Kiss. Anyway."

She was doing so damn good, slowly getting back her language, though she still forgot a lot of the connector words. Stacey said they would come back eventually as her brain relearned their importance.

I kissed her throat. "Well, maybe I'll resist this time." Both her and Stacey snorted in disbelief. Okay, that was fair.

Stacey had called, stalked, and threatened every neurologist she could google to create a recovery plan for our girl, and Enit's parents had been happy to let Stacey handle her recovery. Apparently, she'd impressed X during the surgery.

As Enit had recovered, other changes had become apparent. She'd damaged the nerves in her right hand, meaning her ability to write was shaky. She was learning to write with both hands now, but she got easily frustrated.

Scariest of all, was she seemed to have damaged the part of her brain that controlled fear and anxiety. We hadn't realized until she'd yanked out her cannula, climbed out of bed and fallen flat on her face. She hadn't been at all hesitant about standing on her broken leg or pelvis.

Stacey had wanted to prove the point, and she'd had me gather every Alpha in my class and bring them to her hospital room. Besides being a little surprised,

Enit had just given us a thumbs up and continued watching TV.

I didn't know if I was happy or terrified for her. I was glad she no longer had to live with the anxiety of being around Alphas, but fear was a necessary thing in life. It kept you safe. That being said, I'd walked into the room as a lion and roared, and her fear responses had elevated, so Doc hypothesized that it was only learned fear that had been obliterated. Which was still scary as fuck. She wasn't going to run in front of cars, or wrestle a grizzly bear, or jump from a plane without a parachute. But she would put herself in situations that she would have run screaming from before the accident. Like a damn room full of Alphas.

But she was still my Enit. When I'd taken her outside to the pond, she'd breathed such a sigh of relief to be back in the sun that she'd just lain against my chest and dozed. She still picked flowers, albeit with her left hand and not her right. She still made happy noises about the ducklings, which were full-grown ducks now. She frowned at the weeds in her medicinal garden, and I'd gotten some of the juniors to weed it.

Now, she bit her lip and held the pen in her right hand, growling when her hand shook. But still, she managed to scratch out a rough E.

"Yes!" she crowed. "Kiss."

I smiled and kissed her softly, and she mumbled

unintelligibly against my lips. I missed hearing her speak, missed having her wrapped around my body in the dark as she talked about everything and anything. But one day soon.

She turned her face to Stacey, who was beaming down at her, despite being the bad cop today.

"Kiss."

Stacey shook her head, leaning forward to kiss Enit softly. When she pulled away, she was smiling, but then turned it into a mock frown. "Two kisses for the one letter? Stop rorting the system and keep going."

Enit scrunched her face up in a pout, but she felt happier. She did a shaky N, and I squeezed her tight around her middle. She kept going and I felt myself swell with pride. Stacey cleared her throat.

"I think you should both move into my apartment."

I froze, and so did Enit. Then she shrugged. "Yes."

See, no anxiety at all. Guess I was going to have to be the worrywart for the both of us for now. "Are you sure? We'd be in your space." If I'd learned one thing about Stacey in our time together this last month, it was that she really appreciated her space and quiet. She got overwhelmed by large crowds and stupid people. I couldn't argue with that.

She hummed low. "Yes. I've thought it over. I don't find your presence unbearable and I lo—" She cut herself off, her eyes flying to Enit.

"Love," Enit whispered.

Stacey hummed. "Yes, I love you," she said softly. "So I think that I would be okay with you two living in my apartment."

I squeezed Enit tighter against my chest. "I'll go where you go, Princess."

Enit looked between us. "Yes."

I beamed at them both. "Looks like we're going to be housemates. I better go pack up my drum set."

I kissed Enit's cheek, slapped Doc on the back and skipped out of the room. I grinned as I heard Doc's frantic, "He's kidding, right? Enit? He's kidding?"

Ha. This was going to be amazing.

16

ENIT

Even in my wolf form, my right paw was broken. I couldn't run any faster than a lope and it was making my wolf insanely frustrated. Both the wolf and the human were happy to be roaming the woods outside the Academy though. With the threat that had been stalking my littermates gone, we were safe to roam around again. My parents had asked me to come home, but I'd managed to convince them that letting me stay in the Academy, where Stacey could do around the clock speech therapy with me, was the best course of action.

Well, Bohdie had convinced them. All I could do was think of complicated arguments and then say two words at a time. I whined, the frustration of the human permeating the wolf. I pushed it away, working on the meditation tricks that Bohdie had been doing with me.

Breathing in through my nose, out through my mouth. Usually when I did this exercise, I was resting against Bohdie's chest and I matched my breathing to the slow thumps of his heart.

As if I'd summoned him, a huge lion appeared like he was made of magic. Screw pulling a rabbit out of your hat, try pulling a lion from the Canadian wilderness and then I'll be impressed.

He tilted his head as if asking *Are you okay?*

I lifted my paw, and he bent down, licking it with his giant tongue. Honestly, it was as big as my damn head, rough like it was coated in velcro, and my wolf wanted to hack a hairball or something. She didn't enjoy the sensation. But human me was fascinated.

As a lion, Bohdie was absolutely massive. Ten feet long for sure, his golden mane was long and shaggy, and his teeth were as long as my paw. His paw was as big as my head. He was terrifying and my wolf wanted to run away screaming.

Then he'd roll onto his back, bat at a low-hanging tree branch like a damn tabby, and I'd be reminded that he was my sweet, playful Alpha.

He let out a low rumble, and the human me purred right back. His tail started to flick and he threw his head at the woods. Oh, we were going to play chasies. My wolf yipped with excitement.

He lay down on his belly, obviously giving me a headstart and I whirled around. I limped and loped my way further into the woods, stepping around fallen logs that I once would have hurdled.

It was good to be out of the infirmary. It was good that my siblings were basically whole again. I was happy about those things, I really was. But sometimes, when it was dark and moonless, I'd let the anger overtake me. Anger that I'd paid for Mouse's choices, and she was out living it up with her new fated mates, while my partners had to baby me while I recovered. We'd barely had a chance to cement our new relationship before the accident. Suddenly, one had to do surgery on my brain and the other one had to help me shower, for fuck's sake. It wasn't fucking fair and I wanted to scream and rage.

This anger was new. It burned in my chest until I wanted to growl and snap in my wolf form. I'd sent Christopher away early on, because his hovering was worse than my parents. His anxiety just made my anger worse, until we were feeding off each other and all I could see was the sadness in his eyes at what he'd lost. His sweet Omega sister who wouldn't have said boo.

Logically, I knew that I had changed. Something in me had broken, and it wasn't just my Broca's area, or whatever Stacey called the speechy part of my brain. It was hard to remember who I was before. I wasn't her now and I don't think I wanted to be her again. As long as my mates loved me, as long as I didn't hurt them, I was okay. We'd adapt, recover, and move on with our lives, even if that might be years after my siblings had recovered.

In those same dark hours, I wondered if Bohdie and Stacey wished I was the old Enit too. The girl from before, the girl they fell in love with. I'd never be that sweet girl again; could they love this damaged creature who rose in her place?

In moments like these, playing under the noonday sun, I knew that Bohdie at least still wanted me. I could see it in his eyes, in his touches.

I could hear his happy chuffing and I picked up my pace. Luckily for me, he wasn't much of a sprinter, preferring to prowl around. But his stride was... insane. Legit insane. Even at a lope, he ate up ground quicker than a human could sprint. And with my snowy white form, I wasn't great at hiding unless it was snowing.

I looked at a small outcrop of rocks, and headed toward it. I could hide, and maybe pounce on him as he strode past. Then he'd take me back to my room and work on his tongue exercises.

I sighed, knowing that wasn't true. He hadn't done anything even remotely sexual. I may as well have a pineapple down there instead of a vagina. I knew he was worried that my head would explode or something if we had sex, but my body had healed. I was *nearly* one hundred percent physically, it was just my brain that was fucked. Hell, maybe he could bang me into the wall and it would fix it. Like banging a DVD player. You know… if people still had DVDs.

As I got behind the rocky outcrop, I realized it was already occupied. A man sat there, his face painted muddy brown. Hmm. I paused, my sore foot raised as the guy spun to look at me. He was kind of pretty. A knit cap pulled low over his ears, a scruffy beard accenting his jaw. Piercing eyes that were a color I couldn't really name straight away.

Maybe he was a hunter. I sat down on my haunches, tilting my head at him.

He tilted his head back. "Man or beast?" he asked me softly, or maybe he muttered it to himself. That was odd. Someone who belonged would know that any animal they found in these woods would be supernatural. We didn't have many lions roaming Canada.

I eased forward. I wanted to smell the pretty man. I should tell Bohdie too.

I lifted my snout to howl.

The guy whipped out a gun and shot me.

He. Shot. Me.

My brain couldn't comprehend it, even as darkness sank in.

17

KELL

The wolf went down and I didn't hesitate. Scooping it over my shoulders, I hefted it up and ran for my truck. They never travelled alone, its pack would be here somewhere. This was an opportunity, but one misstep would end in me dead.

The truck came into view and I almost sighed with relief. I dropped the wolf heavily into the back and hogtied it, taping its jaws shut. I didn't know how long the tranq would work for, and I wanted to be well away from this compound before it woke up. I didn't want to destroy years of work by fucking it up at the last minute.

Tying it off quickly, I jumped into the driver's seat and gunned it out of the woods. I needed to make it back to the freeway.

A bloodcurdling roar echoed through the woods,

and I knew that I didn't want to face whatever made that sound. I skidded down a firebreak, the potholes throwing around the wolf in the back. Hopefully it didn't bounce right out and make this all for nothing.

Finally, I saw the turnoff back to the road, looking in the rearview mirror and seeing a motherfucking lion. Holy shit. Any doubt that I had the wrong place was thoroughly squashed. Unless the circus was in town and had an escapee, this was Eden. Fucking Eden.

After years, I'd found it.

Pushing the truck to its speed limit, I drove away from this backwater section of Alberta. I needed to get as far away as I could, otherwise I had no doubt that the monsters of Eden would find me. And then they'd do what they were made to do.

Kill.

I had a safe house for this moment. Off grid. I'd interrogate this monster in the back of my truck and then I'd plan. I'd finally have my revenge. My father's revenge.

My brain shied away from thoughts of my father. Instead, I cranked up the radio, listening to the music so loudly it threatened to burst my eardrums. But it kept the circling thoughts away.

An hour into my drive, I pulled over to a rest stop, grabbing a syringe from my glovebox. Leaning over the bed, I looked at the wolf. No, not a wolf. A werewolf. It was snow white, and bigger than a normal wolf. Definitely male, given its size.

I jabbed it with more tranqs, because the last thing I needed was a drugged-out wolf falling off my truck in the middle of the highway. Then I covered it with a tarp, so animal rights activists didn't call the Department of Wildlife Services or whatever they had up here in Canada. Explaining why I had a snow white fucking wolf in the back of my truck would be difficult.

Once the tarp was over the monster, I got back in my truck and drove solidly for another six hours. Those drugs would put out an elephant for a day, and my contact was pretty sure it would keep a werewolf out for a day or so.

The sun set, the darkness out here so all-encompassing that it was like driving through the abyss.

My phone screen lit up.

Frost: Did you do it?

Me: Mission success.

Frost: Holy fucking shit. I thought you were insane but you actually got one?

I'd met Frost on the dark web; he was scarily smart and also kind of fucking weird. But he'd believed me when I'd told him that monsters existed, and he'd been invaluable in helping me track shit. He believed in the mission. Believed in what I was doing.

ME: Yes. Going dark. Call you in twelve days.

THAT'S how long I thought I'd need to break the monster in the back of my truck. My father had taught me everything he'd known about these monsters, about Eden. I'd learned under his own hand how to make people talk, and I was going to make sure the wolf in the back sang like a canary before I was done.

I was light-headed and sleep-deprived when I pulled into the parking lot of a diner off the freeway. There hadn't been any movement under the tarp since I put the wolf back there, so apparently my contact was true to his word. I would stop real quick to refuel on coffee and food, just so I didn't drive into a tree.

Walking into the small diner, a pretty girl stepped up to me. "Morning, Mister. Table for one?" she cooed, her eyelashes fluttering.

I gave her a wide smile. "Thanks, near the window if I could."

"Sure thing."

She led me to a booth right in front of my truck and I thought I might tip her extra. I looked at her pert little ass under her denim skirt. Maybe I'd give her more than the tip.

"Can I get you coffee?"

I nodded. "And eggs, over easy. Extra bacon."

Her eyes watched my lips as I spoke, and I didn't need to be a mind reader to gauge her interest. When she brought back my coffee and put it on my other side so she could rub her breasts across my arm, it made it pretty fucking obvious too.

It was like five a.m. which was too damn early for flirting, but it had been a long time since I'd last got my dick wet, so maybe I'd take her up on what she was offering. The fact that there was hardly anyone in here except the odd trucker meant the food came out damn fast, and if I wasn't staying under the radar smuggling supernatural creatures, I'd give it a damn good Yelp review. As it was, I called for the check and the girl pouted at me. Her lips were cherry red, and her skin was smooth as cream. She looked tasty.

"You sure there isn't anything else I can get you?" she purred.

I looked her up and down, snagging on her breasts as she leaned over my table. "Sure, just looking for the bathrooms."

She eyeballed my face a little longer. "They're around the back. Let me show you."

I followed the woman—fuck, I didn't even know

her name—out of the diner and around the side of the building.

She looked over her shoulder and grinned. "Here's the ladies' restroom."

I laughed low, stepping into her body. "I ain't no lady, sweetheart."

"Oh, I know. Me either."

She grabbed my shirt and dragged me into the first cubicle. I had her skirt up and my dick buried deep before you could say "keep the change."

Today was really my fucking day.

THE SUN WAS COMING up before I turned onto the long road that would take me to the cabin I'd bought a couple of hours out of Yellowknife. I'd bought it with cash, it was entirely off grid. It was little more than a run-down shack with a fireplace, but it was all I needed. I was far enough away from any form of civilization that no one would hear a thing.

I pulled up in front of the cabin, burned up adrenaline running under my skin. I was so close to keeping my promise. So close to the end. Where I could just live my life for me, and not for a ghost.

I drew my gun, walking slowly around to the back of the truck. The drugs might have worn off and the last thing I wanted was to get mauled to death, or worse, turned into a monster too. I pulled back the tarp and sucked in an ice cold breath.

Fuck.

Oh fuck, fuck, fuck.

There wasn't a wolf in my truck anymore. There was a girl—she couldn't have been more than twenty, and she was naked. Worse still, she was blue. I touched her skin and it was like ice.

Shit, shit, shit. I'd killed a girl.

In the back of my brain was my dad's voice, telling me that it wasn't a girl, it was a monster, and one less of those in the world was a good thing. Still, I couldn't question a corpse, and she might know something useful.

I felt for a pulse, and exhaled the breath I'd been holding at the slow thump. Not dead. Thank fuck. I pulled her from the truck far more gently than I'd put her in there, shucking my jacket and wrapping her up in it. She was a tiny thing, and I could wrap her up tight.

I walked her into the cabin and laid her gently on the couch. I needed to start a fire and warm her up slowly. Dropping her in the shower would shock her heart or some shit. I wasn't a prepper, I was a bounty hunter, for god's sake. Still, I lit the fire as quick as I could, setting it to burn hot and hard. Then I grabbed all the blankets stored in this shithole cabin and dropped them on her.

I knew body warmth was best, but my mama hadn't raised me to take advantage of unconscious girls. Especially naked, unconscious girls. She was just going to have to warm herself, and I'd do what I could from out here.

I buried her so deep in blankets that I couldn't see her. And if I couldn't see her, I couldn't see the evidence of my mistake. My father used to say something was only a mistake if it could look you in the eye and tell you so. Everything else was just collateral in life.

He'd made it very obvious that he was talking about me when he was imparting that piece of life wisdom. I was his mistake.

Well, I was until he realized he could use me to exact his revenge against the monsters who had stolen his ability to walk. Who'd molded him into the man he'd become before he'd died. Mean. Bitter. A little too generous with his backhand.

The girl—I mean, the monster—made a noise, and my hand went to my gun. But she didn't even move. This was a clusterfuck and it was making me jumpy as hell.

I set another few logs on the budding fire, and already the chill was being chased away from the tiny cabin. It was just one room, with a bed, couch and fireplace at one end, and a kitchen and dining table at the other near the front door. That was it. The toilet was off the back porch, just an outhouse with an impressive hole in the ground.

When I'd bought it as a "rustic getaway," they hadn't been kidding.

Another snuffling noise drew my gaze back to the couch. The blankets shifted and then I was looking at bright blue eyes, so clear they were like looking into the heart of a gemstone.

Then she screamed behind the duct tape.

18

ENIT

It was good to know that the part of my brain that had broken my speech wasn't so damaged that I couldn't scream. I screamed and screamed as I drifted out of the foggy, drug-induced blackness, like I was wading through mud. But when I saw those dark eyes staring down at me, I knew I was in trouble.

As if the duct tape across my mouth didn't give it away. My lips felt raw and chapped, and I felt like I was suffocating behind it, even though I knew I wasn't. The man, the hunter, grimaced as he looked at me.

"I need to take that off, but you have to stop screaming. No one can hear you here, so all you're doing is making your throat hurt."

My eyes felt too large in my head as I stared up at him. It was the same hunter from the woods outside the Academy, I was sure of that. A shiver wracked my body. I was so fucking cold. My muscles ached, and my joints felt like they were frozen until I was nearly moaning in pain. What the hell had happened to me?

I also realized I was naked, and a whole new horror dawned on me. I'd been completely unconscious. Did this man, this human, take advantage of me when I was unconscious?

I wailed, pulling the blankets tighter around me like they could protect me.

"Oh shit, no. I didn't... I wouldn't do that," he growled, sounding offended.

I snarled at him, as he turned, grabbing a shirt from a duffle near his feet. "You were a fucking wolf. You were meant to be a man, not some tiny fucking girl." He grunted like it was my fault he'd abducted me. He threw me the shirt and turned his back. "Put that on. Don't try anything stupid. I mightn't rape women, but I'll still shoot you dead if you try to run."

Terror crawled along my skin, and I grabbed the shirt and pulled it over my head. Apparently, my fear response wasn't so broken that I'd forgotten the terror of a gun. Some fears were ingrained in your DNA. Fear of a predator, and when you were the top of the food chain, the fear of a gun barrel in your face was a visceral response. But when I looked at the man behind the gun, the fear was just gone.

Yep. I was still broken.

I crawled closer to the fire, seeking its warmth. I

was so fucking cold that I didn't think I'd ever be warm again. When he turned around, I was almost inside the hearth. "Move back or you'll burn."

He grabbed the blanket and dropped it over my head, but didn't make me move from where I was. His eyes were cold, but he *felt* like something different. He felt like regret.

I'd always been good at reading people. It wasn't some magical process, where I could read their heart's desires or some shit like half the Academy thought. No, it was more an extension of my Omega powers. An extension of the feelings everyone had.

He watched me with wary eyes, like I was about to jump up and tear his throat out. It might have been possible in my wolf form, but he was more likely to die from frostbite wherever the fuck we were. And I knew we were a long way from home.

I couldn't sense my siblings, the connections I'd had forever.

The air smelled different, crisper, less convoluted without scents of shifters and cars and people. It smelled like nature and the man in front of me.

He was tall, nearly as tall as Bohdie. He was broad, like he spent a lot of time working out. There was a small scar on his lower lip that looked like he'd been punched in the mouth and the split had healed rough.

"What." I growled at myself. I wanted to yell, "What

do you want? With me? With Eden Academy?" but the words wouldn't come.

He paused, waiting for the rest of the sentence but I just held his eyes. I gritted my teeth. "Why. Take?"

He frowned. "You don't speak English? You understood me before?"

I clenched my fists. I wanted to pound his face in, as my face flamed with embarrassment and rage. I lifted my hair, which was an inch or so long now, and showed my scar. "Accident. Brain."

His hand moved toward me like he wanted to trace the scar that wrapped around my skull but I flinched away.

"You've got brain damage? Fuck. Just my luck. I had to grab a fucking broken one," he grunted, and that rage that was simmering underneath the surface burst through my skin and I was springing up before I even recognized the action. I launched myself at his face, wrapping my legs around his waist as I pummelled him with my good hand, my broken hand gripping him uselessly. I got two good, crunching hits in before he peeled me off, tossing me back to the couch. He pulled his gun again and aimed it in my direction.

"What the actual fuck?" he yelled and I curled my lip.

"Not. Broken."

"Fuck me, fine. You're not broken. But you're fucking worse than useless to me. You're a damn liability. I should take you out and fucking put you out of your misery."

My body froze. Maybe that would be best. Bohdie and Stacey would mourn me, but they'd move on. So would my littermates. This strange, terrified half life would be over.

But even as part of me contemplated letting this hunter kill me, another part of me rebelled. Bohdie wouldn't be okay, because I was stolen under his watch. I knew enough about my Alpha to know that it would haunt him forever.

Stacey would never allow herself to love another person again.

Christopher and Carmen would both blame themselves, especially if they couldn't find me. I'd always be the missing piece of their lives.

My parents would tear apart the world looking for me. I knew that as well as I knew my own name. Mom especially would never recover if they found me dead. If they found me too late.

No, I couldn't give up. I needed to run.

I looked up at the man in front of me. He looked as cold as my bones felt. I looked toward the fire, and he followed my gaze. Then I launched myself at the door. I needed to get out of here, and once I was in the woods I could shift to my wolf.

I hurdled the back of the couch and made it to the door before a strong arm banded around my waist and another curled around my chest. I was a fucking wolf shifter, surely I was stronger than a human. But the weakness in my dominant hand meant that I was just flailing around.

"Stop or I'll jab you again," he growled.

I went dead limp. I'd rather be docile than that vulnerable again. He dragged me back toward the fire. He dropped me in front of the hearth and pulled his gun. Holding it on me, he reached into his duffle bag and pulled out a long chain. At each end of it was a cuff.

"We can do this the easy way or the painful way," he said in a hard tone. "This is silver. You're going to put it on, whether you want it or not. The difference will be that in one scenario, I give you this protective leather guard to wrap around your wrist so it doesn't burn through your flesh. I'm happy for it to go on either way, the rest is up to you."

I glared at him, and held my hand out for the brace.

I went to put it on my useless right wrist, but he whistled. "Other wrist, little monster. I've noticed you favoring one over the other."

I bared my teeth at him again and tried to wrap it around my left wrist with my useless right hand. With the shaking and my still numb fingers, it was an exercise in pointlessness. "Can't. Hand fucked."

He snorted a laugh, and then I watched him visibly

swallow the sound down. "I'll do it, but honestly, if you bite off my hand, I won't be so nice."

I scoffed but I held out my arm, refusing to look at him. Like ignoring my damn abductor was going to bother him. This wasn't fair, but since when was life fair? I felt the heat of the silver go around my wrist, and while the effects of silver on shifters had been largely exaggerated by Hollywood, it did sting a little. More like an allergy than poison. Plus, it inhibited our ability to shift. It was more of an inconvenience— unless you shot us with it. A bullet was a bullet, no matter your species.

Then he surprised the shit out of me by securing the other end of the four foot long chain to his wrist. "Just in case you get any ideas about shooting me. Good luck trying to run through the wilderness dragging my ass."

I was so fucking screwed. He pointed at me with the gun again. "Go over there and warm yourself." He sat on the couch as I kneeled in front of the fire, keeping one eye on him behind me. How the hell was I going to get out of this?

I looked around the cabin, which was barely more than one room. It would be hard to sneak out of a single room. Who was I kidding, it would be hard to sneak anywhere.

I didn't think anyone would come to find me soon

either. This guy was… maybe not a professional, but he was organized.

I looked back at him and repeated my question. "What. Want." The situation was making my speech worse.

He seemed to understand fine though. "Eden is made of monsters. Those monsters destroyed my life. Now I'm going to destroy them."

I looked at him incredulously. I tried to judge his age. Maybe mid-twenties? Not very old, I didn't think. Maybe Eden, the organization that founded the Academy, had done something before they'd come to Canada. But I knew Micah, Alistair, and Locke. I knew they wouldn't hurt some random person for no reason.

"Lies."

The guy snorted, waving me away. "You're just brainwashed." He fell silent and I reached out to my littermates, hoping our bond would work over these long distances. But there was nothing. I pulled my knees up to my chest and wrapped my arms around them.

"I need to know how to get to them. How to break apart their world like they did mine," he said softly, more to himself than to me. "You were meant to be a guy. I could torture a guy for information. Not some pretty, waifish girl who can't speak." He raked a hand down his face.

I glared daggers at him. "So sorry."

He laughed, and then smothered the sound again. "Get up. I'm hungry."

As I stood, his shirt falling down to my knees, I watched his eyes travel up my body, snagging on my surgery scars. I may as well have been wearing a circus tent, but I searched his face for anything lecherous. But he just turned away and walked toward the kitchen, dragging me along like a faithful puppy.

I was so screwed.

19

Bohdie paced back and forth through the room, temporarily as a man and not as a lion. He'd lost control of his shifting after Enit had been taken, and he was just as likely to shift into a lion in the middle of the conference room as he was to stay human.

For the first time in nearly fifteen years, a bounty hunter had stolen a member of Eden. The fear in the room was a palpable force that kept stealing my breath. The room was filled with people, including some of Enit's parents, plus her pseudo-grandfather and Convocation member Alexander, who was a goddamn dragon. He scared the shit out of me and I was worried that he was going to snap, and rip Bohdie in half.

Bohdie was on the phone too, and whoever was on

the other end was trying to appease him but the Alpha lion was without his Omega and he was spiraling hard. I was spiraling hard.

"Get Talbot on it. Yeah, Reese is here too but Vance, I need this. I'll owe you whatever you want. I'll become a soldier or come home or fucking pledge my allegience to the Sleuth, but I need to find her. She's my Omega, my mate. I need her," he growled and I paused. So did everyone else in the room.

His mate. I didn't think they'd actually made the leap yet to perform a mating ceremony, but it was good to know that he was thinking forever, because so was I.

If we ever got her back.

Whatever the guy at the other end of the line was saying calmed him a little, and I drew my gaze from him to the rest of the people in the room. Half the vampires were missing, searching the surrounding area and the cities further out. The Alpha of the Nîso Pack was also missing, along with Carmen's mate Bobby, as they searched the woods for a scent trail.

Everyone was doing something, except me. I was lost. I didn't know how to help. All the founding members of Eden were here, including all my parents but Layla, who was home with the kids. The humans who had funded Eden were all here: Lincoln, Reese, and Vincent with their mate Celeste, who was a snow leopard shifter. Lincoln was on the phone to some contacts in the States and Reese was on a computer, doing whatever the hell he did.

If there was a human who could keep up with me, it was Reese. He was a genius, especially when it came to technology. It wasn't my area of interest, but I could appreciate the art of his creations.

As if he could feel my gaze, he looked up. "Stacey, come and look at these. Maybe your mind will pick up a pattern that mine is missing."

I doubted it, but I was happy to have anything to do. I sat down beside him, looking at what I assumed was a log of security incursions.

"This shows everything that bounces off our secure firewalls. The numbers beside them are origin VPNs and their location. The better the hacker, the more difficult it is tracking their origin location." There were hundreds, from random spam to more tactical attacks. But I couldn't see any patterns as Reese scrolled through the logs. "I'm hoping I can find something to trace from here while Talbot puts a crawler through the dark web for any reference to Eden or shifters. It'll take time to sift through all that metadata though."

He may as well be talking in another language, but I could do patterns. I watched the numbers scroll down, as my brain did what it did best.

Finally, after what could have been minutes or hours, I shouted, "Stop." Everyone turned but I ignored them. "These all say New York."

Reese nodded. "Yeah, it's a popular location to bounce through because there are literally hundreds of millions of VPNs just in that city. It would be hard to pinpoint any one person in that mess."

I grabbed his mouse, and he gasped a little. Lincoln huffed a laugh under his breath.

"Here. These suburbs are all within a twenty-mile radius of each other, like he's bouncing their first location somewhere close to home. Can we triangulate that?"

Someone muttered something about a nineties technothriller, but Reese was already on it. "I didn't think about triangulating differing VPSs," he grumbled to himself. He pulled the data from a bunch of logs and then pinpointed the locales on a map, narrowing it down more and more until he found an exact location.

Celeste shook her head. "The internet is a scary place..."

"The house belongs to a Cedric Frostmore," Reese said, but Alexander was already on the phone.

"I need the occupant of this address brought to me. Now." Alexander's voice was an order, and even without being a shifter, I wanted to follow his command.

He looked around the rest of the room. "Now we wait."

·   ·   ·

WE ALL LOOKED at the photo of an average human on the screen. He had a black eye, and you could see a hand holding him by the scruff of his shirt. What you couldn't see was Enit anywhere.

Alexander had given his contacts terse orders to get the guy on a jet and bring him to Eden immediately. I thought I knew everything there was to know about the Academy, but apparently there was a holding cell deep within the lower levels of the compound. Below the infirmary, which I'd thought had been the lowest level.

Apparently, I was wrong.

I was a healer, and I knew that I should have a visceral opposition to the idea that this guy would be tortured when he reached us, but I couldn't find it in me to care. Even if he had nothing to do with Enit's disappearance, he was a human who was up to something. You didn't repeatedly try and break through a firewall without a good reason. I was nervous and anxious, and when Bohdie reached out to hold my hand, I grasped it like it was my last lifeline.

Enit had been gone for an entire day. Twenty-four hours in the hands of god knows who, someone who could be assaulting her. Torturing her.

Micah looked toward me and Bohdie. "Go get some rest. We'll call you if there are any developments. Stacey looks like she's about to drop."

I wanted to argue that I was fine, but logically I

knew that my body was exhausted. I could feel it in the heaviness of my limbs. I also knew that Micah was getting Bohdie to rest in a way only another Alpha understood—he was telling him to take care of his Pack. I was his Pack.

The idea filled me with more contentment than I thought it would. Once we got the heart of our Pack back, I wouldn't take it for granted.

Bohdie led me from the room, across the drive and into my apartment. No one had told me that relationships would feel like this, that they'd be fraught with so much drama.

Though really, drama had chased me since I was a child. Maybe I wasn't fated to be truly happy.

We stepped into the living room, and my thoughts spiraled darker and darker. Maybe I was cursed, though I was a scientist and didn't believe in that shit. But still, it was kind of hard to argue. Maybe it was Enit who was cursed. Maybe it was the whole supernatural race, though I assumed there were those who had average lives.

Bohdie grabbed me by the shoulders and turned me to look at him. "We'll get her back, Doc. And then we'll be there as she heals, just the same as last time."

I looked up into his face and did something I hadn't done since I was four. I cried. Great, soul deep, aching sobs that bubbled up from my diaphragm and spilled over my cheeks. Bohdie stared at me agape for a second and then dragged me into his arms. I stood in them stiffly, as embarrassed as I was devastated. I was crying like she was dead, but I'd know if she was. Not because we had a metaphysical bond—that was more likely to be Bohdie's domain one day—but because I would hear Christopher and Carmen's grief hit them like a palpable blow. They were metaphysically connected. Enit had told me that when they were younger, they'd been able to talk to each other using ESP, like a Pack bond created from necessity. They'd grown out of it as they aged and had settled into easy lives filled with love, but in times of great stress, the connection could still operate over short distances. And they knew she was alive. They mightn't be able to communicate with her, but they could feel she wasn't dead. It wasn't much of an assurance, but it was the best we'd get.

I let Bohdie hold me, knowing he needed this connection just as much as I did. He needed to hold what remained of his Pack, otherwise he'd feel even more adrift than I would. At least, that's how I justified it to myself, this complete collapse of decorum. I was a healer, and I knew the only thing that would make the Alpha better was the return of his Omega. Taking care of me would be like putting a bandaid over a bullet wound, but it was all I had to offer him at the moment.

"It's okay, Stace. It'll be okay," he soothed, stroking my back like I was a child. There was nothing sexual about the contact—we still didn't feel that way about each other and I doubted we ever would. Enit was everything, for both of us.

If she never came back...

I doubted that either of us would survive. Oh, we'd live, but we wouldn't *live*. We'd be shells of the people we were, because Enit had made me who I was today. She'd been my touchstone for longer than she knew.

She needed to come home. They needed to rescue her *now*.

Because I needed her more than anyone knew.

20

KELL

I didn't know what to do with the broken werewolf who was still sitting on the rug in front of my fire like a faithful fucking hound.

She hadn't spoken to me since I'd made her a peanut butter sandwich. Not that she'd spoken to me much before that anyway. I eyed the scar that crowned her skull, just visible under her stark white hair.

"How'd you get the head injury?" I grunted, mostly because the silence was getting to me. Her blue eyes flashed but she stayed stubbornly silent. I ground my back teeth, trying to rein in my glare. "I could make you talk, you know? It might be slow, but I don't have anything else to do for the next twelve days."

Her body froze. "What then?" she asked, her voice rough from lack of use.

It took me a while to understand she meant what

would happen after twelve days. I shrugged, mostly because I didn't have a fucking idea either, but I hoped it looked more mysterious than stupid. "That's up to you." She snorted, and I narrowed my eyes. "What's that supposed to mean?"

"You. Dead. Just don't know."

I reared back in surprise, firstly because that was the longest sentence she'd said to me yet, and secondly, because of the look of pity in her eyes.

"Better you kill."

What the fuck was wrong with this girl? "Are you actually sitting there trying to convince me to kill you? Because that's the exact opposite of what normally happens."

She raised an eyebrow, her expression saying "Kidnap many girls, do you?" But her face dropped into a grimace. She pointed to herself. "Parents. Deadly."

This was the worst cryptic shit I've ever heard. "Fuck! If I get you a pen and paper, can you write to communicate?"

Her eyes got big and wet, and I thought that maybe she was about to cry. It surprised me, because this whole time, she hadn't cried or pleaded or any of the other girly bullshit you'd expect to happen when you *kidnapped* someone.

She blinked away the dampness in her eyes, and

lifted her hand. She was holding it wrong, her fingers trembling. "Broken."

The desolation in her voice tugged at something in my chest, and I smothered it down. She was my captive. A monster. Instead, I cleared my throat. "I've got time. Talk as slow as you damn well need." I leaned back against the couch, the silver chain snaking over my thighs and up to my wrist like a deadly adornment. "So your parents are deadly? Werewolves too?"

She screwed up her nose. "Shifter." She pointed to herself. "Wolf shifter."

A surprised laugh burst past my lips. "Are you chastising me about the correct terminology right now?" She shrugged, her eyebrow raised. "Apologies, little monster. Are your parents wolf shifters too?"

She shook her head, and the smile she gave me would have looked just as natural on a wolf. "Vampires."

Ice flooded my veins. Oh fuck. Fuck, fuck, fuck. Her eyes taunted me with just how bad I'd fucked up by plucking this wolf from the woods.

I didn't know a great deal about the supernatural world. It wasn't something you would search in an encyclopedia in your local library. The information I'd gleaned had been from my Dad before he'd died, and from the dark web, courtesy of Frost.

And the one thing that both these sources agreed on was that you did not fuck with vampires.

They were virtually indestructible, insanely blood-thirsty, and everything a human was not. She wasn't wrong—I didn't stand a chance against vampires, if she was telling the truth about her parents. She was also right in that I probably should just cut my losses, kill her now, and escape far across a large body of water while I still could.

"Why the fuck do vampires have a wolf as a daughter? Are you like, an afternoon snack?"

She bared her teeth at me, fire in her eyes that lit up her whole face and made my heart thump in my chest. Not in terror, but in something else that I knew would result in me being dead if I examined it too closely.

"Rescued. Skin traders."

My eyebrows shot up to my hairline. "Vampires rescued you from the black market? The fuck? You realize none of this makes any sense, right? Like when you see those lions adopt baby lambs. It's weird."

She shrugged. Maybe she was lying, but what did she have to gain from that, really? There was a better chance that I'd now kill her and run, rather than letting her go. She'd be a loose end that would defi-nitely result in my death if I just let her go.

The idea of killing her was getting harder to think about though. "Are you going to tell me how you got your head injury now?"

She shook her head, pointing at me. "Why?" She

waved a hand around the room, and I didn't think she was referring to the meaning of life. "Why take me?"

I turned away from those eyes that seared into me. "What the hell is this, twenty questions? We aren't playing any elementary school games right now, Wolf."

She turned back to the fire and I battled the discontent that overwhelmed me. "I can't answer your questions, because otherwise I'd definitely have to dispose of you and I don't make a habit of kidnapping and murdering girls."

She gave me a droll look, like she thought I was an idiot. I was inclined to agree today. "Fine. Do you have a name at least?"

She turned back to me, her head tipping to the side, exactly the way the wolf had done twenty-four hours ago before I shot it full of tranqs. I didn't like seeing comparisons between the girl and the wolf. Because while she was sitting there, on my rug, in front of my fire, I could pretend she was just a pretty human and not one of the monsters that had destroyed my life.

She hesitated a moment longer, before breathing out a sigh. "Enit."

Enit. I mentally rolled the name around in my mind; I liked it. It was almost old-fashioned but not quite. It spoke of gentleness and tranquility. I wasn't sure if the girl in front of me represented either of those things for me.

She looked at me expectantly, and against any sane judgement, I said, "Kell."

Then she smiled at me and it was like she'd punched me in the solar plexus. Her smile lit her whole face, making her eyes sparkle and her cheeks round and her pretty cupid's bow lips curl. She was already pretty when she was glaring, but right now she was a work of art.

For a moment, it was like I hadn't fucking stolen her from the organization I'd vowed to punish. We were just a man and a woman.

She lifted her chin. "Pretty."

I cleared my throat and tried not to blush like a loser. "Thanks."

Then she turned back to the fire and I attempted to get my pulse—and my goddamn mind—under control. We sat in silence for a long time, until it grew late into the night and I was fighting to keep my eyes open. I'd been running on adrenaline for an entire day and my body was starting to crash.

"We should go to bed," I murmured, and her whole body froze up like she'd been taxidermied. "I'll drag the couch closer and sleep on it, and you can have the bed."

She lifted her cuffed wrist. "Take off, sleep wolf?" she said hopefully, and it was my turn to snort.

"Unlikely. Come on, I'll push, but I can't be dragging you along too." I stood, looming over her in a way that made my heart thunder. "I promise I won't hurt you. We both need sleep and I promise you'll be safe."

I expected her to snort, to argue, to call me a liar. But she just stared at me for a moment and then nodded.

"Pee."

I flushed red. "Uh, yeah. Of course. Come on, unfortunately it's outside." I looked down at her feet, knowing she'd have to walk in the freezing conditions barefoot. I tried to tell myself she was a captive. A monster. One of the people I'd vowed to exterminate to avenge my father's death.

But another part, a softness I'd inherited from my mother, that I'd thought was well and truly dead, reared its head. This girl wasn't the enemy. She was just another victim.

We walked slowly toward the door. "How old are you?"

She eyed me suspiciously, then nodded. "Eighteen."

I blew out a breath between my teeth. I was twenty-six, even though I felt like I was ninety-six somedays. She was so fucking young. I didn't say anything else, and when I threw open the back door, the cold air swirling around us made her skin rise in goosebumps. I'd drop my vendetta for a night. Just one night. We both needed rest. Tomorrow, I would make the hard decisions.

"If you like, I can carry you down to the bathroom. I don't have any spare boots."

She gave me that long look again, staring at her own feet. They were cute. Someone had painted her toenails baby blue.

She nodded and raised her hands. I scooped her into my arms and walked through the snow to the latrine.

Her nose twitched, and she gave me a look somewhere between disgust and disappointment. "Smell like sex."

I was glad we were outside in the dark so she couldn't see the red of my cheeks, or the shame that probably clouded my face. Instead, I just cleared my throat. "A guy has needs."

She was tense in my arms, and she basically threw herself out of them as soon as we reached the toilet. She slammed the door in my face, the chain stretching underneath it, and I took the moment to move around the side of the small building and take a piss.

I was just stuffing myself back in my jeans as she marched out of the outhouse and up the path toward the back door. I took long strides to catch up. Her feet must have been like ice and I looked at her face, at the hard line of her jaw, confused as fuck. "Want me to carry you?"

She gave me a sharp shake of her head as she marched over the porch and pulled the door open. In the light of the room, I was still confused. I thought we'd, I don't know, built enough of a rapport that the next eleven days weren't going to be a shit fight, but maybe I was wrong. It was probably too much to ask, seeing as I stole her.

She watched me move the couch and then climbed into bed without another word, her cuffed hand behind her and her back to me.

It was better this way. Rule number one of being a fucking vigilante was don't get attached to your hostages.

But as I watched her tense back muscles ease into sleep, her body softening and her breaths coming in even little puffs, I knew that that would be harder than it sounded.

ENIT

I would never truly understand my wolf. I mean, she was me and I was her, but still, our instincts were sometimes wildly different. Like pouting because your freaking abductor smelled like sex with another woman? That was absolutely ridiculous, not to mention possibly deadly. The wolf was meant to protect me, even from myself—especially as an Omega—but maybe she was as broken as the rest of me.

Still, I hadn't spoken to Kell since last night, accepting the food he gave me with a grunt and walking through the freezing snow in my bare feet so he didn't have to carry me. Granted, he hadn't pushed anything since last night, studiously ignoring me like I wasn't there. Fine by me. We could do this dance until my parents arrived. I had no doubt that they would be here in a few days. I'd been gone forty-eight hours.

Christopher would be going crazy, Brody would be tracking me across borders by now. I shuddered to think of the killing spree that Lucius and X would be on, and could only hope that Nico or Judge was there to temper them before they inadvertently started a war.

When Kell handed me another peanut butter sandwich, I screwed up my nose and shook my head. The guy didn't know how to make anything else and as hungry as I was, I couldn't stomach my seventh sandwich in two days.

"Too good for a sandwich, little monster?" Kell teased, and I looked up at him.

I tilted my chin up haughtily. "Yes."

He threw back his head and laughed, and it was a sound that skittered down my nerve endings and made them tingle.

"Kitchen's yours. If you can do something better, go for it. Pretty sure some of that canned food rolled out with the first computer, but you're welcome to it." His tone said he didn't think I could, but I'd inherited the same stubbornness as the rest of my littermates, even though I kept it better tempered. Well, I had before.

I stood, smoothing his shirt down my thighs. I probably needed a shower, but I didn't think I wanted to be naked in a shower attached to my kidnapper. Though, I guess as far as abductors go, he'd been okay.

And he was kind of hot. Though I wanted to growl at myself for even thinking that.

I strode over to the kitchen and looked in the cupboards. Most of the cans didn't even have labels. Kell stood behind me so that the chain was slack. But then he was the one who'd made me put the cuff around my good wrist, so he had to be close.

I grabbed a container down and opened it. Flour. Nice. I could work with this.

Kell cleared his throat, and I turned to look at him. Pink flushed his cheeks and his eyes looked too bright. "Here, I'll hold this for you," he said, grabbing the canister of flour.

I grabbed a silver sachet that had the ambiguous title of "stew" printed on the side. That was it. Well... I could work with that too.

"Stand," I said, pointing to a few feet away from me, because I was finding his scent intoxicating. He was beginning to smell delicious and it was ruining my good sense.

I made a dough out of the flour and some warm water, happy that I could use my bad hand enough that it didn't make much difference to the mixture. I left it off to the side and opened the stew. It smelled a bit like dog food, but hopefully I could season it and it would be fine.

I worked silently, taking a ball of dough, rolling it flat in my palm, adding some filling and then closing it up. I pointed to the pile of dough, lifting my chin to tell Kell to do it too.

"Seriously? You make it look easy but I have my doubts."

Still, he gave it a go, saying fuck more times than making a stuffed flatbread really needed, and I had to admit, his first one looked a little mangled. I gave him an encouraging smile and he tried again.

This was so damn messed up. But I was starving for something hot and not stale, so I'd look past the fact that I'd probably had some kind of crazy mental break in thinking this was okay.

It might have been that my wolf was broken and was insanely attracted to him. Might have been that the Omega in me was drawn to the sadness that hung around his eyes, even when he was smiling. It might have been because of his dark hair that seemed to be artfully messy all the time, plus he had a jawline so sharp I lost my good sense. What I had left after the accident anyway. He was a type of danger that had stalked me my entire life, and now that I was too broken to feel fear, something else had popped up in its place. Lust.

Finally, I had a plate filled with tiny, floured flatbreads and even Kell looked impressed. He picked up the griddle and some oil that had been hiding in the back of the cupboard, and I grabbed the plate of food.

He reached in to put the griddle directly on the

coals of the fire, slopping a bit of oil in. At least he wasn't completely useless. But as I stopped in the middle of the room, my wrist spasmed, my hand going dead and the plate falling to the floor.

"No!"

I dived for it, but missed, and the stuffed breads landed all over the floor. A mess. Like my fucking life. "No. No," I whispered, dropping to my knees and peeling them off the old, dirty floorboards. Sadness welled up in my chest, and it wouldn't be contained.

Not about the food. Or the fact I was being held hostage. Or even the fact my body was fucked from the accident.

It was *everything*. The sadness wailed past my lips and spilled from my eyes.

Kell was suddenly there, righting the plate. "Hey, no, it's okay. They'll be okay." He sounded nearly desperate as he grabbed them and piled them high on the plate again, ignoring the black specks of dirt and other stuff I didn't want to think about. "The fire will burn all this off. Enit, it's okay."

I shook my head. It wasn't okay at all. Not even a little okay. I just curled into a ball, my body bowed over my knees, and continued to cry. He took them over to the fire, dropping a couple in like he could prove to me that it was okay. Like it was just the bread that I was crying over.

I could smell them cooking, but sadness had

curdled my stomach. Arms wrapped around me, picking me up like I weighed nothing. He dropped me in front of the fire, grabbing out a flatbread, holding it in front of me.

"See, totally fine," Kell said, as he juggled it from one hand to another. He took a bite, breathing around the hot bread. "Holy shit, this is amazing."

I turned my face away, trying to make myself stop crying but I just cried harder.

"Fuck, Enit. Don't cry like that." He sounded almost pained, and then he surprised us both by dragging me onto his lap and wrapping me in his arms like I was a child who'd fallen over and gotten a boo-boo. His arms looped around me, my tearstained face pressed into his chest. "It's going to be okay."

The outrageousness of that comment made me drag in a ragged breath. "No." I turned on his lap, realizing we were now sitting on the couch. "Not okay. Maybe never okay."

I just wanted fucking connecting words and whole sentences. To be able to speak without having to pause and force my lips around it. I wanted to be able to hold a plate. I wanted to be at home in the arms of my partners and not in the arms of a stranger who made me feel things I had no damn right feeling.

His face shuttered, and he heaved in a breath. "Okay. You might have a point there. But this moment, right here, right now? I can fix that." He lifted the fried bread to my lips and I opened my mouth instinctively, taking a tiny bite. I ignored the intimacy of the action, especially in supernatural culture, and just enjoyed the warmth of the crisp bread against my tongue.

I made a small hum of satisfaction, and I felt his chest rumble. "See? They might not be perfect, but we can make them work."

I wondered if he was talking about the food or the situation we found ourselves in. Because there were only ten days to go on his timeline, and he hadn't told me what his endgame was. Maybe he was a freaking sociopath and toying with me like a cat would a mouse. I nodded, because what did I even have to say to that really?

I slid from his lap and sat in front of the fire, placing some more flatbreads on the griddle. I had to close off that small part of me that hoped my life would be anything but a shitshow, and just take it as it came. If you had no expectations for tomorrow, then you couldn't be disappointed.

I felt Kell's eyes burning into the back of my head as I easily flipped the flatbreads. Cooking was something I'd always used as a coping mechanism, right back from the very first time X had sat me on the kitchen bench and made pancakes with me. I clung to the methodical actions of cooking. Measure, stir, cook, cool, eat. I worked in the Immortal Cupcake as a baker during the holidays too. It was therapeutic, like a safety blanket.

"I'm not going to kill you or anything." He sounded pained by the fact. "I... can't. It wouldn't be right and it's not what I signed up for."

I finished the bread and pointed to them. Instead of grabbing them and moving them back up to the couch, he climbed down onto the floor with me. We sat cross-legged, eating silently, until I stood up and pointed to the bed.

Kell didn't argue that I was dragging him to bed at what was probably seven, but it was dark out. He stoked the fire a bit, moved the griddle onto the hearth and put on a large log. Then he followed me to the bed, lying down under the thin blanket on the couch while I snuggled under a slightly thicker down one on the bed.

I lay there in silence, pretending to sleep, until I wasn't pretending anymore. I was in purgatory, and sooner or later, I was either going to die or go back to my life.

I just couldn't stand the waiting.

22

BOHDIE

I'd argued with Alexander until he'd allowed me to stay. Arguing with the head honcho of all head honchos probably wasn't a great idea for a shifter—not to mention going toe to toe with a dragon—but I wanted to be here. I wanted to see the fear in this guy's eyes and listen to every single word he had to say.

Within minutes of the chopper setting down, the guy had been bundled downstairs and put into a holding cell in the very lowest level of Eden Academy. You had to input a special code in the elevator to even get this low.

I was waiting with my back pressed to the wall of the interrogation room, and I jumped as the heavy metal door slammed open. Three guys in tactical gear dragged in a hooded figure, who seemed to have bloodstains on the front of his shirt and made the air reek of fear. They shoved him in a chair and pulled off the hood.

Although he smelled of fear, he hid it well, his eyes bouncing around the room until they landed on me. Or more to the point, the Academy crest on my shirt. Then his eyes got real wide.

"Holy-freakin' shitzle. Eden. You guys fucking exist. I mean, I knew you existed but I thought you were just some preppy little school for rich kids, but you aren't, are you? He was fucking right, but this is insane." He sucked in a deep breath, and then kept going. "Are you guys all, you know, supernaturals? What kind of supernaturals? I mean, I've heard glimmers about it on the dark web, but there are people on there who claim to have seen Elvis too, so you can't just trust their unverified information, but this?" He waved a hand. "This definitely verifies everything."

He paused, his eyes traveling all over the room like they were detached from their sockets. It was like he was trying to catalogue everything all at once.

"Are you Cedric Frostmore?" Alexander asked, probably a little redundantly. The guy's eyes flicked back to Alexander and he froze, his eyes getting even wider, until I could see the whites around his irises. Yeah, looks like his hindbrain just caught up to his situation.

Enit's mother, Raine, stepped toward the guy. Even

I could admit she was pretty, and it was hard to remember she was Enit's mom when she looked around my age.

She smiled sweetly at him, but there was a hint of something darker in there. "Cedric, isn't it? You know, he was my favourite character in Harry Potter. Such a shame when he died."

Cedric screwed up his face in confusion. "You mean that old book series from like, the early 2000s?"

Raine reared back, horrified. "You know what, we should just kill him. Save humanity from itself."

I snorted a laugh, which had everyone turning to look at me. "What? It was funny. Want me to try?"

Alexander waved a hand. "Go for it. I'm going to retrieve my tools."

He strode from the room, and the guy turned his eyes to me. "Are you meant to be the good cop? Try and relate to me until I spill my guts?"

I stepped up close to him, until I was bathing in the scent of his fear. "No." I circled his chair until I was behind him and leaned in close to his ear. "You stole my mate. What I'm going to do is break all your fingers. When that doesn't work, I'm going to get my Pridemate in here, and she's going to open you up and remove pieces of your liver until you talk. I've never had a liver biopsy without anesthetic before, but I can't imagine it's pleasant. And if anyone knows how to do it without killing you, it's her."

The guy shivered. "Okay, that's terrifying as hell, but could you not whisper in my ear? It's turning me on and confusing my dick."

Raine threw her hands in the air. "You're gay? Fuck, we should have just led with Judge and we'd be out of here by now."

Cedric Frostmore's eyes flicked back to Raine. "Not gay." His eyes skimmed down her body. "Definitely not gay."

Raine looked over at me. "You know, I really respect this generation's ability to embrace their fluid sexuality. Do you know three of Carmen's mates are bisexual? Why choose, right?"

I hummed in agreeance. "Each to their own, but I'm straight as an arrow."

Cedric blew a raspberry. "Boo." His eyes lit up at Raine, but she waved him away.

"I'm too old for you."

His face screwed up in confusion. "You're what, twenty? I'm like five years older than you."

She smiled at him then, her fangs flashing in the fluorescent lights. Finally, the color drained from Cedric Frostmore's face and his fear turned to absolute terror.

I huffed. "I threaten to remove his liver, and get nothing. You flash some fang and he looks like he's going to piss himself. Vampires have such an unfair advantage."

Raine sashayed over, patting my cheek. "It's cute you thought you even stood a chance in the competition." She turned hard eyes on Cedric. "Are you going to tell me what I want to know? Because the guy who just left? He's a fucking dragon, and he makes even vampires scared. You stole his granddaughter. He's not happy."

Cedric was shaking his head, and as if Alexander had been listening at the door, he strode back in, holding a bone saw and a fucking dinner plate.

Honestly. It was terrifying.

"I don't have her!" Cedric yelled, finally struggling against his bonds. "I was just researching. I didn't even think you guys were real. I promise, I don't know where she is."

Alexander rolled his eyes. "Well, we have nothing but time, and you have a lot of body parts."

"Seriously, it wasn't my vendetta."

I tilted my head. "Whose vendetta was it, then?"

Cedric swallowed hard. "I won't tell you. But he won't hurt a girl. His dad used to beat his mom, so he won't hurt a girl. He wanted..." He trailed off like he knew he was about to dig himself deeper.

Raine put a hand on his arm. "Trust me when I say it's best to get this all out before her fathers come home. Because the last person who hurt our family? Got his heart ripped out and eaten. The one before that, chopped into a thousand pieces. Trust me, you don't want that fate. Pretty sure the guy didn't die until the ninety-seventh slice."

How Cedric didn't wet himself was almost courageous. I'd heard about Lucius the vampire. He was a boogeyman under your bed. For years, he'd been an unchecked sociopathic hedonist. He'd eaten whole villages, drained whole Packs. Raine had steadied him, apparently, and from what I'd seen of him, he seemed... okay. Not homicidal, but he danced on that knife's edge like he enjoyed the pain of being cut.

Cedric shuddered. "Look, I won't give you his name. I know he's as good as dead if you find him."

No one refuted his words. We wouldn't lie to the human about it.

"I don't even really know why. All I know is that Eden did something to his family, and he promised his dad on his deathbed that he'd avenge him."

"The same father who beat his mother?" Raine asked, and Cedric shrugged.

"Guess so? Anyway, he put out feelers and at first, I thought he was insane. But he was hot, and a certain level of insanity is okay if they have a sharp jaw, you know?" Raine made an understanding humming noise. I guess she really would know. "So I looked into it for him; I thought nothing would come from it. But the deeper I dug, the more questions I had, until I stumbled across you guys up here in the wilds of fucking Canada. And then to be bounced off a military grade firewall? May as well have held up a giant flashing sign that says 'Nothing to see here', because I'm going to try and find a peep-hole in that wall, you know?"

I rumbled low in my chest. Enough with the fucking conversation. "Where is she, Cedric?"

He looked back at me, and I knew the lion was really close to the surface.

"I don't know."

"YOU FUCKING LIE!" I roared.

He blanched even more, and I was a little worried he was about to pass out. "I mean it. Somewhere up north. He's gone dark for twelve days. But you have to promise not to kill him. Or me. He's just screwed up, his dad was a violent fuck, and he twisted him up inside. He's a good guy. Promise you won't kill him. Or me," he added again.

No one made him that promise, because it depended on Enit. If this guy had so much as bruised her pale skin, I would tear the fucker limb from limb. The lion snarled in my mind and I knew I wouldn't be able to help myself, no matter what promises I made right now.

"Where?" I said in a low, quiet voice.

"Outside Yellowknife. In the Northwest Territories."

That was all I needed to know. I punched Cedric once in the face, knocking him clean out—he deserved it. His actions had resulted in *my* girl being kidnapped. Scared and alone somewhere up north, with a fucking psycho as a kidnapper. If I thought about what he could be doing to her... I swallowed hard.

She would be okay. She would.

But that other fucker? I was coming for him and his days were numbered.

23

KELL

My phone flashed at 5:02 in the morning, the screen lighting up the darkness of the room. It made my heart pound and the blood rush straight to my ears. I was meant to be dark. No contact. No random messages in the middle of the night.

Which meant only one thing. Frost called it *Kaboom*. It was his doomsday protocol that wiped his computers, his entire life, and he'd set it to send me one final message. I scrambled for my phone.

Opening it, there was just an emoji of an explosion. That was it.

Fuck. Fuck, fuck, fuck.

They'd gotten Frost.

I dragged myself off of the couch, panic running down my veins. Had they killed him? He was my friend, arguably my only friend, the only person with me in this fucking suicidal crusade. Had Enit's vampire parents torn his throat out? Were they on their way here now?

Rage consumed me and I dragged Enit from the bed by her ankle. She screeched, and I ignored the way the sound made my heart lurch. All this had been for nothing. Frost's death had been for nothing, and why? Because I'd captured a fucking girl and was too soft to make her talk. But her kind weren't soft. They were fucking monsters and it was time I remembered that she was one too.

"Kell!" Her voice was scratchy with sleep, and it came out more like a distressed squeak than a yell, but I hardened myself against it. I picked her up by her arms, dragging her to the table as she kicked and struggled. I could almost feel the presence of her wolf in the room, only inhibited by the silver wrapped around her wrist. I twisted the excess chain around her, and she went limp.

"Tell me! Tell me how to get past Eden's wards. How to get to the leaders. Tell me what their fucking weaknesses are so I can kill the bastards!" I screamed the last part and she was shaking and wide-eyed in front of me.

"Can't."

"YOU CAN!" I shouted it this time, the window-panes rattling with the sound. Tears started streaming down her cheeks and my racing heart pounded in my ears. I dropped to my knees and grabbed her upper arms. "You can. You know. You said yourself, your parents are influential. They'd know the leaders of Eden. You know something!"

"No. Kell, no."

Everything I worked for was crumbling. Everything. And all because of this girl.

Frost was dead. Because of this girl.

I had failed. Because of this girl.

I would have to run, have to hide, because of her.

"They killed him. Frost. I know they did. Just like they killed so many before him. Like they killed all The Hounds, and injured my father until he was twisted and bitter and cruel. It's their fault. Theirs and I..." I dropped my head to my chest, because I knew that I couldn't do this. Couldn't hurt her for information. Couldn't use her to get my answers. My body shook with rage and pain. Grief.

Enit bent forward and rested her cheek on my head, humming something that was probably meant to be calming but only made me want to cry for the first time in as long as I could remember.

"Be okay," she cooed. "All okay."

I looked up, straight into those sparkling blue eyes. Behind the terror, there was something softer. Something that promised exactly what she said; that everything would be alright. I lurched up and did the one thing I shouldn't do.

I kissed her.

Not a soft and tentative peck. I kissed her like there was a hunger in my soul that only she could satisfy. I kissed her like she was the very thing that could make me live. That could save me.

She sat stunned and wooden underneath my lips and then suddenly, she was kissing me back. She reflected my anger, my rage, my grief. She fed it back to me with her lips and tongue, showing me her own sorrows. I stood, briefly breaking the kiss to unwind the chains. Once she was free, her arms snaked around my neck, holding me in her own chains as she curled against me. She took my lips again, kissing me back and I stood tall, dragging her up to my height as her legs wrapped around my hips.

I growled my appreciation, my hands gripping her tight to me as I walked back toward the bed. I pushed all thoughts from my mind and just felt. I revelled in the feel of her perfect ass beneath my hands, the soft little moans she was making against my lips that threatened to bring me undone.

She wasn't a monster and I wasn't getting revenge. In fact, she was my prisoner, and I was currently devouring her like she was a flame. Right now, I was the monster. I was stealing something from her, even if she thought I was giving her something in return.

I broke away from her lips and laid her down on the bed, kissing my way down her jaw, then her throat. When she turned her head so sweetly, I knew it meant something, so I sucked at her pulse point and she rolled her hips against me. I could feel the wetness between her thighs where it pressed against my tightening tactical pants.

Scraping my teeth against the column of her throat, I moved down, bunching the collar of the t-shirt in my hand, I pulled it lower, kissing along her collarbone. But I couldn't reach and taste all the things I wanted in my mouth with that shirt in the way. I dragged it over her head, pulled it down the chain between us.

Her eyes flicked briefly to the chain, such a blinding reminder that she wasn't free here. But I took her nipple between my lips and sucked, bringing her attention back to me. Her hands gripped my hair, holding me close, my own hands wrapped around her tiny waist. She was insubstantial in my hands, like if I squeezed too hard I'd lose her forever.

Moving to the other nipple, I bit gently and she screamed, her legs tightening like a vice around my hips.

"Kell," she breathed, and my name on her lips destroyed any ounce of control I still possessed. I gripped her thighs, tugging them apart as I dived for her pussy, licking and sucking and fucking her with my tongue until she was writhing against my face, fucking me right back. She came all over my face, her thighs clamped so tightly I was slightly worried she'd re-break my cheekbone.

I wouldn't care. It would be worth it.

I pulled back, but she grabbed me with needy hands, pulling me up her body, her eyes suddenly desperate. "Kell," she whispered again, and she pleaded at me with her eyes, even as she kissed me. Her hands flew to the button of my jeans and she yanked them open, freeing my aching cock.

She stroked me and I groaned, grabbing her wrist.

"I've taken too much from you already." My dick was cursing my name, but I had a fucking code of honor. And that code didn't include fucking a girl who was my captive, who was still chained to my wrist.

She gripped my wrist with her other one, using the little strength she had to push our hands down and roll her hips up, sliding the head of my cock against her slit. "Please," she whispered.

I couldn't have said no now. As soon as I felt her wet heat against me, there was no turning back. I notched my cock against her entrance and slid all the way in with a single thrust.

I grunted at how good she felt around me, like I was finally fucking home, cradled in my little monster's hips. She moaned and urged me on with her heels pressed tightly into my ass, and I set a punishing rhythm. Punishing us both, really, because there was no way I would forget the feel of her beneath my body, or the soft sounds she made as I bottomed out, balls deep. That was going to be permanently etched in my memory forever, tainted around the edges by guilt.

Gripping one of her thighs, I lifted it up and out, curling her body and reaching spots that made her scream. I slammed home hard, again and again, as if I could somehow tattoo myself inside her, a permanent reminder of this moment. She came on a scream, her teeth biting down into my shoulder to muffle the sound, milking my cock. I gritted my teeth against the sensation, my technique getting jagged and rough, until my balls drew tight and I came inside her with a gasp.

I collapsed against her, my face buried in the pale white of her hair, breathing her in. We both panted into the silence, and guilt hit me like a fucking baseball bat. This was wrong. Fuck.

The Kaboom Protocol, the loss of Frost. The minor fact that my life was now forfeit. It all came back on a tidal wave of guilt.

I rolled off of her and onto my back, automatically tugging the chain between us out of the way. Breathing into the darkness, I did the only thing I knew how to do. I built my walls back up.

I stood, pulling up my pants and rezipping them. I reached into the small zippered pocket and pulled out a key. Undoing her cuff, I removed it from her wrist.

She gasped with relief and I felt all sorts of shit. It had obviously been paining her, but she hadn't complained. No, she'd taken the shit I doled out like a fucking champion, and I had been little more than a villain.

But there was still time to fix this.

"It's over, Enit. Go home. You should be able to shift again."

Her eyes got real big and I tried to pretend I didn't know why they were filled with tears. That I didn't know what that odd burning in my own gut meant.

"Kell..."

I shook my head, walking toward the door and throwing it open. "Your parents are probably already on their way, I don't have time for sad goodbyes. Shift and leave. There's a town about ten miles from here. You'll be warmer and safer in your wolfskin."

Safer from predators like me, who would consume her completely and leave nothing but heartache and misery in their wake.

I didn't make the mistake of looking into her blue eyes again, instead bustling around the cabin, throwing shit into my duffle bag. I couldn't leave anything behind that they could use to trace me, but these were supernaturals—they'd probably be able to track me anyway.

I'd so royally messed this up, and my greatest mistake was still kneeling in the middle of the bed, looking like I'd just torn out her heart and stomped on it. I hardened my face and pointed at the door. "Go. You're wasting my time."

Her face twisted in pain, but she finally dragged herself from the bed and shuffled toward the door. We both ignored the fact that my release still ran down her thighs. She gave me a sad look and then stepped onto the porch.

"Goodbye." The word was so soft it threatened to be stolen by the wind, but I'd heard. It was the final nail in my coffin, the final sin that I would use to crucify myself. Faster than I believed possible, a white wolf stood where Enit had been moments before. It tilted its head at me, almost exactly the way it had looked at me four days ago, except this time, its eyes were mournful.

"Get out of here," I growled and slammed the door in her face. I slumped back against it, not breathing until I heard her nails clip down the front steps. I let out a shuddering gasp, sliding to the floor, my chest threatening to implode at the sound of a mournful howl at the edge of the woods.

"She's a monster. A monster. You could never be with a monster. They ruined Dad. You can't love them," I told myself, but my chest gave my head the middle finger. Dad had been the monster; I'd thought I could be better than him, I could write my own story, if I just shut the door on the past. By fulfilling my promise to a man dying in pain. By ending Eden.

How fucking wrong I'd been. If I'd shut a door during this shitstorm, it was more like slamming it on my own future and getting my dick caught in the process.

Standing, I moved around the room in a haze. I needed to get my head back in the game, otherwise I was going to be dead. I was going to be an entree for a vampire.

I had to forget about the beautiful monster who'd taken a sledgehammer to my defenses and concentrate on what I did best.

Surviving.

24

ENIT

I ran as fast as my injured paw would allow me to run, the wolf taking over, pushing the girl with all the confused feelings to the back. The girl felt the rejection of the man who'd just worshiped her body. Felt his rejection like she was somehow defective. The girl was close to panicking about how she was going to explain fucking her captor to her other mates. Why she smelled like another man, when they were probably frantic at her disappearance.

It was safer to be a wolf. The wolf watched for the physical predators, normally blind to the emotional carnivores. But even the wolf felt wounded this time, the effects of the betrayal at Kell's hands hurting even her.

I roamed through the fresh snow, my coat perfectly adapted to blend in with this surrounding. I stayed off the road, but followed it into town, toward the smell of humanity. Destruction, refuse and death. That's what humanity had to offer the surrounding woods.

I kept my senses alert, and my connections open. I wanted to be rescued now, but on the flip side, I hoped my family didn't catch up to me for a day or two, giving Kell a head start. Because he wasn't wrong—he was a dead man if they caught him. I might be heartsick, but I didn't want him in the ground. I wanted him to live and find the happiness that was so obviously lacking in his life. The ache in my chest got worse, and I just wanted to crawl into a hole and lie there.

Instead, I pushed on, although I didn't know what I'd do when I got to the edge of town. I had to stay a wolf because I had no clothes, no shoes. No money. Being a wolf so close to civilization had its own perils, mostly men with guns trying to protect their stock. I was no threat to their livelihoods, but they didn't know that.

It wouldn't be my first time starving for a few days. Christopher, Carmen and I were often starved as pups, our parents too neglectful to remember to feed us. The last litter in a long line of litters, we were an afterthought, fed scraps under the table at best. Christopher would always give up his to me and Carmen, even when we were little more than toddlers. The Alpha instincts emerged young in wolves.

I missed my littermates. They'd be frantic as well.

We'd never been this far away from each other; the loss of their connection was like a chasm in my chest.

I felt like I'd been trudging through the snow for hours when I passed a rocky outcrop, boulders moved millenia ago by some unseen force, creating a little nook of space.

Chances of it being uninhabited were slim, but as long as the occupant was something smaller, I could barge my way in there for a while. If I went easy, maybe I wouldn't have to kick the natives out into the snow.

I stepped in, raising my snout into the air, twitching for a scent. Bear.

I froze, and sniffed again. The scent markings were old, like it had found this shallow crevice not quite comfy enough and moved on, but even the hint of predator was enough to warn other animals away. No one—not man, beast or shifter—fucked with a bear. The Moon Goddess must have been shining down on me because I settled on the old leaves, the slight swirling breeze cold but not as cold as it was outside. I couldn't live here for long, but long enough to be rescued.

I scented the den entrance, just enough to warn off anything else that wanted to seek shelter in this little den. Plus it would make it easier for the shifters to find me. The wolf happy with that, she curled in a ball, retreating back, letting the human out more. We were the same person, obviously, but my instincts as a wolf were skewed.

I was exhausted. Mentally, physically, emotionally. I was wrung out. It had been one thing after another and I couldn't take it anymore. Misery bubbled up in my chest, and a whine emitted from my throat. I just wanted to sleep and sleep and sleep, and if I never woke up? I guess the Fates would have the last laugh after all.

Enit.

My nose twitched at the sound of Christopher's voice in my dream, calling to me.

Enit.

I blinked sleepily, my body feeling frozen. I couldn't move, though I wasn't sure if it was stiffness or the beginnings of hypothermia.

Enit.

I perked up, raising my head, my ears flicking. It wasn't a dream. *Christopher?*

The rush of relief coming down the connection with my littermates threatened to overwhelm me completely. I didn't realize how flimsy my hold on my courage had been until that moment. I let out a shuddering wail that reverberated down our bond and I could feel Christopher's Alpha essence wrapping around me, like a warm blanket made of thorns. To comfort and protect. Soothe and savage.

We're coming, Enit. Carmen's voice sounded weaker, more shaky than Christopher's but it was no less soothing. I missed them so much. As much as I missed Bohdie and Stacey. *We're almost at the border.*

They were getting more strained, as if the connection we hadn't had since we were kids was satisfied. We were all okay, and it could cut those strings again. Magic was fickle like that. But they were coming and I knew I'd be on my way back to Dark River in the next twenty-four hours, away from this town, that cabin and him.

I pushed the feelings that crept up my chest back down. I had no right to have feelings for the guy who *stole* me. I stood, shaking off the snow that had blown through the gap in the crevice, and paced back and forth between the back wall and the entrance.

Like I was compelled to do so, I turned my head in the direction I'd come from, seeing if I could pick up the scent of Kell. I didn't know how long I'd been curled up in an exhausted ball. I couldn't even detect a trace of him on the wind, maybe because he was too far away, but hopefully it was because he was long gone. Hopefully I'd never see him again, but I didn't know why that made me want to tip my head back and howl.

So I did. I pushed all my loss, sadness, frustration

and anger into that howl. I howled mournfully at the moon, and somewhere far away, a natural born wolf howled back in solidarity. Never alone, no matter how lonely I felt right now.

Unlike Kell.

Twelve hours later, there was a lion in the doorway of my little cave. He let out a ear-shattering roar and then he transformed into a very naked Bohdie. The sight of him there, in front of me, close enough to touch, made me spring toward him, transforming from wolf to girl as I went.

"Enit, baby, god," he mumbled, pressing kisses all over my head and face, his arms banding so tightly around me that I was worried he'd crack a rib. I cried into his chest, no longer needing to hold myself together at all. I relaxed back into my Omega designation, happy to let my Alpha—the man I loved—take care of everything right now, just like he promised over and over against my hair.

He inhaled deeply and stilled.

I knew what he smelled, and I began to shake. Heat flooded my cheeks, shame at what I'd done, and guilt that I didn't regret it. I could almost hear the questions rotating through Bohdie's mind, but he stayed blissfully silent. He stood, lifting me easily into his arms. I snuggled my face into his neck and breathed in his reassuring smell. The smell of home and safety. The smell of happiness.

"I found her," he yelled into the snow white tundra around us, trudging us both barefoot and naked through the snow. I wiggled to get down so we could both shift, but he just held me tighter. "It's okay, Princess. I don't want to let you go yet. Just want to hold you and convince myself you're really back in my arms," he murmured, his breath fogging over my cheek. "Even if my dick freezes off."

"The snow isn't that deep and your dick isn't that big, Lion," a voice said from behind us, and I looked over at X.

His trademark snark was there, but the relief in his eyes was so immense it was like a physical wave. He shucked a backpack and threw me and Bohdie clothes. "We figured you'd probably escaped as a wolf, so we brought you clothes." He turned his back while we both changed.

I got dressed quickly, and then threw myself into the arms of my dad. He gathered me close, like I was a tiny pup again.

"Don't do that again."

"Get abducted?"

He nodded. "You and your sister are going to give me grey balls. I'm too young for frosted testes."

I screwed up my face. "Ew, Dad."

He kissed the top of my head a couple of more times, and then passed me back into the arms of

Bohdie. But by then, more people had appeared out of the woods, including Christopher and Carmen.

They barreled out of the woods, twin streaks, and didn't stop until they were on top of me, knocking me onto my ass in the snow, licking and kissing my face, whines rumbling from their chests. Happiness and relief came off them in waves. Then I was dragged out of the puppy pile and into the arms of my parents. All of them.

Raine smooshed me into her arms, even though I was a few inches taller than her now. "God, baby girl, I thought you were gone forever. Did he hurt you? Are you okay?"

Brody emerged from the woods as a tiger, and I knew shit was serious. Like there was any doubt, but the tiger was Brody's power animal, the one that let the world know the Alpha of Nîso meant business.

He curled around my legs, chuffing, and then he stilled, sniffing the air around me.

He let out a roar that was one hundred percent outrage on my behalf. He leapt into the woods before I could say another word.

He had Kell's scent and the wrong idea. Brody was the best tracker in North America; he would catch Kell and tear him to pieces.

I turned to X, whose face was hard. You didn't need to be Dr. Doolitle to know what had made the tiger so outraged. "Dad, no. I wanted to."

Bohdie stiffened behind me, and the guilt threatened to eat me alive. I tried to step away, but Bohdie wouldn't relinquish his hold on me. But he held his own body like marble behind me.

X narrowed his eyes. "I don't give a shit. I hope Brody tears him into a million pieces. No one takes one of ours. No one," he growled, his eyes dead and his lip pulled back in a snarl.

Yeah, pleading with the Executioner was not my brightest idea. I turned my eyes to my Mom.

"Mom... Please."

Her eyes searched my face, like she was looking for damning evidence of my mistreatment or something. Finally, she nodded. "I'll try to intervene. But he's coming back to Eden, and letting Brody kill him might seem like a mercy if Lucius gets hold of him," she warned.

I had to take that risk. Hopefully he was well and truly gone, but if he was still in North America, Brody would find him. Then he'd kill him.

My knees finally gave out and Bohdie scooped me into his arms. He didn't look at me, but he held me close. Carmen reached out and grabbed my hand. She'd shifted and put clothes on at some point. "Come on, E. Let's get you home, back where you belong."

Yeah, I belonged back in Dark River. But a small part of me was worried I was leaving a chunk of myself behind in a tiny cabin in the wilds of Canada.

25

STACEY

Although the guards outside the interrogation room stared at me with cold, hard eyes, I walked into the room like I owned it. Which I guess in the big scheme of things, I perhaps did. When I was a child, they'd called me the Duchess of Eden. A completely ridiculous moniker—it made me sound like a poodle—but elementary school kids were cruel. My parents had seemed like the Monarchs of this place—they were the first teachers, the first disciplinary council, the first everything. If there was a ruling family of Eden, it would be mine.

It had set me apart even more so as a child; I'd had little chance of fitting in anyway.

Still, I channeled the ideal as I walked in, doctor's bag in hand.

The guy in the corner was still bloody, but it was

crusted and dried. There was a gash on his cheek and above his brow, like he'd walked into a door frame, and they both still oozed blood gently. He looked up at me, his brows drawing together.

"Look, I told the pretty vampire lady everything I know. They're probably in Yellowknife now, gutting my best friend." A shudder wracked his body and I realized it was emotion. I couldn't tell if he was crying or shaking, but both slightly tugged at my heartstrings.

I set my bag down at his feet, grabbing his chin and raising his face. He had a pretty face, I realized, beneath the swelling and the blood. Almond-shaped eyes warred with pale white skin, and I decided he was Eurasian. Some melting pot of genetics that had created a visually impressive offspring.

"I wouldn't be so sure."

He frowned again, making the wound near his eye open more and blood start to drip down his temple. He hissed at the sting of pain. "What do you mean?"

I opened my kit and pulled out gloves and a suture kit. "I mean that your *friend*"—I couldn't keep the derisiveness out of my voice, despite my assertion to myself that I would keep my cool—"stole an Omega. She is soft by nature. Forgiving. Loving. *Healing.* If he is somehow worthy of your sadness, she'll have seen it too, and she will argue for leniency. It's in her nature, despite the fact that he took her from her family, from the people who loved her, to torture her for information."

He just watched me as I set up my kit. "Your eyebrow and cheek need stitches. Any other injuries I should know about?"

"My ribs."

I grabbed my stethoscope, lifting his shirt and looking at the bruising that was distinctly fist-shaped. You did not fuck around with the King of the Shifters. I lifted my stethoscope to his back to ensure one of his broken ribs hadn't injured a lung.

He continued to stare at me, his eyes running over my face. "You're very pretty."

I gave him a dead-eyed stare. "Gay."

He shrugged. "Just an observation." He took a shuddery breath and winced. "I'll tell you what I told them. Ke— My friend, he wouldn't hurt her. If she'd been a guy, we might be having a different conversation; he has a lot of anger towards men. Not as much as he has toward Eden, but he'd never hurt a girl."

I snorted. "How noble."

I put some numbing cream around the areas I intended to suture. I didn't think he'd like me coming at him with a big needle filled with local anesthetic. It needed time to work though, so I stepped back and appraised him.

He appraised me right back. "What kind of supernatural are you anyway?"

I shook my head. "Not supernatural. Just a human."

He raised his eyebrows, making his wound ooze more. He had an expressive face, and it was like his eyebrows couldn't help their movements. "A human? What are you doing in a school of supernaturals?"

I weighed up my answer. He obviously didn't have the blind vendetta his friend had, but then again, he could just be a very capable spy. "They took me in when a fanatical organization killed my family."

He tilted his head. "Kell believes Eden steals children and kills humans. You being here doesn't really counteract his claims."

Silence was heavy between us, and I could see him grit his teeth at the fact he'd just slipped.

Kell. The name of his friend, the one who stole Enit, was Kell. I filed that away, but I'd reward the slip with a little truth of my own.

"In a way, I guess they did. But those children they stole? Cast out from their families and Packs, or worse, orphans thanks to bounty hunters and skin traders. The Hounds, an organization of zealots, killed my family and stole me and my brother. Kept us in a glass cage and studied us. They were humans. If Eden stole us, they stole us from a lifetime of imprisonment."

The guy—Cedric Frostmore, according to his file— went totally pale. "The Hounds?"

Now it was my turn to tilt my head. Hmm. He knew more than he was letting on about this world.

I picked up the needle and began to suture his face. "The Hounds were, I mean are, an organization as old as history itself. The North American branch is gone, wiped out by Eden, but there are more worldwide." He winced as I tugged the thread into a knot. "They originally just wanted to eradicate all supernaturals, but as time passed, they succumbed to greed like everyone else, and realized there was better money in selling them. Unique supernaturals could be sold for millions of dollars, shipped all over the world like chattels. More mundane supernaturals, like shifters, were usually sold as sex slaves or into underground fighting rings. Some, they kept to study for scientific or breeding purposes." I swallowed hard as old horrors rose up and threatened to consume me.

He chewed his lower lip, even though it already had a split in it. It opened again and blood welled at the edge. "But you're human, you said so yourself. Why would an organization that specializes in supernaturals want a human?"

I scoffed. "So narrow-minded. We call ourselves, as a collective, preternaturals. Anything out of the ordinary is a commodity. I have hyperintelligence. My brother has telekinesis. Working with human samples is far easier to replicate with modern science than the magic of other supernaturals. Who wouldn't want an army of telekinetic and hyperintelligent soldiers? We were an investment."

"You're a genius?"

I didn't know if I should be amused or insulted by his shock. "Mmhmm. Certifiably."

"Uh, cool." He worried at his lip again and I flicked at it with my fingers, tugging it gently from between his teeth as I would do to an errant child. "Look, uh... You didn't tell me your name?"

"Stacey."

"Look, Stacey, what I've heard of The Hounds and Eden is a lot different."

I just bet it was. "And where did you hear these stories? Because if it wasn't from someone who was there, who was so indoctrinated to the idea of having her blood drawn, to only seeing the sun once every week that she thought it was a treat, then your information is wrong."

He was silent then, his eyes distant as I finished the last few sutures in his cheek as well. My stitches were neat and precise, and I was happy that they would barely scar.

I stepped back, packing up my equipment for disposal. He frowned as he watched me work. I grabbed my surgical scissors and walked behind him. "Being immobilized for so long is bad for your blood flow. If I release you, do you promise not to attack me? Because I can promise you, there are things from your very worst nightmare that would kill you in a hundred different ways, very slowly, if you hurt me."

He shook his head. "That's not my thing. I'm a pacifist. I do my guerilla warfare from behind a keyboard. Blood makes me want to puke."

I weighed the variables: the fact that he was human, there were no weapons, and at least ten highly trained shifters were right outside the door. I cut his bindings.

He wrenched his hands in front of him, shaking out his palms. He looked up at me. "What will they do with me?"

I shrugged. "I don't know, Cedric. You're a human who knows too much, who worked against Eden. That's still a possible security threat."

"Call me Frost."

It kind of suited him, with his pale, almost Nordic skin. Would it be rude to ask him his heritage? Probably. I inclined my head. "You pose a threat, not to just Eden, but to the supernatural community as a whole. What you don't realize is that Eden lives up to its name. The people here have always striven to make this a place of sanctuary. The rest of the supernatural community? Less gentle."

That was an understatement. You would be hard pressed to find an older supernatural without blood on their hands, supernatural or human. Just the vampire Lucius alone would have spilled enough blood to drown in.

But no more than humankind spilled of its own

blood every day. I wouldn't sugarcoat it for him. "Like any society, human included, the preternatural community has good and bad forces. Despite what The Hounds preached, we aren't inherently evil. But a lot of us do believe in collateral damage, especially when it comes to sacrificing what a good portion of the supernatural community consider a food source anyway."

Frost looked pale, so pale I stepped forward in case he passed out. "I don't want to die..." he whispered. Something about him tugged at the heart I didn't realize I had. Enit was making me soft.

It would be a waste of life, and that was something I'd vowed to preserve when I took my oath as a doctor. "I'll do what I can, Frost. We aren't monsters, and we have consciences. I'll argue on your behalf. But if he's hurt her, not even God will save you from the wrath of the immortals."

With that, I left. I needed to message Bohdie and see if he had found our Enit yet. They should be nearing the border by now, and I hated that I was stuck here, waiting for news. She was my girlfriend too. But I would only be a lead weight holding them back from getting to her faster.

Still, I wish they'd hurry. I needed to feel her back under my palms, taste her lips once more.

26

BOHDIE

Since I found her, I hadn't been more than three steps from her. My lion panicked everytime she moved out of sight. We had been the ones to lose her, and the anxiety about that happening again was overwhelming.

I lay curled against her in the dark, the soft snores of Stacey on her other side as she clung to our mate soothing both me and my beast. But I couldn't sleep. Running on adrenaline for the last week had burned out my nerves. It didn't help that Enit stank of guilt and sadness.

She was restless too, and I felt the moment she drifted back out of her listless sleep.

I wrapped an arm around her hips, pulling her closer to me. I kissed her short, spiked hair. "Are you okay?"

She shook her head. "No."

Stacey reached for her in her sleep, and I'd never tell Doc this, but she looked kind of adorable in her periodic table pajamas. Sometimes I forgot that she was so young; her demeanor was of someone so much older. She'd seen loss and the worst of humankind way too much in her short life, even more so than the rest of us.

Enit put her hand over Stacey's, where it rested on her stomach, and then I put mine over the top, sending my protective Alpha pheromones through the room, soothing their restlessness. It was a promise to keep watch, that I would protect them so they could sleep easy.

But my Omega, she wasn't resting easy.

"Do you want to talk about it? If not to me, to Doc?"

I felt her stiffen, and then her body seemed to curl in on itself in defeat and I hated it. Hated that I couldn't just fight whatever dark thoughts had chased away her sleep.

"I had sex with Kell." Her words were even and measured, like she'd put a lot of effort into her confession.

Kell Arborson. Eden had pulled his history to pieces, knew everything about the man who had taken the very light from my life, right from under my nose. Everything, except why he would have a grudge against Eden. He was human, that much was obvious.

Washed out army grunt. Deceased parents. Mother of suicide and father of cancer a few years later. He was nearly too young to even remember Eden before it was an Academy.

I curled my fingers around hers, rage and jealousy sparking in my chest, but I breathed through it. She didn't need violence and retribution, although both Nico and Lucius were still out hunting for her abductor. She needed understanding. Reassurance.

"I know, Princess. Shifter senses, remember?" I squeezed her tighter to me. "It was consensual?"

If he'd taken advantage of her, I would tear out his eyeballs and stuff them down his windpipe. But she nodded, even though I could see her eyes squeeze shut in the darkness. Unable to cope with the waves of guilt pouring off her, I leaned forward and kissed her face. "It's okay, baby. Anything you feel is perfectly okay, except this self-loathing. Nothing you could do would make me feel any differently for you. I loved you the first moment I saw you, and I'll love you when my saggy old lion balls drag on the ground."

She let out a choked laugh. "Love you."

Those words were like an arrow in my chest every time. They tore the breath from my lungs.

"Liked him," she said softly, and I didn't know if it was her nature or some weird abductee psychology bullshit, but only Enit would see the redeemable qualities in a person who'd literally kidnapped her.

I slid out of bed, and she tensed. "Come on, Princess. There's something I want you to see. Go get dressed and I'll tell Doc we're going out for a bit. She'll freak out if she wakes up and we're gone." Stacey would never admit it, because it wasn't logical, but I caught that same panicked look on her face as I got whenever Enit was out of sight. Like we could misplace our heart again, and we wouldn't survive without it this time.

Enit nodded, not even questioning me. She grabbed my hoodie off the ground and slipped it over her head, then rummaged through her dresser for pants.

I leaned down and shook Stacey gently. Her eyes snapped open, then they bounced around the room until they landed on Enit's white hair, a beacon in the darkness.

"Everything alright?" she asked, her voice croaky.

I nodded. "Yes. I'm taking her to see him."

She frowned. "Are you sure that's a good idea?"

Not really, but Enit needed to know that she wasn't the only person who didn't hate Kell Arborson. "I think it will help."

She nodded, moving to sit up, but I placed a hand on her shoulder. "Sleep, Doc. I've got it. You need to rest."

She yawned again, her eyes tracing Enit's back as

she tugged on yoga pants. I could see her brain warring with her body.

"I won't let her out of my sight, Stacey. You have my word. She'll never leave us again."

"Alright, Alpha. Be careful with her." Then she was dragged back into sleep. She was truly exhausted.

I pulled on my shirt and tiptoed toward the door, not even bothering with shoes. Clutching Enit's hand in mine, we walked down the near silent halls, though the odd nocturnal supe roamed. We hopped into the elevator, and I typed in the code that would take us down to the very depths of Eden. Enit gave me a quizzical look, but didn't say anything, and I pulled her closer to my body on the way down. I just wanted to feel her warmth against me and let her scent fill my lungs.

As we stepped out into the bottom floor, Enit's eyes took in everything at once. The perspex cages, the interrogation room, and the locked metal cabinets that I'd found out were an armory. It held an impressive range of weapons, from swords to rocket launchers.

I lifted my chin in greeting to the soldiers guarding the doors, who were both shifters, and watched them tilt their heads as they breathed in the Omega in the room. I curled my lip in warning, and they both dropped their eyes. They were well-trained soldiers, but they weren't Alphas.

Enit seemed oblivious as her eyes connected with

the sole prisoner on this floor, asleep in his perspex box. She drifted over on light feet until she was staring down at the sleeping man.

"Who?"

I stood behind her, my body shielding her from any threats. "Cedric Frostmore. You might know him as Frost."

Enit gasped, her hands slapping against on the plastic barrier. "He's alive?"

The sound startled Frost from his sleep. His eyes slammed open, and he jerked upright a moment later. He gazed around, unseeing, for a moment, before his eyes landed on me and he settled.

Apparently, he didn't see me as a threat. Foolish.

When his gaze dropped to Enit, his brows drew together in confusion. He looked at my hands, the way my body crowded hers, and understanding dawned on his face. It was followed by sadness and fear. Understandable. He'd lost his usefulness as an information source, and now they'd have to figure out what to do with him.

That couldn't end well for Cedric Frostmore.

"They got you back," he said softly, his gaze boring into Enit's like he could read her secrets. "Is he dead?"

The sadness in his voice tugged at me. I could see how big and wet Enit's eyes were in the reflection of her face in the perspex. She shook her head.

"Not yet," I murmured, then I could have kicked

myself when they both stiffened. "I mean, he let Enit go. We mostly just wanted her back."

Mostly. The vampires weren't likely to just let it go, neither were Eden.

Frost's eyes travelled over Enit's face. "I can see why. You look like a lamb to slaughter—he wouldn't have been able to hurt you if he tried. Bet he was mad." A sad smile crept over his face, like Kell Arborson was already dead, and he was remembering the lost.

She drew in a deep breath. "Can't speak good. He was unhappy." Her words were as slow and modulated as she could make them, and I was impressed by how far she'd come. She was a fucking miracle, and I loved her so much that sometimes I thought my heart would explode in my chest.

Frost looked at me, seeking explanation. "Enit was in a car accident and suffered brain damage. She's had to learn how to talk again."

Enit pointed to the scar, her face still sad. Frost tilted his head and stepped closer to the perspex, so there was only a foot and a three inch thick slab of plastic between them. "Ah, you would have been his kryptonite. A broken little bird for him to save, even when he was meant to be the villain."

She tugged her lip between her teeth. "Kaboom. Thinks Frost dead. Let me go."

Frost shook his head, his floppy hair falling over his eyes. "Does he? Was he sad?"

Enit nodded. "Yes. Loves you."

Frost snorted. "That'd be right. Probably not the way I loved him though." It had been entirely obvious to everyone that Frost had a crush, at the very least, on this Kell guy. He was fiercely loyal, even though he seemed to be a good person who knew that kidnapping nice girls wasn't the right thing to do.

But he'd never outed his friend.

Enit just shrugged, not willing to speak for their mutual acquaintance. Frost put his hands on the perspex and leaned forward. "He's really a good guy, you know, under all that gruffness. He wouldn't have hurt you."

"I know."

"I don't want him to die."

Enit's face dragged down but she raised her hand to his. "Me either."

Frost slumped forward, his head resting on the plastic. "Then you're the only one who can save him."

Tears tracked down Enit's cheeks, and I pulled her away from Frost and back into my arms. She cried softly against my chest, and I held her tightly.

"If he's lucky, he'll continue to run and never come back," I said, but for the first time, it didn't feel like a threat. I hoped I was right. Because supernaturals had long memories and I had a feeling that one more thing inside my girl would break, should Kell Arborson die.

Somewhere in Eastern Europe

In my dreams, she is on her knees, looking up at me with those brilliant blue eyes filled with pleading lust. I'd wrap my hand around her throat, collar her with my fingers, but she wouldn't look at me with fear in her eyes. No, instead she'd part her pretty pink lips and beg me to kiss her.

But every time I'd squeeze just too hard, and her face would turn this godawful blue, almost the same blue as her eyes. I wouldn't be able to open my hand, no matter how much I'd yell and scream, or how much she'd struggle beneath me. Then she'd die and it would be my fault.

I rocketed up in bed, the chill of the air fogging my

breath in the moonlight coming through the window, and breathed through the nightmare. Every night she came to me. Every night I woke in a cold sweat. Frost would say that it was my guilty subconscious, and I was pretty sure he'd be correct. All my greatest regrets centered around Enit.

"Hello Kell."

I went for the gun I kept under my pillow, but there was suddenly a vampire over me, his fangs bared as he gripped my wrists easily. His eyes reflected my painful death, and my body froze.

Another vampire sauntered over, and he looked exactly the same as the one holding me. Twins.

The one who spoke looked less monstrous, but his eyes still promised my death.

"I am Nico. This is my twin, Lucius. You may have been acquainted with our daughter, Enit."

My whole body went limp with defeat. They'd found me. Even if I had my gun, or my blades, I wouldn't have been able to kill both of them. It wasn't in my nature to just gently accept my death, but a part of me, the part that kept feeding me those nightmares, believed I deserved what was coming to me. And maybe that part was right.

"I'm ready to die," I said hoarsely, making the crazy one holding me grin.

"Ah, but I'm not ready for you to die yet. The fun has only just begun."

Nico looked at him, frowning slightly. "Mmhmm, my brother is mostly correct. We aren't ready for you to die yet." He sat down on the side of the bed, his cold skin touching mine. "I think we should have a little conversation first, before we get to the tearing and rending."

Lucius huffed and let me go. "Always were a killjoy," he grumbled, wandering back to the shadows in the corner of the room. I might no longer be held down, but I didn't fool myself into thinking I wasn't still a prisoner. They could move faster than I could see. Still... I looked at the nightstand. I had a stake in there. Maybe I could take down at least one.

Nico looked at me with disappointed eyes. "I wouldn't bother. Lucius is looking for an excuse to snap your neck, and we gathered all your weapons up while you were sleeping." The idea of them being in the room while I slept made chills break out across my skin. Surely they hadn't found...

"Yes, even the one beneath the mattress."

Air hissed out through my teeth. I was royally fucked. This was my end, and instead of going out in a blaze of glory, I was going out filled with regret in a shitty motel in a shitty village in a shitty country in Eastern Europe, the kind where people don't ask questions if guests just disappear.

I sighed, sitting up in bed. If I was going to die, I preferred not to do it on my back. No one turned on the light, and I was at even more of a disadvantage. Their faces were cast in shadow, and the shades of grey made them look even more monstrous. "Let's get this over with."

Lucius barked a laugh from the corner. "So eager to be cut into tiny pieces. Maybe I'll be kind and only cut you into four. For every day you stole her from us."

I wanted to apologize, but I wasn't really sorry for my actions. I was just sorry it had been her.

Nico looked over his shoulder. "Calm, Lucius. This will be over soon and we can return to Raine." He turned back to me. "Excuse him. He's been off his meds for a few months as we tracked you across Europe. It makes him... unstable."

I'd felt his hand flexing around my throat. I had a feeling he wasn't particularly stable on his meds either.

"I, however, took a vow not to kill humans. Though I might make an exception for the man who stole my daughter." That tiny glimmer of hope disappeared. Nico laid a hand on my arm, and I tensed. "Tell me, Kell Arborson, son of Stephen and Astrid Arborson, why did you steal our Enit?"

"I didn't mean to," my mouth said before my brain even had time to catch up. I snapped it shut, and the look that Nico gave me was incredibly shark-like.

"Explain? It's not like you tripped and fell, then accidentally tossed her into the back of your pickup truck, did you?"

I ground my back teeth, trying to keep my mouth shut, but I couldn't. He was compelling me to speak and I couldn't fight it. "She was meant to be a guy. If she'd been a guy, I could have pressed for information about Eden with more, uh, hands-on methods."

"Torture," Nico prompted.

"I think he had his hands on her more than enough," Lucius growled, and I knew that I wasn't coming out of this alive. They knew I'd slept with Enit. I knew how it would have looked, like I'd forced her, raped her. I mean, I'd had her chained to me with silver in a cabin in the middle of nowhere. Consent, I guess, was a dubious concept right there. I deserved what they dished out, I knew it.

Lucius was suddenly in front of me. He leaned forward until his lips were beside my ear. "I am going to tear off any part of you that touched her."

I just nodded.

Nico huffed, tilting his head at his twin, who obediently went back to his corner. "What information were you after?"

I dropped my chin, turning away from his face like that could numb his effect, but it did nothing. Words tumbled out of my mouth, betraying everything I'd worked toward. "Information about Eden, the key players, easy ways to get in and out of the Academy. Weaknesses."

Nico made an absent humming sound, like we

were having a therapy session rather than a little mental coercion. "And what were you going to do with that information, Mr. Arborson?"

"Kill the monsters. The Lycanthropes."

Lucius laughed. Like, really laughed, to the point of hysteria.

"You and what army?" Nico cooed.

"The Hounds."

Their laughter stopped abruptly. Lucius snarled. "Even with The Hounds, you wouldn't stand a chance. However, there are no Hounds left in North America. They are dead," he said wistfully. "That was quite a good day."

I tensed. His words rolled around and around in my head. He'd been there for the destruction of The Hounds facility fifteen years earlier, the day my father...

I cut the thought off. I didn't think they could mind read, but I wasn't going to give them more than they could take.

But the reasonable twin was just looking at me pensively, like I was a puzzle and he knew he was missing a piece. No matter how I might try to hold onto my secrets, I was fairly sure they'd wring me dry before they killed me.

He tilted his head to the side and continued to study me, then he looked out the window, at the light brightening the sky. "Thank god it's almost dinner time. I'm starving." He turned back to me, and his eyes said I might be dinner. "Did The Hounds approach you?"

I shook my head.

"Did you approach them?"

I clenched my jaw, because maybe, just maybe, if they believed there was an army coming for me, they'd cut their losses. But that was a foolish dream.

"No. I was going to bring them a plan for retribution."

"So they don't know about Eden? Does anyone know?"

I gritted my teeth again, trying not to betray my only friend. But it was useless. I hung my head. "Only my friend, Frost."

As the light started to pour in, I could see more details of my captors, including the tribalistic tattoos that dotted their faces. They were old. Like bone-achingly ancient.

So. Fucked.

Nico shook his head. "Ah, yes. Cedric Frostmore." He let out another sigh, and walked to the window. Weren't vampires allergic to the sun? Maybe I just had to hold out a few more hours and the sun would solve my problems for me. Nico turned back toward me, taking a seat in the only chair in the room. "You know, the person you abducted was really your blessing and your doom. Enit is... well, she's the best of us all, really. She's the sweetness and light that you tend to lose when you are an immortal. She genuinely cares. She argued for the life of your friend Cedric. And she is hard to say no to, so he's hers now."

Shock froze the air in my lungs as I processed what this vampire was trying to say. Frost was alive. Enit had saved him. Had she saved him because she was everything Nico said she was, or did she save him for me?

My eyes bounced back to Nico's ancient ones. "She argued for your life too, but we are less forgiving. There is only so much leniency I am willing to grant, and your friend Cedric used it all up."

I huffed out a relieved breath. Frost was alive. I hadn't been the cause of his death. I could die today with an easier conscience.

Yet Nico wasn't done. Though he wasn't touching me anymore, so perhaps I could resist his questions. "What I really want to know, Mr. Arborson, is why you care so much about Eden? Micah, Alistair and Locke have racked their brains about what they could have done to a small child, but they have nothing. Which leads me to believe it isn't about you at all, is it?"

"No."

"Tell me what it is about then. Make me understand."

I'd been fooling myself that this ancient vampire

needed physical contact. I was an open book to him, a nut that he wanted to peel open and get a good taste of the inside.

"My father was a soldier for The Hounds. He was a good man, he used to dance around the kitchen with my mother, and would take me to the park." Nico's lip quirked but he motioned for me to continue. "He was there at the battle—when The Hounds fell. He saw friends torn apart by monsters, he watched those he'd sworn to protect be stolen."

Nico snarled. "Those people were already stolen, Mr. Arborson. From their families. Off the street. They were stolen so The Hounds could sell them for a profit." He took a deep breath and calmed himself. "Please continue. I know he didn't die there, that your vendetta isn't a blood oath. He died seven years later from cancer."

I didn't want to continue, to hash up all this bullshit from the past. But right now, I was unable to help myself. "You're right, he didn't die. He was injured though, and those injuries plagued him for the rest of his life. But it was the mental scars that affected him most. He started hitting my mother in the kitchen instead of dancing with her. He stuffed me in closets for days on end rather than take me to the park."

Lucius rolled his eyes. "Did he feed you to an angry god that demanded blood, turning you into an immortal killing machine? No? Stop whining."

Nico threw him a worried look, then turned his gaze back to me. The sunrise bathed him in its rays, and there went my idea that they'd just burn to a crisp.

I looked back at the good twin. "When I was ten, I came home to my mother dead in her bed from an overdose of sleeping pills. After that, my father realized what had caused our life to spiral out of control. Eden. He began to train me to become a soldier. When he died, he made me promise to live out his vendetta on the people who ruined my life."

Nico was silent and I was sweating, memories pouring out of the recesses of my brain, torturing me all over again. He stood, walking toward me, staring down at me in pity. "The monster who ruined your life is already six feet underground, Kell Arborson. Killing the Lycans, bringing down Eden, none of that will make the betrayal go away." He turned toward Lucius. "Let us go home, brother. Raine waits for us and I am done with this chase. Besides, if we spare him, we will be Enit's favored parents again."

Lucius looked like he wanted to fight—his brother, me, this entire city. He visibly shuddered, trying to get himself under control. Then he sneered at me and strode out the door.

Nico paused on the threshold. "You probably have Enit to thank for saving your life. There are few things that Lucius loves more than bloodshed; she happens to be one of them." His face fell into a scary mask that made all the tiny hairs on my body stand on end. "Attack us again, and I will personally cut you from groin to gullet and feast on your entrails."

With that, the door slammed shut and I leaned over the bed and vomited into a waste paper basket.

28

ENIT

I lazed on the banks of the pond, ignoring the expectant looks of the ducks standing near us, staring. The sun beat down on us, and my head was in Stacey's lap, mostly so she could nudge me whenever I stopped reading.

"He kissed me until the stars left the sky and spread across the back of my eyelids..."

My mouth didn't stumble over the words anymore. It was smooth and modulated, even if I did still have to concentrate on the way my tongue moved. My hand didn't shake where I held the book, and I was almost back to normal. Except for the ache that seemed to be permanently in my gut.

Frost was lying on his stomach, his head pillowed on his folded arms. "I'd bang Dallas Hellson six ways to Sunday and twice on Thursdays," he murmured lazily and I laughed. Stacey just shook her head at him and he grinned up at us both. "You guys look so sweet together, you know? As sweet as any romance novel anyway."

I flushed, and although Stacey tensed slightly under my cheek, she didn't stop stroking my hair. It was at a weird length right now, and I kind of looked like an early 90s heartthrob. Or at least that was what my mom had said. I didn't know who the hell Devon Sawa was, but she got all dreamy when she talked about him.

Bohdie was at Alpha Studies, and they'd arranged for his Omega friend to start tutoring me next year. My freshman year at the Academy had passed so fast, but it had been a crazy nine months. My second year at the Academy would be better.

It really couldn't be fucking worse.

I guess some good things had come out of it, though. I looked up at Stacey, lifting my head for a kiss. She briefly touched her lips to mine, still not a huge fan of public displays, and I grinned at her. She huffed, tugging my hair lightly. "Read."

I continued on, but my mind was wandering. That was another milestone, though it wasn't quite as visible. The ability to read without consciously thinking how to move my lips to form words.

Frost rolled onto his back and I took a moment to study his sharp jawline. He was really very handsome, and funny. Months ago, when I'd petitioned Alexander for clemency, he'd given it to me, because I'd had that big dragon wrapped around my little finger since I was five. But there were strict guidelines. He was constantly watched, even when it didn't seem like it. Even now, although he probably wouldn't realize it with his human senses, there was a wolf in the woods with their eyes on us. He wasn't allowed around any technology more sophisticated than the elevator. He wasn't allowed to leave the grounds until everyone—and I meant everyone, including the Eden Board of Directors, my parents, Alexander, maybe even Sergei the janitor—was convinced he wasn't a threat.

He was a prisoner at the Academy, but he didn't seem to mind. He said he didn't have any family. Nothing was waiting for him back home except his laptop. Not even a goldfish. It made me incredibly sad for this vivacious man. Honestly, he wooed as easily as he breathed. He just had this way of making you feel like you were his whole world in that moment. Even Stacey liked him, and she hated everyone.

"We should go get some lunch," Stacey said softly. I wasn't hungry, but I rolled to my feet, standing to brush the grass off my butt. Stacey was looking up at me, her brows drawn together. "You're losing weight."

It wasn't a question, at least not one that I could refute. My clothes had begun to hang off my frame, my hip bones a little more prominent.

"Stress," I said softly. "From exams. We're going home for the summer, and I promise that Beatrice will take it as a personal affront and make it her duty to fatten me back up."

Stacey didn't laugh like I thought she would, still looking at me pensively. "I'd like you to come down to the clinic so I can do a few tests. I'm worried that I've missed something."

I pulled her to her feet and stepped into her arms. "I promise I'm okay, but if it will make you feel better, I'll come down and let you stick me with whatever you want."

Frost snorted. "That's what she said." When I stepped back from Stacey, Frost wrapped an arm around my shoulders. "Come on, I'm starving."

A group of Nîso shifters walked past us, lowering their heads at me respectfully. Frost shook his head in exasperation. "You know, once upon a time I thought I was attractive, but this place is ridiculous. Why is everyone so beautiful? Is there some kind of secret pool somewhere that makes you physically appealing? Because I'm ready for my bath."

Stacey rolled her eyes, but I giggled, leaning into his warmth. He tightened his arm around my shoulders and squeezed me affectionately.

"You're very handsome and you know it, Frost."

"You think I'm pretty?" he gasped, and heat flooded my cheeks. He was beyond pretty really. It wasn't just the outer package either, though that was very appealing with his sharp jaw and the grin that lit up his entire face. Not to mention the lean muscle of his body. He raised an eyebrow at my blatant appraisal and I flushed a little.

"You know you're pretty, butthead."

He laughed and kissed my temple. No, it wasn't just the outside of Frost that was pretty. His inside was pretty great too. He was funny and generous, as well as smart enough to keep up with Stacey, most of the time anyway. Sometimes, he knew when to let me be lost in my silence, something that Stacey and Bohdie struggled with. They remembered the Enit of before. We just all had to come to terms with the fact that I wouldn't ever be the same, even after I healed.

People waved to us, even to Frost, who had seemed to make himself at home here. The girls especially loved him, his humanness something exotic in this institute. I ignored the stab of jealousy that speared my chest at the thought. I had enough on my plate. I didn't need to feel possessive about a man whose heart belonged to someone else. Though sometimes I caught him looking at me in a way that wasn't just friendly. No, it was definitely something hotter than that. But it had only been three months, and I didn't think that Frost was going to get over his heartache quite so quickly.

Three months since I'd been rescued.

Three months since I'd seen—

No. I shut the thought down. I didn't need to dredge that shit up today. It plagued me enough when I slept. Lucius and Nico had returned, but they refused to tell me if they found Kell. I wasn't sure if I really wanted to know, but somewhere deep down, I knew he wasn't dead. It might have been wishful thinking on my behalf, something to help me sleep easier.

AFTER MY AFTERNOON LECTURES, I found myself in Stacey's clinic getting vial after vial of blood drawn.

"Goddess, Stace, are you going to leave me any?"

She gave me a slight frown. "You would need to lose far more than this to exsanguinate, Enit."

I'd quickly realized that there were two sides to Stacey. The Doctor and the Lover. Down here, surrounded by her sterile surfaces and medical equipment, she was very much the professional.

She released the tourniquet and I rolled down my sleeve. "I'll run some tests and see if I can't work out why you are wasting."

I rolled my eyes. "Stacey, I'm hardly wasting."

She made a disapproving noise and moved toward me, putting her stethoscope in her ears. I sat still, breathing when she told me to breath, moving and stretching as directed. "Everything sounds fine."

She was beginning to sound frustrated, and I pulled her around so she was standing between my knees. "I'm fine," I lied, once again glad she wasn't a shifter. I gripped her chin, making her look at me. "I love you, Stacey."

She froze in my arms, her eyes searching my face for any hint of untruth. She swallowed hard and leaned forward, closing her eyes as she kissed me softly. "Love you too, Enit. Always have."

I kissed her back, nibbling her full, soft lips. "I know. I'm sorry it took me so long to realize what was in front of me all this time."

She deepened the kiss and I moaned as her tongue stroked mine. How an asexual woman knew how to kiss this well without practice was a mystery. I smiled against her lips as she owned my mouth with the precision of someone who had studied the hell out of this. She pushed at the edges of my sundress, slipping the straps down my shoulders. My nipples peaked under her gaze as she drew away and stared at them.

I grabbed her chin again. "Stace, we don't have to do this."

She smiled at me. "I want to," she whispered, lowering her head to my breast. "I've researched this."

I stifled the laugh, because of course she had. And when she wrapped her pout around my nipple, I sucked in a breath. My fingers weaved into the curls of her hair, holding her to me as she sucked and nipped with just the right amount of pressure. "Stacey!"

She moved to the other nipple, giving it the same treatment, maybe a little rougher, like she was experimenting to see what I liked.

I watched her face, and her eyes were alight in a way I rarely saw outside the lab. Like she was proud of herself.

Her hands ran up my thighs, and she gently tugged them further apart. She hooked her stool with her foot, and pulled it closer to the edge of the table. Apparently, I had a doctor fetish, because just at the sight of her looking up from between my thighs, completely put together except where my hands had tugged out some of her curls, I moaned.

She bit her lip, looking nervous for the first time. I was up on my elbows, not wanting to miss the way her soft fingers rubbed circles on my thighs, or the way her hungry eyes watched my face for my reactions.

I frowned, about to tell her again that she didn't have to do this, that I loved *her*, not the physical pleasure she could bring me, but as if she sensed my impending words, she pushed my dress up around my waist and slid her fingers against my damp underwear. I sucked in a breath.

She gripped the waistband and slid them down my thighs, and I lifted my ass to make it easier.

She huffed out a breath that brushed over my over-heated core. I was trembling on the edge of the treatment bed, my body on the precipice of something. That moment when you know pleasure is coming, the way your whole body goes tight as it waits for it.

Then finally, when that moment dragged on for so long I thought I was going to explode, her tongue flicked against my clit. I squeaked out a moan, and she did it again.

"Goddess," I let out on a breathy whisper, and I didn't know if I was praying to the deity or talking about my beautiful girlfriend.

Probably both.

She'd done her research. She sucked my clit and I rolled my hips up into her face. She did it again and I made a long, low moan that echoed around the room. When she slid a finger inside me, I couldn't help myself, gripping her head tighter. "Stacey!" I gasped, and she pushed another finger inside me, rolling them in a wave motion that was making me see stars.

The door burst open. "Doc, have you seen..."

I relaxed when I realized it was Bohdie. He stood there in the door, looking between us. "Oh shit, sorry, I'll, uh, fuck I'm going to go—"

"Stay, Alpha. I'd like your input."

My whole body flushed. Did she mean...

"You want me to watch as you eat out our girlfriend?" he said, his voice an octave higher than normal, and he cleared his throat. He looked between us, dropping his voice low. "Are you sure?"

"Yes. I want to make her ejaculate." As if to make her point, she sucked on my clit again, and Bohdie locked the door, stepping further into the room.

"You want to make her come," he corrected.

Stace made a humming noise on my clit and every muscle in my abdomen clenched. "Stacey," I moaned, and I could feel her smug smile.

She curled her fingers, looking over her shoulder at Bohdie. "No, I want to make her squirt, as it's colloquially known. I read a research paper on the phenomenon."

We both stared at her with wide eyes, and then she curled her fingers again, going back to swirling her tongue around my clit. I dropped my head back as she ate me out like I was a mission, careful not to slam my thighs closed and keep her there forever. Jesus, she knew how to research. Her fingers were like a wave inside me, rubbing my g-spot like she could see it on the outside.

My orgasm built until I was gasping for air, coming as I rolled my body against her face. I screamed her name as I came, and it was too much for Bohdie, who came over to taste my pleasure, kissing me hard and catching my moans.

But Stacey wasn't done. Oh no, she looked up as

Bohdie pulled his lips from mine and took my nipple in his mouth. She nodded in appreciation.

Her other hand came up to massage my sensitive clit as the rhythm of her fingers changed, and she tapped at my g-spot firmly, then stroked, then tapped again. I started to pant out weird noises somewhere between a moan and a stifled scream, and Bohdie covered my mouth with his.

It was too much, my whole lower body tensing as the coming orgasm filled me up. Tears leaked from my eyes, pleasure making my body tremble, and when she did that tapping again, I came like a tsunami.

I came and came and came some more, soaking the treatment bed and Stacey.

Holy shit. *Holy shit.*

Bohdie stepped back as I dragged Stacey onto the bed with me, kissing her hard. I slid my hand between us, but she grabbed my wrist.

"That's not what I want from you. You just gave me everything I needed."

She was perfect. "I fucking love you," I whispered against her lips, and she lifted a still wet hand to my cheek, smearing my release on my face as she held it gently.

"Never as much as I love you."

29

BOHDIE

My parents wanted me to come home for the summer, but I didn't want to leave Enit. I could always take her with me, but Stacey definitely wouldn't leave her lab and I was fairly certain Enit's parents would gut me if I even suggested it.

Which was how I came to be sitting in a bustling cafe in a small town completely filled with vampires. The cops were vampires, the business owners were vampires, even the sanitation workers were vampires. The only non-vampires were somehow related to Enit. Her dads, a cousin, Carmen's mates—including a fucking Wendigo and my best friend who was now a freaking jaguar shifter. That still blew my mind.

We all sat around one big table at the back of The Immortal Cupcake, and I ignored how most of the vampires eyed us with something like forlorn regret, kinda the same way a pregnant woman eyes sushi. It was against the rules to eat us, but man, we looked all the more appetizing for it.

"You get used to it," Sammie said, stuffing a pastel pink cupcake in his mouth with absolutely no finesse. "You ignore it but never one hundred percent let down your guard. Walker—that's Enit's dad who's the cop—says everyone here pledged not to feed from living beings on penalty of death, but you know... accidents happen."

While the residents of Dark River eyed us like juicy steaks, they looked at Enit like she was the best thing that ever happened to the town. Inside the borders of Dark River, she was the safest person alive.

Guilt that I'd made her stay in Eden with me and Stacey hit me again. If she'd been here, she never would have been taken. She would have recovered, been happy again, and not haunted by whatever happened up in that cabin, the things she still wouldn't talk about.

Enit wandered out of the kitchens, her apron smeared in flour and frosting, and the smile that lit up her face when she saw me struck me dumb. I grinned back, my eyes drinking her in like I hadn't seen her for a decade, rather than just a few hours.

Jesus, I was so fucking whipped, it was sickening.

But in the back of my brain, Stacey's words about

her losing weight were playing in my mind. She was right, of course. Enit's cheeks were a little gaunter, her curves a little less pronounced. She was wasting away, and I knew that was part of the reason that Stacey hadn't joined me in Dark River today.

Something was wrong with Enit, despite her declarations to the contrary, and Stacey didn't like a mystery. Frost had to stay at the Academy, so he was keeping her company down in the labs today. I wasn't sure if she was happy or annoyed about it, but I felt better that I wasn't abandoning her there by herself. The Academy was nearly empty during the summer break.

I kind of missed Frost too. He'd fallen effortlessly into our friend group, and he made Enit happier, which made me happy. He was human, so my lion had decided he was no threat to our standing within the Pride.

Enit sat down on my lap and I nuzzled her cheek. She smelled like sugar and deliciousness, and I wanted to find a closet to devour her in. But this was her family's business, and we were in a town filled with overprotective vampires, so I'd keep it in my pants.

Still... I kissed her gently, tasting the powdered sugar on her lips. "You smell like something I want to eat," I whispered softly in her ear, and she shivered.

I gripped her hip, unable to ignore the feel of her hip bone. I'd talk to my parents about it. If Stacey couldn't find something medically wrong, it had to be magical in nature.

Carmen, who had been waitressing, came over and sat in the seat between the looming Wendigo and Sammie. Monster hadn't spoken a word, but Sammie seemed comfortable with him. Plus, he looked at Carmen like he'd tear out the heart of every person in the room, just for her. Which was, you know, romantic in a crazy serial killer kind of way.

They both kissed her, and then she turned her gaze to me. Enit's sister was fucking nuts, so they were all a pretty good match. Sometimes, if there was a sudden cold snap, my nose still ached where she'd broken it.

She looked softly at Enit, her eyes equal parts worried and excited. "I have news."

Enit tensed. "Are you pregnant? The dads are going to shit a brick."

Carmen threw up her hands. "Why does everyone keep saying that? No, I'm not pregnant. Sheesh." Enit grinned, and I realized she'd been teasing her sister. I chuckled silently, squeezing her closer.

Carmen looked between us. "No, that's not what it is. Bobby asked me if I would be his mate. Officially, I mean. We're going to have a mating ceremony. I want you to be there."

Enit squealed, her face going through a comical amount of emotions: surprise, happiness, but my eyes snagged on the longing on her face.

Soon, little Omega, I'll make you mine forever.

She launched herself across the table and into her sister's arms. "Of course I'll be there. Where else would I be?"

They fell into conversation about ceremonies and dresses and all that stuff, and I pulled her back down on my lap so I could just appreciate her closeness. Apparently, having her stolen had messed me up a bit too.

When she had to get back to the kitchens, I felt her absence like a physical ache. Carmen watched me with narrowed eyes. "Keep looking at her like that, and I won't be the only one having a mating ceremony soon." She watched her go as well. "There's something wrong with her."

My eyes snapped back to the beta. "I know. Stacey is working on it, but Enit insists she's fine."

Carmen shook her head, sliding out from between Sammie and Monster. "She'd insist she was fine even as you put her body in the ground. Figure it out, Alpha. Prove your worth." With that, she swung her long, dark hair over her shoulder and marched off.

I looked at Sammie. "Your girlfriend is scary as hell, man."

Sammie gave me a goofy, lovestruck look. "I know."

.   .   .

As Enit rode me, moonlight dripping down her skin until she looked like a goddess, I bit my lip and thought of the Queen of England naked so I didn't blow my load right then. In the corner, a fully dressed Stacey watched on, her eyes appreciating the long lines of our girl's back, the way she tipped her chin to the sky, pushing her pretty tits in the air.

Ever since that day in the infirmary, when I'd walked in on literally every guy's fantasy, Stace had watched me make love to our girl. We'd become closer before that, banded together while Enit was gone, but this was another step.

And I loved it. Loved that someone else could see how well I treated my mate, how I made her come all over my cock, how fucking amazing our bodies looked rolling together in the darkness.

Stace and I didn't have a sexual relationship, and we never would, but we had a mutual desire to make Enit as happy as possible, and this scenario fulfilled something for us all.

I grabbed Enit's waist, thrusting up roughly, and she mewled my name in the darkness, begging me for more, or hell, maybe pleading with me not to stop. She didn't have to worry. I had myself locked down.

"Come on baby, you're almost there. Come for me, Omega," I purred, and like the good girl she was, she fucking shattered all over my dick, her sweet little pussy milking me. I gritted my teeth through the pleasure. I wasn't done yet. I wanted to wring one more orgasm from her before we called it a night. She slumped against my chest, and I wrapped one arm around her shoulders, holding her to me as I flipped her onto her back.

She looked toward Stace in the corner, and I kissed her neck, moving slowly, building her back up again.

I heard Stacey's whispered, "Beautiful," then Enit's eyes were back on me. They were dazed and filled with satiated lust, and her body rolled gently against mine, meeting my gentle thrusts. I slipped her legs over my shoulders. I snapped my hips as she begged and gasped, holding out until one final orgasm shook her body, and we were both sweaty and panting.

I collapsed beside her, stroking her floppy white-blonde hair from her face. "I love you, Enit Baxter," I whispered into her shoulder. "One day I'll mark you and make you my mate."

"I love you too—"

"That's it!" Stacey was bounding to her feet, moving to the bed in a single jump. "That's what's wrong. Why the fuck didn't I think of it earlier?"

I blinked dumbly, mostly because all the blood in my body was still working its way from my dick back to my brain. Plus Stacey had said fuck; she never swore, it wasn't in her nature. "What?"

Stacey grabbed a panicked Enit, turning her face so

she could stare down at her. "When you had intercourse with Kell Arborson, did you bite him?"

My whole body froze like I'd been stunned with a cattle prod. She couldn't be implying...

Enit started to shake in my arms. "I can't remember. It was all so fast and—" Her eyes shifted back to me, like she was waiting for my anger. "I don't remember."

Stacey met my burning gaze, and then looked back at Enit. "You created a mate bond with the human. You're pining away without him."

Enit gasped. "I don't understand."

Stacey softened her voice. "You mated the human. We need to find him, or you'll die."

Enit tore herself from the bed, running into the bathroom and locking the door.

In my shock, I just let her go.

Something was wrong, but everyone was pretty tight-lipped about it. It didn't help that everyone was off doing crap during the summer break and I was stuck on campus, so I had nothing else to obsess over. I mean, it could have been worse after I got caught. I could be dead or in a dank cell somewhere. But Stacey had been right—Enit was too soft to let that happen.

Speaking of which, Enit and her two mates were stepping out of their house right now, and I lifted my hand in greeting. Enit looked pale. Well, paler—on a good day she already looked like a snowball in the sun.

I moved to meet them, but a girl stepped into my view.

Somehow—and honestly, this shit was as surprising to me as it was to everyone else—I was catnip for supernatural girls. They wanted to climb me like I was a damn tree, and it was a surreal experience.

"Hi, Frost. I just wanted to invite you to my party on Friday night." The girl stepped closer, her body almost pressed against mine.

I took a small step back. "Uh, thanks, uh..." Fuck, I'd forgotten her name.

"Teesha."

"Oh right, stupid human brain." I slapped my forehead. "Unfortunately, I can't leave the Academy grounds, you know?"

She was definitely a barnacle shifter, because she was stuck to my ass once again. "That's okay. We'll have it in the woods at the back of the grounds." She fluttered her eyelashes. "Or we can skip it altogether and have a party in my dorm room."

Holy crap. The desperation level of this chick was about to go supernova. Still, I didn't want to be rude. "Look, you're really hot and stuff, and I'm sure you go off like a cat in a sack in the bedroom, but you're not really my type."

"Because I'm a shifter?"

"Because you're desperate and easy."

Teesha's face went bright red. She opened her mouth to probably give me a tongue lashing, and not the kind she wanted to give me, when a throat cleared, and Teesha looked over her shoulder.

"Oh look, it's the losers." She looked up coyly at Bohdie. "Except you, Bohdie."

With a speed I couldn't fathom, Bohdie's hand was around her neck and he was squeezing lightly until her eyes bulged. "Enit is my mate. Stacey is my Packmate. You will not speak about them in that manner ever again. Do you understand?" he growled, and Teesha nodded. He let go, and I swear to god, she licked her lips at him and sauntered away slowly.

I mean, no shade to Teesha, because damn bitch, I got it.

"Not going to lie, that Alpha shit makes me hard as a rock. Choke me, Daddy," I cooed and then cracked up laughing at the look of absolute horror on his face. None of them laughed; they were all wound so tight, they were about to explode.

I needed them relaxed.

I wrapped my arm around Enit, and she nuzzled into my chest. It was a completely innocent gesture, but it didn't help the hard ache of my dick. Enit was unlike the rest of the supernaturals, and I think it was possibly because she was an Omega. She was distracting.

She melted into my arms and I held her tight. Looking over her white head, I gazed between Bohdie and Stacey.

"What's up? Why do you guys look like someone just kicked your puppy?"

It was Stacey who spoke. "What do you know about shifter relationships?"

A lot, but I played dumb. I'm pretty sure it would be awkward for everyone if they realized how much I knew about the shifter world. The internet was a highway of forbidden knowledge, you just had to know how to navigate the dark alleyways.

"Uh, not much?"

Stacey looked like she was about to give me the birds and the bees talk, which was bound to be hilarious. "Well, shifters create bonds with other beings by sharing blood and saliva during intercourse. In, uh, the heat of the situation, it seems that perhaps Enit has created a mating bond with Kell. The fact he has been gone for so many months is causing her body to waste away." She sighed. "The physiological effects are obviously more complex than that but you get the idea."

"She's dying... for the D?"

Enit snorted, and that snort turned into a belly laugh, which then turned a little strained. We all looked at her like she was losing it. Hell, maybe she was.

I pulled her into my arms again, squeezing her shoulders tightly. "Soon, this won't even matter. It'll just be a bad dream."

She let out a hiccuping little sigh. "How do you figure?"

"Because Kell Arborson will come to his senses,

then come back to beg for your forgiveness." Bohdie huffed and I grinned against the top of her head. "Then probably get eaten by a lion, but you know what? Worth it." I looked over her head at the other two. "What's the plan?"

Bohdie reached out and put his hand on Enit's lower back, always touching her. Must have been nice to be raised in a community where touch was acknowledged as being as important as food and shelter. Only touch I'd received growing up had been at the other end of a belt. "We were hoping you'd know where he was, so we can go get him and bring him back. There are ways to break the bond."

Enit tensed in my arms, and I gave her another squeeze. "And if breaking the bond isn't an option?"

I was really poking the bear—er, lion—but I didn't get where I was today by being a pussy. And that was said with the utmost respect to vaginas. And cats.

Bohdie's eyes fell to Enit. "Then we start working out how we're going to live with the situation, I guess. Do you know where he is or not?"

I shook my head. "No idea." I felt Enit sag against me. "But with a computer, I could definitely find him. No person is trailless. If he's so much as bought a beer, I'll be able to find him."

Stacey frowned at me. "You're banned from technology."

"A rule is just a suggestion until you break it."

She tilted her head at me. "That makes absolutely no sense."

Bohdie's jaw tensed. "You can borrow mine."

I grinned, my fingers aching to touch the keyboard again. May chaos reign supreme.

I all but skipped back to their apartment, scooping Enit up into a piggyback ride, making her laugh. She had a pretty laugh, light and airy and only mildly touched by pain. I pirouetted just to hear the sound again.

"Cedric, stop for a moment. I have to get to the lab and I'd like to kiss my girlfriend," Stacey said, stepping closer.

I slid Enit off my back, and stepped away. "I will never say no to a bit of girl on girl action," I teased, just to see Stacey's warning look. It was kind of adorable, like your kindergarten teacher and a naughty nurse all rolled into one. It was a pity she only swung one way. She kissed Enit tenderly, and then raised an eyebrow at the both of us. "I will see you all later."

We walked into Stacey's house, which looked exactly how you would expect it might look. Clean white lines, a lack of clutter. Antique medical equipment and modern art were the only decor. She really was an interesting person. But elements of both Enit and Bohdie had made their way in too. A vase of bright yellow daisies. A pair of running shoes by the door and a gaming console connected to the TV.

Bohdie kissed the top of Enit's head. "I'll just run upstairs and grab my laptop."

He was gone, leaving me alone with Enit. As much as I appreciated all the physical affection, I would miss being truly alone if I'd been raised supernatural. My upbringing had been the exact opposite. All my time was alone.

"Do you want a drink? I could make popcorn and we can watch a movie?"

I gave her a soft smile, because that's the only kind that was worthy of Enit Baxter. "Sure, that sounds great." She went to move away, and I grabbed her fingers. "Come and sit with me first."

She nodded and I led her over to the surprisingly plush couch. Settling in, I patted the space beside me. She sat down close, and I leaned into her. "How are you feeling about the whole mate thing?"

She chewed on her lip and shrugged. "Deep down, I kinda knew. There was this... ache, I guess. It was either a mate bond or I was pregnant, and I can't begin to tell you how glad I am it wasn't option number two."

I blew out a breath. Kids were cute, but kinda gross. "Hell yeah."

"What about you? Are you settling in okay? Are you sure there's nobody back home who'd be missing you?" she asked once more like I'd finally remember that someone actually loved me or something.

I resisted the urge to pull her onto my lap. Looking

at her big, innocent eyes, it was hard to remember that she wasn't human. She just had this innocence that you didn't associate with monsters.

"Nah, no one will be calling the cops on my behalf. I mean, I have family, but we aren't close. I have acquaintances too, but I'm not sure any of them would come to my funeral unless there was free booze at the wake, you know?"

She shook her head, and I guess she really didn't know. People had torn apart the world when she went missing.

"Lucky. But yeah, as far as prisons go, this is a really nice one," I joked, pulling her to my side again.

Bohdie returned, his eyes taking in my position, but he didn't tear my head off. That was something, I guess. He sat on Enit's other side and passed me the laptop. He pulled her onto his lap and I let her go.

"My precioussss..." I hissed, making her laugh again. Argh, I'd missed this, even if it was only a shitty off-the-shelf laptop. I could make it purr like a whore and give up all its secrets.

They both shook their heads, and Enit tilted her head back and kissed Bohdie's chin. "I'm going to make popcorn and watch a movie. Want to stay and chill with me?"

Honestly, they were so cute I was going to throw up all over this inbuilt, clunky keyboard.

"Sounds good."

I started downloading the tools I would need to make this shit work, looking over at the lion Alpha who was watching Enit like she was the best thing in the world.

"You are so fucking whipped—you know that, right?"

The grin he gave me lit up his face. Fuck me, they were a pretty couple. I wondered how I could get invited to be the marshmallow in that gooey s'more sandwich.

He shrugged. "I know it. It's the best feeling in the world."

Lucky bastard.

KELL

The girl behind the bar pushed another drink in front of me and walked away. I hadn't asked for one, but I guess since I'd been sitting on this stool for at least four hours, it was probably a given now.

It'd been months, and this ache hadn't left my chest. Months in which I'd thought I could forget all about that giant clusterfuck and move on with my life. Appreciate my second chance.

That's what it had been. One of those vampires could've torn me to pieces, I knew that. Against two? I would've had no chance. I'd slunk out of Eastern Europe with my tail between my legs and disappeared off the face of the earth. Kell Arborson no longer existed. I was Pieter Arnold. Out of work farm laborer. One of many in today's society.

It wasn't just that I'd been transplanted far from home, or the fact that thoughts of Enit still plagued me. Taking down Eden had been my life's goal since I was a kid. The one promise that had governed my choices for so long.

I didn't know what the fuck to do with myself now. There were groups I could join, that killed for money or on some rich guy's word, but I didn't want to be a mercenary. I could really embrace my new alter ego and become a laborer, back-breaking hard work but honest. But I'd be poor forever.

Alone.

I downed the beer in front of me and the girl behind the bar tsked.

"If you do not slow down, I will get Bjorn to throw your ass out," she said in heavily accented English.

I nodded and threw fifty euros on the bar. I tipped an imaginary hat and left on unsteady legs. The old Kell would have tried to get in her pants, but now? I couldn't get it hard for other girls. Like my cock had seen nirvana and it didn't want to go back to dirty fucks in dark alleys.

I stepped out of the only pub in the tiny village where I was staying. Small enough that it was easy to pick people who didn't belong, but with enough tourism that while I stuck out, it wasn't unusual for me to be here.

So when I saw a guy looking at his phone, leaning

against the wall opposite the bar, I was instantly suspicious. His clothes said he wasn't a local. His six-hundred dollar watch said he wasn't from around these parts at all. I turned the opposite way to the little bed and breakfast I was staying in, looping back around toward the stream that ran through town. I watched the plate glass windows, and noted when the guy started walking along behind me. Another one peeled off further up ahead and now I knew I was being ambushed.

Fuck.

They weren't supes, that was for sure. They didn't walk like shifters, and if they were vampires, I would already be dead. I stilled my feet, and watched the guy in front of me stop and look into a boutique window.

"Let's stop with the foreplay, hmm?" I said loudly, and apparently to no one. The passing villagers gave me the side-eye but didn't stop. The guy checking out the women's boutique turned around, striding toward me. I didn't make any sudden moves, but I brought my hand a little closer to the holster on my hip. I turned so my back was to a wall, and I could keep an eye on the converging men.

Finally, Mr. Fancy Watch was in front of me. "Mr. Arborson, we come on behalf of an organization that has similar values as you."

The Hounds. These guys came from the European branch of The Hounds.

"They believe that sardines are the Devil's food?"

Neither of them so much as twitched an eyebrow. "Hilarious, Mr. Arborson."

I shook my head. "Look, I think you guys have the wrong person. My surname is Arnold. Close, I know, but not quite the same. I have no fucking idea what you guys are talking about."

The second goon huffed, but Fancy Watch just stared at me. "Please, don't insult our intelligence. There are whispers in the wind that you found Eden."

I snorted. "All I found was a pretty girl and the end of an angry father's shotgun. Proverbially speaking."

Technically true.

"You're trying to say you ran to the middle of fucking nowhere to escape an angry father? I'm calling bullshit." Goon Two was super irritating.

I shrugged. "Her Daddy was rich, paid me very well, and was very graphic about what would happen to my balls if I didn't leave the country. I happen to like my balls. Besides, I wanted to see the homeland of my mother."

They stared at me. "Your father was once a member of our organization."

This time, I dropped the congenial act. "Your organization abandoned him. He beat my mother until she committed suicide and then beat me instead. Trust me, my father isn't the way to garner my cooperation."

Neither of them twitched again. "You don't want to be our enemy, Mr. Arborson."

I pushed off the wall and grabbed my gun. I was done with this shit. "I don't want to be your anything, asshole. I want to rot away in this tiny village and forget my life up until this point even happened. I'm not interested. Find yourself another spy or mole or fucking patsy."

Mr. Fancy Watch laughed. "Oh, we have, Mr. Arborson. But you know what they say—a bird in the hand is better than two in the bush." He turned and strolled back down the cobbled streets like he was a tourist. "Leave Europe, Mr. Arborson. If we see you again, it won't just be your balls you have to worry about."

Goon Two stepped close and nailed me in the stomach. "I hear Australia is nice this time of year."

Then he walked away whistling, as I gasped for breath. I walked quickly back to my B&B and started throwing all my shit into my bag. Those fuckers might have sounded like a fortune cookie, but their meaning was clear. They had someone on the inside of Eden Academy, hell maybe they'd always had someone on the inside.

I had to warn Enit. The rest of those bastards were on their own, but the idea of anything happening to Enit made my chest feel like it was being torn apart. I got online, booking a ticket to Australia as The Hounds had suggested. I'd change ID too, become someone else. Last thing I wanted to do was lead them straight to Enit.

Did my heart beat faster at the idea of seeing her again?

Yeah, it did, and that scared the fucking shit out of me.

Carmen looked beautiful. In a sapphire blue dress that matched her eyes, she grinned up at Bobby like she was exactly where she wanted to be. I snuggled in closer to Bohdie, who kissed my head. I held Stacey's hand on my other side.

Bohdie knew what this meant in the shifter world. Mating with someone, especially another shifter, was more than a human marriage. It was like twining your soul with someone else's. The way her other mates were looking at her though, I knew that we'd be attending a few more of these ceremonies for her in the next year or two. But the first one, this first moment, would cement them all as a Pack.

My dad, as Alpha of the Nîso Pack, performed the ceremony, and he looked overwhelmingly proud. "Carmen, Bobby, today you bind your lives, your hearts, and your souls together for eternity. As fated mates, there was never any doubt that you would be together; separately, you were merely parts searching for their whole. Together, your bond will make you both, as well as your Pack, strong. You'll produce strong cubs that will carry on the lines of Nîso. But not for a while yet, okay?" he added quickly and everyone laughed. "Carmen, do you take Bobby as your mate, to run with under the light of the full moon and to stand shoulder to shoulder with during life's battles?"

"Abso-fucking-lutely," she basically shouted, and I laughed, even if Mom ran a hand down her face in exasperation.

Dad shook his head. "Bobby, do you take Carmen as your mate, to run with under the light of the full moon, and to stand shoulder to shoulder with during life's battles?"

The look the Alpha-Heir gave his new mate made tears pool at the corners of my eyes.

"I promise. I will love you every day I draw breath, Carmen Baxter," he whispered.

Brody cleared his throat. I might have been mistaken, but even he looked a little misty. "Pack, I present to you Nîso's newest mated pair."

Stacey squeezed my hand and that was when I realized I was openly crying. Tears of happiness mostly, because Bobby and Carmen had been destined to be together since they were teenagers; they'd both just been way too stubborn to get out of their own way for a long time. Carmen had been there for me through everything, had protected me long before she had any concept of what an Omega was, had loved me unconditionally. She deserved happiness with her mates, who were as fiery and intense as she was—and that wasn't hyperbole in the case of Flint, her Ifrit mate. He was literally fiery.

But deep in the recesses of my heart, where that constant ache sat, was the knowledge that I might never see my mate again. That instead of making me stronger, my mate bond was slowly killing me.

To say it made the day bittersweet was an understatement. Everyone stood, the steady hum of conversation bouncing off the trees in the grove where we held mating ceremonies. I wouldn't call it sacred or anything; it was just beautiful. I gripped Bohdie and Stacey's hands as we wandered back through the trees toward the giant feast that would be held in the square. We'd go back to Dark River tonight, and have another feast with the townspeople, because despite us being wolf shifters, they loved us as if we were their only offspring. I might have had eight actual parents, but my family were innumerable.

The actual creation of the matebond would happen tonight, probably, if they hadn't done it already. That was a private thing, like consummating a marriage, and I certainly didn't want to bear witness to that.

Everyone was here, which was kind of nice. Ghost, Nîso's snow leopard Enforcer, was juggling a baby snow leopard, which could only be one of Celeste's. Celeste and her human mates lived on the grounds of Eden Academy, but they visited Ghost up here a lot. It was nice how they'd become family, adopting each other like siblings. Life was funny like that.

Actually, most of the founders of Eden Academy had come, because our lives had become entwined with theirs somehow. We'd grown together, I guess, from the very early years of the Academy until now. Miss Pea was there, as well as Ramer. The Lycans, Micah and Alistair, were there with their mate and the worlds nicest person, Layla. Her third mate, Locke, was carrying a baby. Actually, he was carrying a baby and two toddlers. I guess they were kind of my in-laws now, and to prove the point, Stacey dragged me toward them.

I blinked rapidly as she pulled me, and by extension Bohdie, to a stop in front of them. "Parentals. You know Enit, my mate. And my Packmate, Bohdie."

Locke laughed, handing her the baby. "Of course we know them, Stace. I knew Enit before you knew the periodic table."

Stacey frowned, and honestly, her holding a baby

kind of did things to me. "No you didn't. I knew the periodic table when I was two."

Locke laughed, leaning over to kiss the top of her tamed curls. "Just a saying, Sweetheart. I'm glad it has worked out for you guys. I couldn't have picked a better person for you to fall in love with," he said softly, and I swear, I almost cried again.

Apparently, we were playing pass the parcel with the baby, because she handed him off to Bohdie like he was a relay baton; Bohdie just held him with complete ease.

Yep. There went my ovaries.

Calm down. You have plenty of time for diapers and midnight feedings. We aren't done banging in every room yet, I told them. That perked them up.

Stacey rounded on Alistair, who was gazing at us all with bemusement. "Actually, I wanted to talk to you about breaking mate bonds."

The whole party went silent and everyone turned in our direction. I went pale, swaying on my feet, and Bohdie juggled the baby into one arm, wrapping the other around my waist. Alistair's eyes bounced between us all, and Micah reached out to extract the baby from Bohdie.

"I think it's best we talk about this at some other time, Sweetheart. A mating ceremony might not be the best place." But even as Alistair was saying the words, I could see him appraising me with a scientific eye, as if he was making the connections.

The founder of Eden was brilliant. I had no doubt he was surmising exactly the right scenario in his head right about now.

The conversation of the party resumed, and when Carmen and her Pack arrived, we were forgotten in the cheers of celebration. Stacey turned to me, her face flushed pink. "I'm sorry, Enit. I momentarily forgot that everyone had supernatural hearing," she said softly, and I leaned forward to kiss her cheek.

"I know."

Shifters really knew how to party. Food was eaten, a crazily large cake constructed by Mom and Nico was cut, and by the time someone cracked the moonshine, everyone was on a good sugar rush.

Carmen kept shooting me worried looks, and I think it was from how pale I looked today, or maybe it was the way my dress kind of hung off me in a way that it hadn't six months ago. We'd all been caught up in our own bullshit, but there was still no one I knew as well on this planet as I knew my littermates.

Which became extremely apparent when Christopher appeared, his eyes a little wild, and his breath scented with the bite of moonshine. Christopher had taken the accident badly, and my abduction even worse. Now I wasn't living at home in Dark River with him, I rarely saw him. He seemed to be avoiding me on campus, and when I did accidentally stumble across him, he hugged me and told me he loved me, then disappeared again.

He was drowning and I wasn't sure I had the emotional capacity to pull him back up anymore. I was just drowning right along with him.

He pulled me into a hug, and I let my Omega essence wrap around him, gentling his fractious spirit. He relaxed a little, though that might have been the moonshine kicking in. "Something is wrong with you, E."

I let myself sink into his strength. It was something I was doing more and more of, relying on other people to keep me propped up. Bohdie, Stacey, even Frost. "I know, Christopher."

His arms squeezed, like he wasn't expecting the admission. "What can I do?"

I shook my head. "I accidentally mated him, Christopher. There's nothing you can do unless he decides to come back."

My brother's whole body froze like he'd been turned to ice. "What?" he hissed, pulling me away so he could look down at me, like I might have been making the world's worst joke. I just looked up at him sadly. "Fuck," he whispered. "Does Carmen know?"

I shook my head, and then pinched him. "And you won't tell her, either! Let her enjoy mated life. There's nothing she can do and we can tell her if things get... dire."

Christopher exhaled deeply. "E, I can feel every one of your ribs under my palms. Things are already pretty dire."

I shook my head, stepping away, feeling self-conscious. "We're working on it, Christopher. Just have to wait and trust the process, you know?"

He nodded, but pulled me close again. "I hate trusting the process," he grumbled, making me laugh.

I rested my head against his shoulder. "I know, big brother. I know."

THAT NIGHT, I lay in between the warmth of Stacey and Bohdie. Stacey had her head pillowed on my chest, and Bohdie had his legs twined in mine, his body pressed as close as possible.

It was calm and peaceful, until Bohdie broke the silence. "I think we should form a mate bond."

I stiffened, my eyes finding his golden ones in the dark. "Why?"

He eased away, propping himself up on his elbow so he could see my face. "I think forming another bond will ease the strain of the one you have with Kell. Like it'll give your soul something to latch onto."

Stacey sat up too, her eyes narrowed as she thought. "Theoretically, it should work."

I was shaking my head. "No. You shouldn't be forced into mating with me out of desperation. That's not how mate bonds should work, Bohdie."

He sat up completely now, dragging me with him. "Enit Baxter, if you think I'm being forced into this, you are extremely mistaken. I knew I wanted you for a mate from the very first moment I saw you. We're just speeding along the timeline a little." He paused, his brow knitting. "Unless you aren't sure?"

Was I sure? It was hard to remember who I was before all this, but I knew I felt the same way as Bohdie. That instant connection that was the Alpha and Omega sides of our natures connecting, and then falling madly in love with Bohdie, the person. If none of this had happened, and he'd asked me to be his mate in a year or two, would I have said yes?

Absolutely.

"No, I'm sure about wanting the bond with you too."

The smile that lit up his face healed something inside me already. "Then let's do it, right now. We can have a big party when all this is over and you're feeling better, but let's cement our Pack—our Pride—right now."

I looked at Stacey, who was watching us intently. "I don't want to bond with you right now," she said softly, and something inside me cracked. "No, don't look like that. You and Bohdie definitely should bond, because the link between Alpha and Omega should be strong enough to slow your deterioration. I am mad at myself for not thinking of it sooner." She paused, leaning her head to the left to kiss my chest, just below the hollow of my throat. "But I want one of your bondings not to be a life or death thing. I want you to have what Carmen had today. Something joyous and a celebration of our Pack. Do you understand?" There was a note of pleading in her voice and I kissed her softly.

"I understand completely. Thank you for thinking of our future. I love you."

She kissed me in return, pouring her love right back into me, shoring up all the cracks that seemed to have left me broken and exposed.

I drew back and looked over at Bohdie. "Let's do it."

33

BOHDIE

My heart was pounding in my ears. "Really?"

Enit nodded again, and that was all I needed. I wasn't going to wait another second. I dropped to my knees beside the bed, bowing my head low. Vance, the bear Alpha of the Cold River Sleuth, had drummed these words into every single Alpha kid he met. I didn't know if it was because he had an Omega mate, or because he was just a touch old-school, but I couldn't have been more thankful in that moment.

"Omega, I pledge my teeth, my claws, my honor and my pride to your protection. You will be cherished by my Pride, respected by my side and the balance of my Alpha." I tilted my head to the left, baring my throat in a sign of submission. It was obvious by her too wide eyes that she'd never heard of this ritual, which made sense. She hadn't even started her Omega Studies yet.

Instinctively, she knelt on the floor in front of me, taking hold of my chin and dragging me forward until she could lay her teeth on my throat. A killing blow, and a sign of submission often reserved for an Alpha. By submitting to an Omega, I was telling her that we were equals. She pulled away without breaking skin, and I kissed her cheeks, her chin, her lips.

"Enit Baxter. I love you. I am honored to be your mate, and I will show you every day until we both join the Moon Goddess."

"I can't wait to be your mate too, Bohdie. Please."

I couldn't deny her anything. I kissed her hard, and then I realized that Stacey had her phone out, snapping pictures. I raised an eyebrow. "For the memories," she said, matter-of-factly.

I was overwhelmed with gratitude for this human who had taken us from being just mates, to being a Pride. "Thanks, Stace. Love you too, you know."

She gave me the bright smile, the one you didn't see too often, but which filled you with happiness when you did. "Love you too, Alpha. Not going to kiss you though. Gross."

Enit laughed, leaning back to kiss her. "I'll kiss her for you by proxy," she said sweetly, brushing her lips across Stacey's. When she curled back up into my arms, my eyes snagged on hers and I was helpless to move away.

"You're going to want to put the phone away now, Doc, or we'll be making a home movie of a different kind."

Enit slapped my arm with a laugh, but it quickly turned to a moan as I gathered her into my arms, plunging my tongue into her mouth. I tugged her out of her nightshirt, shucking off my boxers as quick as I could. Then I sat back on the bed, and dragged her back into my arms. Thoughts of the future, even of Stacey, took a back seat as I reveled in the feel of my mate. She sat on my lap, facing me, her legs wrapped around my waist, as close together as we could possibly be. Nose to nose, heart to heart.

I kissed her, my hands on her perfect ass, as she ground against my hard cock, nothing between us but skin. I pushed a hand between us, my fingers finding her wet pussy. Already so wet for me.

I growled against her lips and she got wetter. I found her clit with my thumb, brushing over it even as I speared two fingers inside her.

"Bohdie," she gasped, and I curled my fingers. Not gonna lie, I'd kinda learned a thing or two from Stacey and The Great Squirtening, as we'd been calling it. Well, as I'd been calling it—the name horrified both Enit and Stacey. But watching from the sidelines, I'd learned things, and those things were making my mate mewl.

"Bohdie," she whined. "Please."

I kissed down her throat, and across her exposed clavicles. "What do you need, Princess?" I purred and she ground down on my cock again.

"I want you inside me."

I wiggled my fingers, making her moan again. "I'm already inside you, baby."

She huffed but it was more of a sexy little sound. "I want your cock inside my pussy and your teeth in my flesh, making me yours."

I growled this time. "Yes," I hissed, manhandling her into the air, positioning my dick at her entrance, and then dropping her down. She screamed and I groaned as she clenched around me, her body squeezing me tight. Her arms around my neck, her legs around my hips and her pussy around my cock, all pressing me close as she made me hers. I moved her up and down my dick, loving everything about this position, but especially the slow intimacy of it. As much as I wanted to flip her over and fuck her on all fours, I wanted to enjoy the feeling of her falling apart around me first.

My hand snuck between us once more, and when I pinched her clit, she came on a scream, her teeth clamping down on my shoulder the same way her pussy clamped around my cock. I gritted my teeth through it, holding back the release that made my balls ache, my thrusts slow and even. When she collapsed against my chest, I untangled her from my body, flipping her over.

I wrapped my arms around her hips, kissing my way down her back until I was kneeling behind her. I dragged her ass into the air and my lion growled. I pushed back into her languid body, and she dragged herself against me, making us both groan.

"Bohdie," she shouted and I slammed into her hard and fast, losing my finesse to the sensation of my mate wrapped around my cock. Slipping my hand from her hip to her clit, I stroked it gently, working her into a frenzy that threatened to make *me* go blind with pleasure. When her pants had become shouting moans, I gave into the urge that had been riding me since the first moment I'd laid eyes on Enit.

I clenched the curve of her shoulder between my teeth and bit down, making her scream and come around me. I exploded inside her, but my teeth stayed buried in her shoulder as we rode the wave of our releases and the sensation of the mating bond snapping into place. I held her to me, unwilling to separate our bodies yet, even as we rolled onto our sides.

I laved my tongue over the wound on her shoulder, the primal taste of her blood on my tongue. The scent of her wrapped around me, quieting my Alpha for the first time in months. She was where she was meant to be.

She turned in my arms, kissing me. I felt the other bond, the tentative tendril that was so faint I could barely feel it, but so important it was literally killing her. Kell.

I grabbed that bond, that tiny mental thread, and yanked it.

Enit gasped, smacking my chest with the ball of her hand. "What the hell was that?"

I kissed down her jaw, then over to her lips, meeting them softly. "That was me reminding your wayward mate that there's more to life than being a self-important jerk. If that doesn't draw him back to you, then we'll go to him. You'll be fine. I have you now."

She huffed but I could feel her relaxing in my arms, exhaustion and relief making her sleepy. I looked over her shoulder at Stacey, who was sitting in her normal spot.

It should be weird. Sex wasn't meant to be a spectator sport, even if your participation was just of the self-provided variety. But while there was heat in Stacey's eyes when she looked at Enit, it wasn't of the "I wanna fuck" variety. It was a desire to see something beautiful, that kind of passion you felt when you were watching something so amazing, you knew it would change your life.

"It's a night for Pack, Doc. Hop in. I promise not to touch you with the magic stick."

Enit snuffled a laugh against my chest, and Stacey gave me a disapproving look.

"Alpha, as a doctor, I can tell you there's nothing magical about your 'stick.'" She walked into the bathroom and returned with a washcloth. "If you wouldn't mind disengaging from our mate, I'll clean her up, so you don't wake up with your pubic regions crusted together."

Laughter burst out of me like thunder, while Enit gave Stacey a horrified look. "You're mellowing in your old age, Stace."

Still, I shifted out of Enit, dragging myself away to the bathroom as Stacey leaned over and kissed Enit, somehow making cleaning up my cum not weird at all. I looked in the mirror of the bathroom, and all I could see were teeth, my grin was that wide. I was possibly the happiest man on the planet right now. Her mark was a raw wound on my shoulder, and I contemplated never wearing a shirt again just to show it off to the world. I sent that love down my bond with Enit, and she sent it back. I was never going to get sick of that sensation, like you could feel the person's love and warmth traveling all over your skin in a tingling wave.

Out of respect for Stacey, I pulled on my boxers before I stepped back into the bedroom. Stacey had pulled the blanket up over Enit's naked form, and she was cuddled against her. My heart swelled as I watched them, and then I tried to imagine another person in the bed. The man who had kidnapped my mate. Would he cuddle up behind her? Who would be pushed to the edge of the bed, no longer able to touch her?

My lion made a disgruntled huff at the idea and the urge to murder the problem re-emerged. Just one crunch and it would be back to how it was always supposed to be.

This brought a whole new meaning to eating your stress.

34

Both Alistair and I stared at the test tube on the bench and the computer screen in front of us. A frown bunched his forehead, his face extra pale, more so than his Saxon roots would deem necessary.

"You know what you've done, right?"

I nodded, my heart thrumming in my chest. "I didn't mean to. I was trying to find a solution to the deterioration caused by strained mate bonds."

"Destroy the files. Destroy every reference that you've ever made to it, every note scribbled on anything. It all has to be eradicated, Stacey. Now."

I didn't argue. I deleted all my files, then deleted the deleted bin, and then put my entire laptop in the x-ray machine. I burned my notebooks in the sink. The whole time Alistair watched me intently, until I'd destroyed everything except the vial on the bench and a single white mouse.

"What do we do with those?"

Alistair hesitated. "Keep it at the back of the vaccine fridge. Like right at the back. Call it something... redundant. Smallpox vaccine or something." The *just in case* hung in the air. "The mouse can come home with me, I guess. Hannah would like a pet."

There was a knock on the door and Reese poked his head around the jamb. Reese was the human mate of Celeste, the snow leopard shifter. He was also the financier of the Academy way back at the beginning. Entirely human.

He gave us a megawatt smile. "Hi guys. Alistair, I just wanted to go over the security logs with you and show you the information Talbot sent up from his crawlers on the dark web. It's... disturbing."

Both Alistair and I shot a look at the vial on the bench, and back to Reese. Alistair cleared his throat. "Let's head up to my office."

Alistair ushered Reese out of the lab and back toward the elevator. Labelling the vial as a vaccine for smallpox and making it generally uninteresting, I stuffed it right to the back of the vaccine cooler. I was going to treat it like that one carrot that's always in the bottom of everyone's fridge. If I put it slightly out of sight, no one would ever think to use it. That being said, it was unlikely that anyone but Alistair or I would be administering any of the drugs stored in the infirmary, so it should be fine.

Yes, fine.

I'd accidentally created something that could change humanity as we know it, but it would be fine.

I grabbed the mouse's enclosure and locked up the lab. I'd drop off the mouse to Hannah like it was her birthday, then I'd go find my girlfriend. She looked better already, a little bit of color back in her cheeks, especially when she was touching Bohdie.

A stab of jealousy that their relationship had outprogressed ours hit me, but I pushed it down. It wasn't a competition. I was content with my decision to wait until happier times to become her mate. I was only eighteen. Well, in two weeks.

I had time, and I had faith in the longevity of our relationship, even without the mate bond.

As if I'd summoned her with my thoughts alone, Enit appeared in front of me, Frost jogging behind her to keep up.

She leaned forward, kissing me briefly before squealing and dropping into a crouch to look at the mouse.

"Look at this cutie, Frost!" Glimmers of the old Enit tantalized the edges of her tone, the softness of her face.

Frost grimaced. "Adorable." His tone said he wasn't

actually a fan, but it was hard not to get caught up in Enit's enthusiasm.

"Where are you taking him?" she asked, poking her finger into the cage. The mouse came over to sniff her fingers, its whiskers twitching. Enit was like a living, breathing Snow White, and I loved that about her.

"He's retiring from lab life." I hesitated. "Do you want to keep him?"

Alistair was going to kill me, but the look of absolute joy on her face would be worth the tongue lashing I would receive.

She stood up, her eyes wide. "Can I really?"

I nodded. "All yours."

I passed her the cage and she danced on the spot. The mouse seemed pleased too, standing on its tiny back legs, front paws windmilling in the air. "Does it have a name?"

Yeah, subject 632. But I don't think that would suit Enit. So I said the first thing that came into my head. "Uh, Lucky."

Frost snorted, nudging me with his shoulder. "Lucky he didn't get exploded in the lab like his siblings."

Frost had no idea.

"Where were you two going?"

Enit smiled, though I wasn't sure if it was for me or for the mouse, and looked over at the human who had somehow become a member of our weird little Pack of misfits. "We were going to raid the dessert bar and then I was going to take Frost to the greenhouse and show him all my medicinal grafts."

Sounded dull, apart from one factor—Enit. She could tell me about the alphabet and I'd be enraptured. Looking at Frost, I caught the same fervent look in his eyes. If I wasn't wrong, I'd say that our resident prisoner had a crush on my girlfriend.

That didn't inspire the jealousy in me that I thought it would. Bohdie was the protection, I was the brains and Frost was the laughs. We worked well, even though no one had outwardly mentioned the fact.

"Dessert sounds reasonable. May I come?"

Frost wrapped his arm around my shoulder, but it was an infinitely more friendly gesture. "Always."

I DRESSED in my finest dress, a rich gold silk that floated down my body to my knees. My hair was tamed into smooth curls and I was even wearing lip gloss. It was all armor to distract from the fact that I was incredibly nervous.

Bohdie kissed the top of my head. "I don't know why you're freaking out, Doc. If they're going to turn anyone into a rug, it'll be me."

I frowned at the Alpha. "I don't find that reassuring."

Enit gave him a frown, but the smile she gave me

was gentle. "You've known my parents for years. It's going to be fine." She rubbed her cheek against mine. "Besides that, you look absolutely beautiful."

I flushed, but I wasn't that easily distracted. "I have known your parents for years, and that's why I'm nervous. A Convocation member, an Alpha, two ancients, two former vampire mercenaries, and Tex."

She grinned. "What's scary about Tex?"

I paused, huffing a breath. "Nothing. Tex is a sweet man."

We were going to Enit's parents' house for dinner, where we'd tell them that she and Bohdie had done the shifter equivalent of eloping and *oh by the way*, Enit had managed to mate public enemy number one and was suffering from separation deterioration. That was what we were calling it. But worse than that, this was the first time I was going to be talking to her parents as one third of her Pack.

And I was freaking out.

Bohdie seemed to be sweating it a little too, despite his jokes. But not the Omega. She just threaded her fingers through both our hands and dragged us to the front door, completely calm. Pushing it open, she yelled, "We're here," and continued pulling us further into the house.

Carmen appeared, Bobby at her back, grinning. "Hey E." She leaned forward and hugged her sister. She did it a lot more now; it wasn't just our little Pack that had been affected by Enit's disappearance. "Hey Stacey, hey Pussycat."

Bohdie let out a rumbling snarl, but his eyes were sparkling. Bobby shook his head and pushed her toward the back door. "Come on, everyone's out back."

I followed them through the house to the large sliding glass doors that opened up into a generous backyard, bracketed on all sides by the woods. All of Enit's parents were there, as well as Carmen's mates.

Christopher sat in the corner, holding a beer and looking entirely miserable. Enit threw me a wink, and stepped up onto a chair.

"Enit!" I hissed, glaring at Bohdie when he had the audacity to laugh.

She whistled, grabbing everyone's attention. "Everyone, I have an announcement."

Brody, her Alpha shapeshifter dad, glared at Bohdie. "If you've impregnated her, I am going to feed you your testicles." The lion Alpha laughed it off, but he looked a little green.

Enit gave her dad a disapproving look. "No, Dad, that's not it at all." She looked around the backyard. "Two nights ago, Bohdie and I became mates." She tilted her head, dragging the collar of her dress to the side so everyone could see the still raw bite on her neck.

There was a rumbling growl and a blur, then

Christopher tackled Bohdie onto the back lawn, snapping and snarling.

"Christopher!" Enit yelled, and then X was there, lifting Enit down off the chair.

"Congrats, Love." He looked over his shoulder at Lucius, who just seemed kinda bored. "I got fifty on the lion."

Lucius snorted. "There's so much pent-up frustration in Christopher, my money is on him. I will take your bet."

Raine strode over, glaring at them both. "You better not be betting on this fight if either of you ever want to get laid again."

I let a snort slip, even though my eyes never left the fight. It was a lot less clean than the fights at Eden on fight night. They were close to shifting, and all the Alphas in the group were wandering over, including Bobby and Brody.

"Have you ever noticed your family seems to fall in love with Alphas starting with the letter B? Their names even sound almost exactly the same. I wonder if that has some kind of Freudian-style reasoning?"

Enit, Raine and Carmen all turned to stare at me. "What?"

Carmen shook her head, pointing a finger at me. "One, ew. Two, you aren't allowed to mention Freud in this house because it sets Nico off on an epic tangent that will go for literal days about pulp-psychology."

I tilted my head. That conversation actually sounded interesting, but I got the impression I was the only one who would think so, so I kept my mouth shut.

Brody waded into the mass of fur and blood, seemingly unperturbed by the fact that there were shifted paws and fangs

"Enough!"

Even I felt the Alpha power in the word, resisting the urge to drop. Both the brawling Alphas ceased, though they continued to glare at one another.

Enit looked between them, and then back up to her mother. "I guess this isn't the time to tell everyone that I accidentally mated Kell Arborson when he abducted me, right?"

There wasn't a sound in the entire backyard until Carmen stepped closer, wrapping an arm around Enit's shoulder.

"Well, fuck."

35

KELL

For all intents and purposes, I was in Australia. I checked into my flight, boarded the plane, and alighted in Sydney.

Except I wasn't in Sydney, I was in Mexico. Sitting in a bar with patchy wifi, trawling through months of message boards and chat groups designed for anonymity. There were mentions of Eden, but they were almost in past tense, like they thought The Hounds had killed them all off.

As usual, the dark web made me want to throw up in my mouth. You had to dig through the refuse to find what you needed, and that wasn't always easy to find. There was a lot of sad, depressing shit on there.

Every hour, I seemed to oscillate about what I was meant to do. Should I just let Eden fall to The Hounds? Even if they weren't really as bad as I thought, they still were monsters. Plus, they'd lived a long time without my interference. From what I knew, The Hounds had money to throw at someone forever. There'd probably been a mole in there for decades. Though, that couldn't be true. Why wouldn't they have attacked before now?

A kid sat down opposite me, passing me another beer and sighing. "You the guy?"

I nodded, because there was a good chance I was indeed The Guy. She flopped a passport and driver's license down in front of me, not even trying to hide the fact we were doing something shady as fuck. It was just the way of it in this town. "Everything you'll need."

I finished my beer in one gulp. "You sure you wanna do this?"

The kid nodded. "I have to get out of here. I can't stay, but can't leave without your help."

About three weeks into my vampire-imposed vanishing, I'd started searching for answers. Not about Eden, but for other people like Enit. She'd spoken about Eden like they'd been saviors, like the world was a shitty place for preternaturals. I mean, I wasn't an idiot. I got it. On the whole, humans were shit and destroyed anything different with extreme prejudice.

However, the more I searched, the more I found. The dark web had been filled with videos of supernaturals being forced into every evil, vile situation you could think of. Dog fights, except the dogs were really people in chains. Snuff films. Skin trading. If you could think of something sick and twisted that humanity could do to itself, it did ten times worse to the vulnerable supes out there. And up until a few months ago, I had been that person, hunting them down like they were animals. Even if I didn't do the shit that was filmed and flaunted on the dark web, I'd intended to torture and murder to get what I wanted. To satisfy the dying wish of a bitter fucking old man who'd made my life hell. I made myself sick.

These weren't monsters. Sure, there were probably some bad ones in the bunch, but I knew firsthand that twisted people were twisted, regardless of their religion, race or species.

So I searched the other side. I went looking for people in situations like Enit had been when she was a child. People desperate for help, for an escape.

Like this girl—I didn't know her name, and I really didn't want to know. I didn't know what she was, only that she was a supernatural. But she was an expert at forgeries, and she needed to get across the border, while I needed a plausible fake passport.

A quick message later, and we had a deal. What would drive a girl, who couldn't be more than nineteen, to need an escape so desperately that she'd risk trusting a stranger on the dark web? I didn't ask. She was an adult and wanted to get out of this shithole. So be it.

She hesitated. "I just have to get one more thing and then I'm ready."

I nodded. "I'll meet you back here in an hour. I gotta tell you, it won't be super comfortable."

She gave me a dead-eyed look. "It can't be worse than staying."

An hour later, I'd picked up the reasonably nice old Chevy that I'd bought for a steal, as well as some fake plates. She didn't need to last long, just enough to get well into California. It was almost a shame to slit open the bucket seat and clip out the springs. Still, I got to work. I had places to be, and none of them were a backwater, corrupt as fuck cartel town in Mexico. I cleaned the edges up around the piping, stuck in some stiff cardboard and voila, I had my own temporary stowaway compartment. It would be tight, but it would work. Once we were far enough over the border, she could sit up front until I got her to wherever she needed to go. Luckily, the girl was tiny. I knew why she couldn't just leave by herself. She had that wild, desperate look which told me that this wasn't her first plan, but a pretty girl, that young? Trying to leave? It was going to raise eyebrows.

Me? I was used to slipping under radars and fucking charming my way out of shit. I had the privilege of being the top of the fucking genetic heap, and I would never take the benefits for granted.

"I'm here. Let's go."

I turned, looking at the girl's "baggage." My mouth fell open. "Oh, fuck no."

She held a toddler in her arms and I was getting well and truly the fuck out of here. Nope. No way. "Is that yours?"

The girl, whose name I *definitely* didn't want to know now, narrowed her eyes. "Yes. We had a deal."

"The risk is too high." And it was. It literally just quadrupled. The kid looked like two, max. Maybe less.

The desperate look was back in the girl's eyes. "Please. You're our last chance."

Fuck. Fuck, fuck, fuck.

"Fine. Let's go before this gets messier. Are you sure you'll be able to keep it contained?"

"Yes," she said through gritted teeth.

What a clusterfuck. Still, I unzipped my bag and pulled out the down jacket I'd stuffed in my bag after leaving Finland. I laid it on the floor of the hollowed out bench seat to make it a little more comfortable for them. "It's about 45 minutes to the border, and then hopefully we'll only be in lines for another thirty, but be prepared for up to an hour that you'll have to be in there. Keep the seat propped open for as long as you can, and hopefully the kid is asleep when we go across."

"She'll be fine," the girl said. I looked around, and nodded toward the backseat. She watched the shadows too for a moment, and I once again wondered what exactly she was running from. She handed me the baby, and I took it like it was made of C-4. It looked up at me with shining brown eyes, a pacifier in its mouth. Kinda cute, if you liked kids. Which I didn't.

The girl got situated and motioned for me to pass her the kid. Gladly. I expected the baby to fuss or something, but she just curled up in the small space like it was completely natural.

"She isn't going to be freaked out about the closed lid?"

The girl gave me a blank look. "It isn't the first cage we've been stuffed in. It's just the first that will lead to freedom. We'll be fine."

I clenched my back teeth, but didn't ask questions. I grabbed a wedge of wood. "I'll chock this open here. When I tell you, pull this into the seat with you and be as quiet as you can."

"Yes."

It was time.

TWO AND A HALF agonising hours later, I pulled into the parking lot of a mall, right in the back corner. Getting through the border had been surprisingly simple. An easy grin, the fact I was a white American, it all got me waved through with only cursory checks.

Still, I'd driven an hour or so in before I stopped. The girl had propped open the seat again, her relief almost palpable, but she'd been right. The kid hadn't made a peep.

I hopped out and lifted the hidden seat, scooping the baby up into my arms as it slept, letting the girl stiffly uncurl herself from the seat. I watched for people, but with a sleeping baby over my shoulder, I looked like every other Soccer Dad in this parking lot.

The girl half crawled, half shuffled out of the car, stretching her body as she regained blood flow.

This was as far as we'd agreed I'd take her, but I found myself hesitant to just leave them here. "Where are you guys heading?"

She eyed me with suspicion, like I hadn't just illegally snuck her across the border and broken several Federal laws. "Montana."

I raised an eyebrow. "Surprisingly, me too. Well, Canada, but close. I'll drive you guys, or you can stay here and make your own way. But I'm going to get the kid a carseat so we don't get pulled over for child endangerment. You guys bring anything with you?"

She shook her head. "I've got money though," she said, jutting out her chin.

"Yeah, okay. But I got this." I slid my keys from the ignition, and strode toward the doors of the Walmart. "Stay out here, away from the camera."

Another hour and a switched set of plates later, we were on the road again. I'd stop when I needed sleep, otherwise we'd just drive straight through. At least the kid looked comfortable. The carseat was between us on the front bench seat, belted in to the best of the car's 1950s capability. I'd bought some baby crap too, and a duffle bag to store it in. I'd also bought the girl some clothes, praising the tech gods for self-service checkout.

We drove through, only stopping for food, so that I could sleep, or so the baby could toddle around in the fresh air, and then we'd be back on the road.

I didn't examine why I was helping this girl despite the fact that it could very well land me in Federal prison. It wasn't a risk I would normally take, despite my turning over of not just a new leaf, but a whole new fucking branch. Couldn't help many people, supes or otherwise, if I was the bitch to some guy called Bubba in maximum security prison. But there was a tiny therapist on my shoulder telling me it was guilt. I'd done what I needed to get back into the US—I'd held up my end of the deal—yet I was increasing the risk by continuing the trip. Maybe this lightened, just a tiny bit, the huge black mark on my soul from what had happened with Enit.

Two long, silent days later, I dropped the girl and all her new stuff at a long-term apartment in Missoula. We barely spoke, but it was better that way. I watched as she dragged all her newly acquired shit out of the car, staring at me intently. "I don't even know your name," she said softly, the first thing she'd said to me in a full forty-eight hours that wasn't a request like "I need to pee." I'd gotten more conversation out of the baby.

Still, I shook my head. "It's better that way. Stay safe." I hesitated. "If you need help, you know how to find me."

"You saved my life. Our lives," she whispered, and what could I say to that?

"It was nothing." Bullshit, and we both knew it.

She nodded, picking up the carseat and dragging it to the door of her accommodation. While we hadn't spoken much over the last two days, the silence in the car had at least been friendly. As she disappeared through the doors, I finally pulled away from the gutter.

This had been a diversion, but maybe it was also a sign. What were the chances I'd picked up the one migrant who didn't want to go to LA, who instead wanted to go all the way to the freaking mountains of Montana, putting me closer to Enit and...

Shit, I knew who it was. The Mole. It slapped me in the face with its obviousness and I swore so loudly that pedestrians side-eyed me.

The need to get to Enit became overwhelming. She was in danger, and I had to get there in time or finally pay for the sins of my past.

Sin. It was something I knew all too well. According to the church my parents had forced me to attend as a child, we were all sinners. Doomed to Hell, in repatriation for the sins of all mankind. Hell, if we were talking about all mankind, I was probably the worst, especially in the eyes of my parent's church. Not just because I lusted after a man, which according to them was a horrific act. No, if they knew I lusted after an abomination too, they'd have me flagellated for my transgressions.

I'd seen it happen once when I was ten. They'd flayed the skin off the man's back when he'd had the gall to say that perhaps we were the abominations.

I'd agreed with him then, but kept my words trapped behind my teeth. Still, my flagellation would come later, and it wouldn't be at the end of a whip.

The words that had faced me when I'd finally been able to access the secure server were burned behind my eyelids.

Do something or we will.

"Frost, are you okay?"

I looked over at Enit at the other end of Stacey's couch. She had her toes tucked under my thighs and her fluffy sweater had rolled up to show off a sliver of her midriff. I gave her a tight smile and prayed she couldn't scent my guilt. "All good." I squeezed her calf and went back to watch the British baking show on TV. Apparently, her parents owned a bakery, which meant Enit knew her way around a cake. So she tutted when someone put too much baking powder in, or didn't layer their puff pastry the right way.

I understood none of it, but I enjoyed watching her watch the show. Bohdie re-emerged from the kitchen with two more beers, passing me one. Stacey was still at the lab, but she should be home any minute. "Look at that rough extrusion. If you're going to make such a mess of the piping, just slather it on like a four-year-old baking with their granny," he sledged, and I laughed.

Enit lifted her head so she could put it on his lap, but she slapped him in the chest for his troubles.

"Shush. They're trying, and that's what counts."

I snorted. "If the top of that cake cracks any further,

they're going to lose the hosts down the chasm," I added.

Bohdie and I had decided that if we were going to watch cooking shows, we were going to treat them like competitive sports. We picked teams, heckled performances. Honestly, it was the most fun I'd ever had.

I knew that despite it being summer holidays, they returned to the Academy every day for me. They easily could have stayed in Dark River, and I knew that Enit had been pestering Stacey to have some time off, but every day they came back here to make sure I wasn't alone.

Being with these guys, Stace included, was like being a part of something I'd never had. Family. Community. Safety. Fuck, the only other person who'd ever made me feel like they cared was Kell, and I couldn't track him down anywhere. Apparently, he'd taken my lessons on how to stay off the grid to heart. But I knew he'd turn up again eventually. Enit had that draw and if I knew my friend, he'd be helpless to resist.

I wasn't sure if I wished for him to turn up right now, or never. That conflicted feeling raced down my spine again, and Enit frowned at me.

She sat up, shifting toward me until she was sitting on my lap, her arms wrapped around my neck. She laid her head on my chest and I buried my nose in her hair.

"It's okay, Frost. I'll talk to everyone, make them see

that you aren't a threat. Then you can leave if you want."

I froze at her words, but swallowed hard. She didn't know how fucking wrong she was. "What if I don't want to leave?" Let her think that was the only reason I was tense.

She looked over at Bohdie, who tilted his head. "Then you stay here with us."

As simple as that. They just accepted me, despite my past. My heart shattered and I forced a smile, wrapping my arms around her and holding her tightly to me.

"Thanks, E."

We went back to watching the baking, but Enit didn't move from my lap, happy to comfort me with touch. I kissed the top of her head, soaking in the warmth that didn't belong to me.

After fifteen minutes of utter torture, I excused myself, pretending to go to the bathroom, but instead heading toward Bohdie's laptop. They didn't even worry about hiding it from me anymore, content that I meant them, and their little world, absolutely no harm. And if life was fair, I wouldn't. I would take what Enit offered and be happy.

But life wasn't fair, especially not to those with less opportunity. People would crush you under their boot heel for one final glimpse of sun on their face, and if you wanted to make it up from the bottom, you would too.

I booted up the laptop and briefly thought about turning it over to Eden Academy's founders. Those fuckers were scary, possibly scarier than what awaited me back in the States. But I knew deep down in my soul that if I became a bigger problem than I already was, they'd dispose of me like yesterday's newspaper.

I missed Kell, but I knew that if I messaged his old phone number, I'd get nothing back. I'd set up those protocols, knew better than anyone his old phone was now nothing more than a brick. I wondered if he was even still alive, but I figured he must be, because Enit would know if he wasn't, right?

I opened up the secure browser, putting in passcode after passcode until I got to the secure

chat server.

Frost: I'll do it.

Those words were like the call of the banshee. I now realized what it was it was like to be lonely and happy all at once. I wasn't waiting for the other shoe to drop. No, I saw that fucker hurtling down toward me from space, and when it reached me, I knew I was dead.

Either metaphorically or physically, no matter how you looked at it.

Out of habit, I checked the private chat server I'd shared with Kell. When I saw a message there, my heart nearly beat out of my chest.

KELL: Be there in three days.

THAT WAS IT. That was all it said. But it was an opportunity I couldn't pass up. Enit would never forgive me, but I had to forget about her, and now would be the time to start. Otherwise leaving would be impossible. Kell was my way out, and it didn't matter that I was leaving something of myself behind. So I messaged him back.

FROST: I'll be waiting.

The new school year started better than the last one had ended. Bohdie had been right about the mate bond centering me, holding me tightly, making sure I didn't drift too far. It was as reassuring as it was frustrating, because there was another part of me that was always straining, trying to move toward my other bond.

The ground shook and Bohdie let out an exasperated rumble. I couldn't help but grin though. The new school year had also heralded the arrival of thirteen immortal half-fae, half-shifter kids, and let's just say, they were a handful. They were cheeky, devious and worst of all, super overpowered.

Honestly, the heads of the school had been putting out fires since they arrived. Some literal, but mostly figurative.

"Fucking kids," Bohdie huffed and wrapped an arm around my waist, anchoring me to his side.

I tipped my head so my cheek ran over his shoulder. I was always subtly rubbing my scent on him, even though our scents were so intertwined now, it was hard to define between the two. Throw in Stacey, and a little bit of Frost, and we were a complex aroma that smelled like home to me.

"I like them," I said, referring to the fae kids.

He shook his head, dipping to take my lips softly. "You would, you closet anarchist."

I snorted, because what a lie. I just wanted everything to settle down so I could get back to my life.

Suddenly, there was a high-pitched whooping noise that could be heard all over the campus, so loud that it threatened to burst my eardrums. Bohdie stood in front of me, like the noise was an attacker rather than the fire alarm. "Fire drill?"

I shrugged. "We haven't had one in awhile, but given the amount of elementals on campus now, there's a chance it's a real alarm."

The senior Alphas of the Academy, and by extension me, all had a role during a fire drill. They'd each been allocated a zone to clear out, the Alphas corralling the younger children out to the safety zone. It helped that younger Alphas would submit to the authority of older Alphas.

My job was to keep everyone calm, especially the

Alphas. In the case of a real emergency, their protective instincts could go haywire and they'd start attacking any threats, including other Alphas.

We were a powder keg of abilities here at Eden, but we had contingency plans. I stuck with Bohdie as we corralled the younger kids from our quadrant to the field. I held one of the tinier members of the school in my arms. "It's probably just a drill. Nothing to worry about," I said to the tiny shapeshifter girl, and she pressed her face against my neck, inhaling my Omega scent. I watched Christopher bring in his bunch, as well as Kingston. Carmen was nowhere to be seen, nor was her fire Djinn mate.

I looked at Christopher, and he came over to hug me. It was like relaxing back into a security blanket. "I'm glad you're here," he whispered, his body sagging with relief.

"It's not a drill?"

Christopher pulled back, shaking his head. "No. There was an explosion on the lower floor. Between the infirmary and the server room—"

He didn't even get the last word out before I was running.

Stacey.

"Enit, wait!" someone called, but I knew it wasn't Bohdie. He was right there behind me. We tore through the gathering adults, whose job it was to keep fires contained. I saw Carmen with Flint, her fire Djinn, and Sammie.

I bolted around people, aiming for the doors, when strong arms banded around my waist. "No, Omega. Stay."

Bohdie used his fucking Alpha voice on me.

I stayed, rooted to the spot, as he disappeared into the doors, ignoring the shouts of Micah as he lurched toward Bohdie.

Carmen was beside me in a moment, holding me close, or maybe holding me back. I didn't know. "She's going to be fine, E. I know it." Her whispered promises were meant to appease me; she couldn't know for certain, but still I clung to them.

Minutes felt like centuries until Bohdie emerged back out of the smoke, holding the door for Frost, who was carrying an unconscious Stacey in his arms.

I rushed forward, Carmen letting me go, as he lurched a few more yards away and laid her on the grass. He dropped down beside her and I fell to my knees.

"Stacey!" She was still out of it, and I wanted to shake her awake, but I didn't. I checked her for burns or wounds, noticing that her head was bleeding.

"Move, Omega." Alistair was there, and I scrabbled out of the way. He knelt beside her, checking her pulse. "Stacey, can you hear me?"

Her eyelashes fluttered as Alistair gently lifted her

head an inch or two, feeling for breaks and wounds. Finally, she blinked them open. Her eyes bounced between us, and she winced.

"My head has a contusion. I feel disorientated," she mumbled.

Alistair nodded. "Concussion. You banged your head by the looks of it. Anything else hurt?"

She was silent for a moment, probably mentally cataloguing herself. "No, I'm fine."

I took that as my permission to kiss every inch of her face, peppering it like I could take all her hurts into myself. "You scared the shit out of me."

She let me kiss her a little more before gently nudging me away. "I'm okay, Enit. I promise."

We needed a fucking break from life right now. From the bullshit and the drama.

Do you hear that, Moon Goddess? Cut us some damn slack.

I turned to Frost, falling into his arms. "Thank you, thank you, thank you!" I kissed him hard on the lips, shocking us both. "Uh, I'm sorry."

His cheeks flushed and then he kissed me back hard once more. He tasted like peppermint and smelled like smoke. It was kind of alluring.

Someone cleared their throat and I dragged myself away. Micah stared down at me, looking entirely unimpressed. "Sorry to interrupt, but could you please get your asses back to the safety zone?"

I dropped my eyes, and stood. Bohdie leaned down and scooped a protesting Stacey into his arms. "Hush, Doc. You scared us. Let me take care of you or I'll lion out right here and piss everyone off."

Stacey huffed but let herself be carried. Frost stood and reached down, holding out a hand, and I looked up into his dark eyes. I placed my fingers into his wide palm and let him drag me to my feet. "Come on," he murmured, his fingers staying wrapped in mine as we followed Bohdie back to the safety zone.

THE DAMAGE to the main building was substantial on the lower floors, but the design of the building and the inbuilt fire safety system meant that it hadn't spread. Still, until someone declared it structurally sound, none of the boarding kids could go back to their dorms, and the outlying family houses were co-opted into temporary dorm rooms.

Which was how I ended up lying in my childhood bed, squished between the huge frame of Bohdie and the petite one of Stacey.

Stace was sleeping soundly, her head patched up. I wanted to continue to wake her every hour because she had a concussion, but she said that was outdated science. I was supposed to just let her sleep and hope she woke up in the morning.

I couldn't sleep though, as my parents were

bustling around quietly in the house and I could hear their conversation, thanks to my shifter hearing.

"...they said it was a bomb. Deliberately...."

Their voices dropped low again and I missed it. But judging by the tenseness of Bohdie, he'd heard it too.

The front door squeaked open and whoever entered purposefully kept their voice so low that I could only pick up hints of words, never quite grasping them.

But one word made me jolt like I'd been electrocuted.

Arborson.

Kell was here.

I was out of the bed before Bohdie could grab me, marching into the living room. Walker, Nico, Brody and my mom all stood there, their eyes shooting to me.

"Where is he?"

My mom just looked at me, wide-eyed. "Who?"

I narrowed my gaze at them all. "Cut the crap. Kell. Where is he?"

They looked around at each other, before settling on Nico. Guess he drew the short straw. "X was walking the perimeter of the Academy, and found him and Cedric Frostmore in the woods together. Looks like they were conspiring to blow up Eden Academy."

No.

No, they wouldn't.

I didn't realize I was shaking my head until Bohdie

came up behind me, pressing me back against his chest. "Seems circumstantial," he said softly, though he didn't outright deny it.

Walker snorted. "The Academy blows up, nearly killing your mate, on the same day Arborson appears?" He shook his head. "Use your head, little one. There are coincidences and then there is evidence. Why was Frostmore down there to rescue Stacey anyway? He wasn't injured anywhere."

I worried at my bottom lip. "They're friends." It sounded weak to me as well. "Where are they now? Are they dead?" I would have known if Kell was dead, but maybe the bond was malfunctioning. X wasn't known for his leniency.

It was my mom who stepped forward. "Apparently, X is getting soft in his old age. They're over at the jailhouse. One abducted you, the other tried to kill you— don't expect leniency where it can't be given." Her voice was harder than I'd ever heard it before. Usually she was the soft one.

I looked between them all. "I want to see them." I didn't stomp my foot, but I wasn't far off.

They did that thing where they looked at each other and had some kind of silent conversation, but finally Walker nodded.

"Get dressed. I'll take you."

I was gone before he'd even finished his words.

Kell glared at me from the other side of the jail cell. He was even more fucking sexy than I'd imagined, and I'd imagined it a lot. I'd stalked his socials, found him on security cameras—hell, once I'd hacked his cam on his computer before I taught him how to clean up his digital footprint. But nothing had prepared me for how smolderingly attractive he was in real life.

"Why are you mad at me? I did what you *tried* to do."

Actually, I'd done what my family wanted me to do, but Kell didn't know that. Didn't need to know that.

He just glared across the concrete floor at me. "Have you met her?"

I didn't need to ask who he meant. I knew in my very soul. She was a fucking obstacle that I'd found myself banging into again and again, until I realized I *wanted* to collide with her. When I craved being in her presence, I told myself I was ingratiating myself with the enemy. But then she'd smile at me, or wrap her arms around me, and I'd forget that she was anything but Enit. How she could be anyone's enemy was beyond me.

Their whole little Pack was disarming, affectionate and inclusive, even though *I* was meant to be the enemy. I bickered with Stacey, which I knew was her way of showing affection, but Bohdie and Enit? Their affection was far more tactile. I'd received more hugs from Bohdie than I'd ever had from my entire family combined, and he had nothing on the affection of Enit.

When I'd finally been able to get online and see the private channel that was made for me to communicate with my superiors, even reading their orders had made me ill. Human Purity was a grandiose way of saying Humans Only. A way for evil people to do evil things and then be lauded for it. Until Enit, I'd believed them.

Until Enit, I'd been one of them.

"Yes."

"How could you think I wanted her dead?"

Now it was my turn to be mad. "How would I know what you wanted, asshole? I thought *you* were dead. Fuck, you may as well have been. I was left here paying for your mistakes. A captive in a pretty cage. So go fuck yourself, Kell Arborson."

"He doesn't need to. He's already fucked me," a soft voice said from the other side of the bars, and we both whipped our gazes toward her.

Enit.

Why would they let her come here? With her was Bohdie, but no Doc.

"Stacey?" I asked softly, hoping she was okay.

Enit gave me a scathing look. "Do you even care? You could have killed her, or any number of other people. You blew up a school. A school filled with *children*. Are you such monsters that you didn't care that they were children?" She moved her eyes to Kell. "Or are we all so dehumanized to you that even a dead child is just one less monster in the world?"

Kell stood, moving quickly to the bars. "You know that's not true. I would have killed you that first day if it was true." Then he paused. "You're better."

Bohdie growled, and I could see the gold flashing in his eyes. I'd been around shifters enough for the last few months to know that this was about to end in claws and teeth. "No thanks to you, asshole," the lion Alpha growled.

Enit put a soft hand on Bohdie's bicep, and his trembling rage dimmed a little. Such a handy trick. "It wasn't entirely his fault, Bohdie. He doesn't understand. The mistake was mine." She looked Kell in the eye, and I felt his whole body go on high alert. "When we, uh, had sex, I accidentally mated you. I apologize.

As a human, it shouldn't affect you at all, other than a small scar."

Kell's brows knitted as he stared at her. He pulled down the collar of his shirt and there it was, the small round mark that denoted him as her mate. I was kind of jealous. She gulped as her eyes burned into that mark. I couldn't drag my eyes away from it either, the jealousy nearly overwhelming. The only thing I couldn't decide was who I was jealous of. I was so fucked.

Kell grabbed the bars, and I could see Bohdie struggling with himself not to grab his arm and wrench it off. "I promise you, Enit, that I had nothing to do with yesterday's explosion. I was here to warn you."

Another snort, this time from a big vampire. "Convenient."

Kell looked between us all, then he told his story. Right from the moment that two ancient vampires told him never to show his face again, to the moment when The Hounds told him they had a mole in Eden Academy. He hesitated about how he made it from Mexico to Canada, but he was fervent.

I held up my hands. "I swear to god, I'm not a mole for The Hounds." That was at least the truth.

Bohdie cut me a look, and it was equal parts murderous and betrayed, and it was like a knife through the heart.

He twined his fingers in Enit's. "We can't believe anything you say. You played us for months. You're a liar."

It hurt, but I deserved it. "You're right. I lied. But I have nothing to gain from lying about this. The only connection I had with The Hounds was him." I tilted my head and Kell scowled at me. I was messed up. Even when he was glaring daggers at me, I wanted him to fuck me like he hated me.

Enit raised an eyebrow. "So you blew up my girlfriend, *your friend,* for what? Fun?"

I took a shuddering breath, slumping back on the bench seat. "No. The only reason I was even at Eden was because you guys dragged me from my apartment and brought me out here, so let's not pretend it was a premeditated thing. But my family has always been a part of an extreme right wing group called Human Purity. They believe that humans are God's chosen children and the rest of you are abominations to be eradicated as quickly as possible." They taught that to you at a young age, usually at the end of a leather belt, and if you stepped out of line, there were more... torturous punishments.

My brain skittered away from those thoughts. Things that happened in the past needed to stay there. "They thought I'd been killed, but when I checked in, they realized I wasn't dead. They... threatened people I care about, telling me that if I didn't do something, then they'd come marching into Eden with AKs themselves. They wanted me to mirror Eden's servers, probably so they could send info about the students to The Hounds, if what you say about them is true. Eden is like a supermarket for supernatural stock."

Kell was watching me now, like he was looking at a stranger. Which I guess he was, but Kell had saved me, he just didn't know it. Lost in the darkness of my past, Kell and his vendetta had been the only thing keeping me alive.

He stepped toward me. "So instead you blew the servers and all that information up?" I nodded, watching his frown as he moved toward me like I was prey. I looked around him at Enit. "Doc wasn't meant to be hurt. She was meant to be at lunch with you guys. You go at the same time every day. In three months, you've become more like family than anyone else in my life. I'd been so fucking alone. I wouldn't hurt Stacey intentionally."

The whole room was silent, and then Enit turned on her heel and left. The rest of the group went with her and my whole body sagged. Kell sunk onto the bench beside me, his shoulder brushing mine.

He looked at me from the side of his eye. "I didn't know all that. I just thought you were a nerd with a gift for research." I snorted. Well, that wasn't wrong either. "You're my best friend, Frost. You're not alone. Even if we die, we'll die together, yeah?"

I nodded, letting myself slump back against the cold concrete wall. Hopefully they were right about reincarnation, because I'd fucked it all up this time around, but maybe next time I'd be happy. "I loved you, you know. Not as a friend, maybe as a savior—fuck, I don't know. I was doomed to feel this." I rubbed the pain in my chest.

Kell nodded. "Yeah, I know." He twined his fingers in mine, but that was it. We were both silent as we awaited our fate.

I paced in front of Enit's door. She'd been in there for three hours by herself, not letting anyone in, and I was trying to respect her privacy. But for every minute that she was in there, the more my lion got riled.

"Calm down, Bohdie."

I looked over at Stacey, who still had a wide, white bandage on her forehead, and that just made me angry all over again. If anything happened to Stacey, Enit would be devastated. She'd never be the same.

And those fuckers rotting in Dark River's jail cell didn't care about that, no matter how much they pretended to like her. They had no idea about the concept of Pack, of Pride, of connections.

"Maybe they've never had the chance."

I hadn't realized I'd spoken out loud, but still,

Stacey's words had me spinning on my heel in surprise. "Don't tell me you're all about forgiveness too? They nearly killed you, Doc. They destroyed your lab, your life's work. They stole Enit and fucked her up in all sorts of ways we'll still be trying to work through for years to come. Please don't tell me you want to forgive and forget?"

She shrugged. "We've spent months with Frost. Eating with him, laughing with him, getting to know him. Do you think that guy was all a lie?"

I gritted my teeth. "Yes. Because while we were chatting, he was plotting ways to kill us all."

She tensed her jaw. "I reject your hypothesis, Alpha. I think he was discovering what true love and friendship should look like. You can't take a chicken, throw it in a pond, and expect it to become a duck, Bohdie. He needed time to understand what he was missing."

I threw my hands up in the air. "And Kell? What excuse are we giving him?"

She met my eyes and held them, my Alpha abilities nearly useless on her. "He was abused, Bohdie. If we are using animal analogies, would you blame the dog that had been beaten every day with a stick, when he didn't understand that it was the man wielding the stick that hurt him and not the stick itself?"

Fuck. I knew she was right. They were both just products of their upbringing. Hell, we all were, even

Stacey and Enit. "But they threatened what belongs to me. You don't understand—the lion wants their blood."

Stacey stepped toward me, lightly touching my elbow. "You aren't just the beast, Bohdie. You're a man too, the kind of man who gently woos a scared Omega, and accepts slightly eccentric humans."

My lip twitched. "Slightly?" She gave me a droll look, and I huffed a breath. "Fine. Why are you so fucking smart? I thought you were meant to be emotionally stunted?"

Instead of being offended, she just gave me a grin back. "Then I met Enit and your ugly ass. You've taught me that feelings don't need to be understood. They can just *be*."

I bundled her in my arms. "Love you too, Doc. Now get in there. She can never say no to you."

She moved toward Enit's door and frowned. "Where are you going?"

I waved a hand as I walked out the back door. The less she knew, the better.

It was the middle of the day, which meant that Dark River was quiet. I strolled across the nearly abandoned public square. It was like a ghost town, giving the whole place an eerie quality. There were people around, but it was quiet. A skeleton crew in case any travelers rolled through and expected the place to be open like any other ordinary town.

Still, when I stepped through the door of the Sheriff's office, Judge was sitting behind the desk, napping. He opened an eye lazily to let me know he hadn't really been asleep.

"What can I do for you?"

I stared at him hard. I hadn't spent enough time with Enit's parents to predict their responses. I went with honesty. Lay it all out there and at least I could tell Enit I tried.

"I'm going to do something stupid, but I do it to save her heart, okay?"

Judge stared at me for a long moment, until I felt like a bug beneath glass. Finally, he stood, rolling his shoulders, and I tensed.

"I'm going for lunch."

Then he left, his keys still on the desk. I wondered if he thought I was going to free them or kill them?

In all fairness, I didn't fucking know yet either.

I grabbed the keys and headed down the hall toward the cells. Kell was up on his feet, and Frost eyed me warily.

It was Frost who spoke first. "What are you doing here?" he asked softly, a slight tremble of fear in there.

"I don't know."

Kell moved closer to Frost. A show of solidarity? Or did he just think there was safety in numbers?

I paced up and down the small corridor, trying to corral my thoughts. Frost stepped closer to the bars, shaking off Kell's hand as it tried to hold him back. In a miraculous display of human stupidity, he stepped right up to the bars, close enough for me to grab him and choke the fucking life out of him.

He sucked in a breath and pushed it out past his teeth, the sound whistling in the silence. "I'm sorry. I know that doesn't mean shit to you right now, that you can't trust the things I say, but I promise you, I would never have hurt her. She's... I don't fucking know. I know she isn't supposed to affect me the way she does you, but there's something about her that makes you want to see the good in the world. Like she's the last fucking good thing left and destroying her would be your one way ticket to Hell."

I stared at him until he turned away. "You both came really close to destroying her though. The fact she's still standing at all is no thanks to either of you fuckers. I'm left behind trying to fix what you guys so fucking easily destroy without a care." They both stared at the ground, but Kell eventually raised his gaze again. If he'd been a shifter, he'd have been a strong one.

Which somehow made it worse. I wanted to climb in there and assert my dominance. I wanted to make him pay for every fucking tear she'd shed on his behalf these last few months. I stuck the keys in the door, and watched them both tense as I opened it slowly.

I sauntered into the cell like I wasn't worried about

being trapped in there with them, which in all honesty, I wasn't. I would always be genetically superior to humans. To Enit though? It didn't matter if we were humans or supernaturals. Whether we'd wooed her or stolen her love like a greedy child.

Something in her had decided on these two, and eventually she'd get over the betrayal. But they would still be her abductor and the spy. They couldn't be trusted here and this world wouldn't accept them. It would be better if I killed them before they had the chance to break her heart even more.

But instead of rending them limb from limb like my lion was screaming for me to do, I stepped to the side.

"Leave. There's no place for you here, but this is where she needs to be. I can't look at either of you without seeing a threat, and I'm hoping that time dulls the urge I have to tear off your dicks and make you eat them."

Frost blanched but Kell held my eyes. I could begrudgingly admire that. I held out a folded sheet of paper from my back pocket. "In two years' time, we will be at this address. Either be there or don't—I don't give a fuck. But I won't let us get stuck in this cycle for another year, do you understand? If you return here, you will die. Frost has our numbers; he accrued them while pretending to be our friend rather than a threat to our entire safety."

"Bohdie..." I turned at the voice behind me, but I wasn't particularly surprised to see Enit and Stacey. I dropped my head, not wanting to see the look in Enit's eyes. She'd only just gotten Kell back, and here I was, making him leave because I was so damn jealous and pretending it was because I was fucking altruistic.

She rested her hand between my shoulder blades, soothing me, before stepping around me and facing down her demons. Or her potential love interests. It was hard to know which was which, after this last year.

Kell stood frozen, like he didn't know what to do now she was within arm's reach. But when it came to moments like these, where it was all feelings and heart stuff, Enit was the Alpha. She stepped up to him until she was completely in his personal space, then she merely leaned her forehead on his chest, over his heart and shuddered with relief. I could feel the bond flare where it ran beside mine, and I gritted my teeth.

She drew back, looking up into his eyes, her brilliant blue ones wet with unshed tears, and... head-butted him in the nose.

The crack reverberated around the room, and she grabbed her forehead with both hands, wincing.

"Argh, Carmen always said no one wins in a head-butt, but Jesus fucking hell," she groaned, and I stared between them wide-eyed. My sweet, gentle Enit had just broken this guy's nose. I didn't know if I should be worried or proud. When she let go of her head—which was going to sport a bruise for sure—she grabbed Kell's shirt, pulling him into a kiss. She didn't care that there was blood pouring from his nose, and neither did he, given the way he was kissing her back.

Finally, she pulled back—her face smeared with blood—and smiled. "Be better, asshole. Wait for me."

He swallowed hard, kissing her once more on the head. "I will, I swear it." He lifted his shirt and pinched his nose, trying to stop the bleeding. Looked painful. I grinned in glee.

She turned to Frost, and her face was now solemn. The betrayal was written all over her face, and Frost looked like he'd been punched too. She didn't say anything, but her face said it all.

Frost moved toward her, ignoring my warning growl. "Enit..."

She held up a hand, not giving him the chance to step closer. "She could have died because of you. It's going to take me time to forgive you, to believe that the man who made me smile, who watched Netflix with me and my mates, who I was falling for, wasn't just a figment of my imagination. Because I can't reconcile the Frost who laughed at my terrible jokes and stroked my hair and looked at me like I was his goddamn salvation, with the man who tried to blow up half of my heart."

I had to admit, Frost looked absolutely shattered. It was hard to fake that raw devastation. "What can I do?"

We all waited then, waited to see whether they had a future with us, or if it would all be for nothing.

Enit closed her eyes and sucked in a breath. "Stay with Kell. Make amends. Show me that you are the man I thought you were."

Frost chewed his lip, his head hung low as her words hit him like blows. She tucked her hand under his chin, lifting it slightly. Leaning forward, she barely touched her lips to his but I knew what it was. A promise. Or maybe the hint of a promise.

Whatever it was, it was a liferaft to cling to when times became hard.

I saw the shine in her eyes as she turned and fled from the cell. No one stopped her, no one went after her. She needed to process, and she deserved the space to do that in private.

I stood aside once more, waving the two men out of the jail cell. "Hurry the fuck up, because this town is populated entirely by vampires, and I'm pretty sure you two are the equivalent of Whiteclaw in a sorority house right now."

They both blanched, and having met X, I didn't blame them. God knows how they even made it to a jail cell and weren't both in a shallow grave in the woods already. I leaned down to Stace, brushing her hair away from her bandage.

I hated that I'd failed her. That she'd been hurt. She mightn't own my soul the way Enit did, but I loved this quirky as fuck human. She was part of my Pack, and if anything happened to her...

"You should be lying down, Doc. Go home and rest, maybe check on our girl. I'll sneak these two out of town before they become a breakfast buffet."

She gave me a small smile. Then she turned to the other two men and all mirth left her face. "I know seventy-three ways to kill you and make it look like natural causes."

With that, she left. I shook my head, looking over my shoulder at the two humans. "Honestly, I love that crazy bitch. She's worth ten of you. Let's go."

I led them from the station and could have kissed Enit for thinking to bring my car. I didn't give her nearly enough credit.

Thirty minutes later, I watched a banged up old Chevy disappear down the highway, and I couldn't work out if I ever wanted to see them again.

Only time and fate would tell, I guess.

Enit

I hadn't been this nervous since the time I asked Bohdie to take my virginity. As the Canadian border retreated behind us, I was still restless. My knee bounced up and down like I was a crack addict, all my nervous energy pooling there until it refused to remain still. We were on our way to Black Mountain, or close enough. We'd decided to start our lives together out of Dark River, because while I loved my family, I've never stood on my own and I needed this.

Convincing Stacey had been harder. She was happy there, at least now that she had me and Bohdie to lean on, but she'd never really lived outside an institution. First the laboratory she'd grown up in, then within the walls of Eden Academy. We both needed to spread our wings, and now was the time to do it.

When Bohdie had let slip about some of the inhabitants of Black Mountain though, Stacey had been right on board. The Four Horseman of the Apocalypse ran a tattoo studio there? She'd basically salivated at the thought of studying them. They were Sammie's parents, so that basically made us family—at least, that's what Sammie had said.

No, it wasn't the move that was making me nervous, or saying goodbye to Christopher, Carmen and my parents, though that had made me anxious. It was the fact that in an hour, we'd get to a crossroads.

If Kell and Frost were standing there waiting for me, I'd have everything I ever wanted. We'd get to finally *start* the life we could have had.

But if they weren't...

Stacey reached forward and grabbed my hand. "Stop worrying so much. They will be there."

It had been 730 days since I'd seen them. The ache in my soul was barely appeased by regular texts between me and Kell, and Frost had started sending me heirloom seeds. The first one had been a purple hyacinth, which apparently was the flower for forgiveness.

While he didn't text me the way Kell did, he sent me a letter and seeds every month. For a man whose entire identity had been based around technology, it felt... important that he took the time to communicate with me in such a tactile way.

Still, despite Stacey's assurances, as well as Bohdie's, I was a goddamn mess. I was as fearful of them being there as not being there.

What I'd had for the last two years with Stacey and Bohdie was perfect. We were a team. We'd been through so much that we were as close as we could be. Adding two more people, especially ones who came with so much baggage and history, was going to be difficult. I felt guilty for wanting them, like I was betraying the mates I already had.

"Get out of your head, Princess, because we're here." Bodhie slowed and pulled over onto the shoulder of the road. "The decision from here on is up to you. We can go forward, we can go back, and Stacey and I will support you one hundred percent."

I gnawed on my lip. I sucked in a deep breath and felt that emptiness in my chest that just couldn't be filled, despite my happiness. I didn't look at them as I nodded, scared I'd see the betrayal in their eyes. "Let's go."

"Omega, look at me."

I couldn't resist the damn Alpha voice and he knew it. I turned to look at Bohdie. "You are the best thing that ever happened to any of us, but you owe us nothing. The decisions are yours, the speed at which we move is up to you. If they have a problem with it, I will pummel them into oblivion."

"I love you both. Just because I want this, doesn't mean you aren't enough—you know that, right?"

He nodded. "We know, baby. Now let's go see if these fuckers have grown a conscience in the last two years and if they are fit to even kiss your feet."

"Or suck your toes," Stacey added from the back seat. We both turned to stare at her. "What? It's a common sexual desire."

I shook my head, my smile finally reappearing. Whatever happened, I had these two amazing people and they would be enough. Bohdie pulled back out onto the road and we stopped at a diner outside some tiny town named Chatsville. Our entire universe was packed into this SUV, including my mouse, Norbert. He was still as spritely as the day Stacey had given him to me, even though the internet said he should die soon. I mean, he lived in the mouse version of nirvana so maybe that was it.

I cracked the window for him a little and climbed out of the car. I fidgeted with my dress, my hair, my purse, until Stacey grabbed my hand. "You look like a vision. Stop."

I took a deep breath and followed Bohdie into the diner. Every set of eyes in the place turned to look at me, but I was drawn to one table in particular, in the back corner. I stopped breathing, but my feet moved without my conscious thought, and suddenly I was in front of them.

They looked older, but of course they did. They were human. They'd age and eventually die, as would Stacey. I was setting myself up for a few decades of happiness and a century of pain. I looked over my shoulder at Stacey. It was worth it though.

They both stood, and Kell stepped from the booth. "Enit..." he whispered, like he couldn't believe I was here. Me either, big guy. Me either. Then he surprised the shit out of me by wrapping his arms around my shoulders and kissing me like he was dying of thirst in the desert. After a moment of shock, my body relaxed into the kiss. A throat cleared, and Kell reluctantly pulled back. "I've missed you so fucking much. I can't... I don't even understand why, but it was like I was missing a limb."

I nodded. "It's the bond."

He gave me a crooked half-smile. "Maybe."

"No, it's you," Frost said from beside me, and I turned to look at the remaining piece of the puzzle.

"Hello, Frost," I said softly, and that was all he needed. He stepped into me, dragging me into his arms and holding me like I was his last anchor to shore. I wrapped my arms around his waist and sunk into his warmth, letting all the doubts, the baggage, just float away.

When he kissed my eyelids, I realized tears were slipping from them. "I'm so sorry."

I shook my head, pressing my lips to his. "It's the past."

I realized the diner was buzzing at the spectacle we made. Frost glared around the diner, but when he looked back at me, his eyes were soft.

Kell grabbed my hand. "Let's get out of here. We can talk in our hotel room at least. Away from the audience."

Bohdie cleared his throat. "I have a better idea."

Bohdie

Technically, I was the heir to everything the light touched. I snorted at the Pride Rock reference, but it fit. Chatsville was home to one of the largest lion Prides in the US, and the Regent of the Chatsville Pride? My biological father. But I wanted nothing to do with this inheritance, and we all knew it. If I took over any Pride, it would be the Black Mountain one, and that was basically just my parents and siblings. They didn't need a Regent.

No, I was happy for the Regent title to go to my half-brother. He'd grown up in the Pride, knew the families, the people. It was understood and as long as no one made us fight, we were totally chill.

He was a great kid, about seven years younger than

me. We'd see if that cool demeanor lasted into his teenage years though; I wasn't holding my breath.

When my parents had realized I didn't enjoy staying in the Pride house, where everyone except my father were just a bunch of strangers, they'd bought me a tiny apartment. I had my independence and privacy, while still getting to know my roots, my biological family. I'd hated the summer trips here when I was a teen, wrenched away from my friends and my real family, forced to come here and relate to strangers. But I understood why they did it. They hadn't known that I had no intention of becoming anyone's Alpha Regent. They were preparing me, but in the end it was unnecessary.

"You just happen to have an apartment in Chatsville?" Stacey asked, her voice having that high-handed air she got sometimes when she thought I was being a numbskull.

I just raised a brow as I unlocked the door. "Why do you think I suggested this town in the first place?"

She shrugged. "It's halfway?"

I shook my head. "Nope, it's because I could bury a body and get away with it." I looked over my shoulder at the two men who were trailing behind me reluctantly.

Enit slapped my arm. "Stop that. No one is killing anyone. Come in."

The place was a little musty—I hadn't stepped foot

in the place in like four years—but still, it was an easy place to rest our heads and hash out whatever the fuck was about to happen.

But I mean, worst case scenario and I did have to butcher a body, I knew a guy.

Kell and Frost looked unconvinced, but I didn't miss the slight reassuring touches they gave each other. Clearly, we weren't the only ones who had grown closer in the last couple of years.

They stepped into the living room and looked around, unsure. Hell, we all looked unsure. This was like a supremely awkward first date.

Enit drifted between the two groups of us like she was a surgeon, trying to weave us together with her presence.

I indicated that everyone should take a seat, dragging a couple of chairs over from the dining table. I sat in one, Stace in the other, leaving the couch for Enit and the other two. They needed to bond and get over this initial awkwardness, otherwise it was going to be a long damn day.

As if she knew the lifeline I was throwing them, she sat smack bang in the middle of the couch, forcing them to sit either side of her. Not that it was a chore. They both sat close enough that the entire sides of their bodies touched, sandwiching her between them. Almost collectively, they exhaled a relieved sigh.

"So tell us, what have you been doing these last two years?"

Frost looked at Kell, who met my eyes and held them. "It's a secret."

The tight ball of anger that I'd managed to keep under control started to grow. "Do you want to be part of this Pride? Because there are no secrets between us."

Frost looked desperate, but Kell continued to hold my gaze. "I want Enit." Frost became as frozen as his name. "And I want Frost. You two are strangers to me."

A part of me could understand his words, but the rest of me? I wanted to claw out his eyes. "Then I suggest you get to know us, because Enit needs us all, and your days of being a selfish fuck are over."

I looked at Frost, but he was gazing between us, the need for us to get along almost a palpable force emanating from both him and Enit.

Kell finally dropped his eyes. "We've been smuggling shifters."

I blinked, because of all the things I thought he was going to say, that wasn't it. Enit sat frozen between them, and I wanted to reach out and yank her away. Stacey laid a hand on my arm as if she could sense my need.

"Explain."

Kell turned to Enit, no longer trying to convince us. "After I, uh, set you free, I ran to Europe. But the shit you said to me while we were in the cabin kept running through my head, so I did some research. Instead of looking for how evil supernaturals were, I started seeing other things. Shifters crying out for help, stuck in places after being sold off on the black market, or born into shitty situations. People who desperately needed to escape but had no one in their corner." He stopped, his gaze catching Frost's over Enit's shoulder. "When you guys exiled us, we decided the best way to pay for our mistakes was to use the only skills we had to right some wrongs. We met up with a guy on the dark web who knew where we could send them, who promised they knew a place they'd be safe. Big bastard. Scary as hell."

I huffed. "Was his name Vance?"

Both of them whipped toward me. "How did you…"

I waved a hand. "I'll explain later. So you've been rescuing supes?" I prompted them to continue.

Frost spoke this time. "One hundred and fifty-seven, to be precise. Some we deliver wherever they want to go, some we've been dropping to Eden, and some down to Nevada."

Eden? They'd been so close so often? Seeing the question on my face, Frost shook his head. "No, we take them to the border. Locke collects them from there."

The silence in the room was intense. How we could get past this awkwardness was beyond me.

Stacey leaned forward. "I think we should have an orgy. To build bonds."

The actual *fuck*?

Stacey

Frost was off the couch and had his arms wrapped around me in seconds. He squeezed me so tightly, my lungs couldn't draw air.

"I didn't mean me. Still not interested in you."

He just loosened his arms slightly but didn't let me go. "I missed you so much." He looked over my shoulder at Bohdie. "Both of you." I wiggled in his grasp and he let me pull away. "I'm so sorry, Stacey. Sorry for everything. Sorry for almost killing you. Sorry for ruining the good thing we had."

His eyes got big and wet and not gonna lie, I kind of panicked. "Oxytocin is released during orgasm and is imperative in the creation of long-term romantic bonds, and therefore I believe that perhaps a group bonding session may ease some of the awkwardness that is bound to occur due to the long separation, and also cement the bond between Enit and Kell, if that's what they want."

Enit looked at me like I was insane. "Are you prescribing an orgy? You?"

I frowned. "Just because I am asexual, doesn't mean I can ignore the science. I am an atypical case study, and obviously have no interest in taking part in the, uh, gangbang."

"Doc, let's never use the word gangbang again, okay?" Bohdie said slowly, like I was dim-witted.

Well okay then, good to know. I stepped out of Frost's space and moved toward Enit. She was looking between us all, completely unsure of where she should be gravitating, but in all honesty, we should be gravitating toward her. She was our Omega. Our center.

I kissed her, not softly like I normally would, but a firm press that hopefully said "you're mine and I love you." "It doesn't need to be us and them. Show them that they can all love you equally," I told her softly.

She cupped my cheek. "And you?"

I smiled. "I'm interested to see the difference in mating rituals between humans and shifters. For science."

Uh huh. Science.

She laughed and I kissed her again. I tasted her, sucking the plump pale pink of her bottom lip into my mouth. Then I grabbed her chin and moved her face toward Kell.

They stared at each other for an achingly long amount of time, then fell into each other like two magnets that had been kept apart too long.

It was almost painful to watch. I looked over at Frost, who was eyeing them hungrily. I vacated my place beside Enit on the couch, tilting my head so he'd take my space. First step—break down the barrier between them and Enit.

I looked up at Bohdie, who looked like he was somewhere between wanting to watch them bring his mate pleasure, and ripping their heads straight off their bodies. I moved beside him, placing a soothing hand on his shoulder. In the last two years, I'd come to love Bohdie too. Not in the way I loved Enit, but like we were two arms of the same creature. He was my counterpart, the jokes to my seriousness. The fight to my flight.

"It'll be okay, Alpha," I said softly. "If she loves them, it doesn't mean she loves you less."

His jaw tensed but he shook his head. "It's not that. What if they hurt her again?" he asked, his voice pitched so low that I could barely hear.

He was voicing what we all felt, but sometimes, you had to take a leap of faith. Enit had taught me that, in her roundabout way.

"What if they make her whole?" I countered softly. "You're her mate. Get in there, establish the pecking order and do what you do best. Make her feel safe enough to be herself."

He strode over to the couch, grabbing up a lust-drunk Enit, and striding away with her. He stopped at the doorway and looked over his shoulder at the two other people in the room. The rest of our Pack, our

Pride, our family—potentially at least. "Are you coming?"

Frost

I looked at Kell, my heart racing in my chest. I wanted this so fucking bad. I hadn't been exaggerating when I told Stacey that I'd missed them all. While I wanted Enit—and if I was honest with myself, Bohdie—like it was a physical ache, I'd missed the hell out of Stace too. She was the friend I'd never been allowed to have, a match for my wit in every way. While Enit was the balm to my soul and Bohdie had tapped into an unknown submissive need I hadn't realized I'd possessed, Stacey had just been the friend without expectations. She didn't expect me to be cool or funny or charming. I could just be myself.

Together, they had been perfect. And I'd fucked it all up in one stupid move that had been inspired by the fear of the kid I'd once been.

The first thing we'd done was cut ties. I'd sold out my family, and their so-called Church quicker than you could say "I'm in a cult!"

We'd moved south, then kept moving. When I'd put out a call on the less savory places of the web, for anyone who needed help, people had reached back. Then the bear shifters had tracked us down at a bar, and the rest was history. We'd done what Enit had asked—we'd been better.

I knew Bohdie and Kell would be uneasy in each other's presence for some time. Bohdie was so Alpha, and Kell had been the master of his own destiny for so long, that they were going to struggle with the dynamic.

I implored Kell with my eyes not to fuck this up over something as stupid as his macho pride.

"Are you coming?" Bohdie asked, and I hesitated. As much as I desperately wanted Enit, Kell had been my friend, lover, and companion for the last two years. If he walked, I would have to as well. It would break my heart, but I'd do it.

Kell swallowed hard and nodded, getting to his feet. A relieved breath whooshed out of me and I threw Stacey a grin. She just rolled her eyes at me and something in my chest healed a little. We'd be okay, I just knew it. We just had to get over this initial weirdness. And if the Doc prescribed an orgy with the girl of my dreams and two hot guys, then I wasn't going to argue. I skipped out of the room and into a bedroom. It smelled musty and unused, but not unpleasant, and the bed was still made up.

I grabbed Kell's arm, turning him slightly toward me. "I know it seems weird, but this is a huge olive branch. Get out of your head and take it, okay?"

He tensed, but nodded. "This is just not how I thought the reunion with my, uh, mate would go."

Bohdie snorted. "I'm not sure any of us thought it would go like this. This is a weird, slightly fucked up arrangement, and we're all navigating in the dark. But at least we all have something in common." He looked down at Enit. "To think I thought that sharing you with Stace was going to be the weirdest thing that ever happened..."

Enit was looking at us all, wide-eyed and honestly, a little nervous. Maybe she was waiting for a fist fight or for Bohdie to shift, who knew. I guess Bohdie knew her best, because he leaned down and kissed her with a passion so fucking hot that I got hard from just watching. I drifted closer, because how could I not?

He had her in the middle of the bed like she was an offering on an alter, and I crawled toward her. She watched me closely, her eyes filled with heat and something else that I couldn't define. I kissed her with the reverence she deserved, and then she surprised the hell out of me. She bit my lip hard, then sucked it into her mouth, punishing and forgiving me with one movement.

"I've missed you too, Frost."

I shuddered and kissed her hard, pouring everything I had into it, trying to explain my complicated, messy feelings with my mouth and my tongue. She moaned gently against my mouth, curling against me in a way that made me moan too.

A hand wrapped into my hair that had gotten slightly too long, and Bohdie twisted my head to the side, biting my jugular gently. It made shivers run down my spine, and I knew it was how an Alpha punished someone lesser in the hierarchy. It was retribution, and a little gentle forgiveness.

Also, it was hot as fuck.

My dick went crazy hard, like diamond hard, and I pressed my hard on against the softness of Enit's belly, making her suck in a breath even as she kissed me again.

"Move over, Frost. Our girl is overdressed for the occasion."

I shifted to the left, and felt Bohdie's hands gently brushing between our bodies as he divested Enit of her clothes. I didn't dare to move away, just in case she never let me come back. As Bohdie peeled off her clothes, I traced the newly revealed skin with my tongue. I'd dreamed of this. Night after night, I'd dreamed of kissing her throat, her collarbone, the soft curve of her breasts.

When I took her sweet pink nipple into my mouth, the sounds she made were better than I'd ever imagined. She gripped my head, holding me there, but I refused to move my mouth away to even tell her there was no chance of me moving anywhere.

Well, except maybe further south. I kissed down her stomach and settled between her now naked thighs. She was completely naked below me and she took my breath away. "So fucking beautiful," I whispered, kissing just above her pelvic bone and then both hips.

I wouldn't admit it to anyone other than Kell, but I'd never gone down on a girl before. Going down on Kell was entirely different to this. But I had a decent IQ and a good porn collection, so hopefully I could figure it out.

I nibbled my way around her outer lips, kissing and sucking, my nose periodically bumping her clit and making her thrust up into my face.

I. Loved. It.

I was never going to move from between her thighs again. I lapped my way around her slit lazily, sucking and licking her clit, thrusting my tongue in and out of her tight little channel until she was wetting my face with her juices.

Honestly? I couldn't fathom how there were men in the world who didn't get blisteringly hard at the sounds a woman made when she was basically boneless with pleasure, or the way her thighs trapped my face, or the way she breathily chanted my name. It was fucking nirvana when she came all over my face, shouting my name.

I felt eyes on me, and I realized Kell had moved up

to kiss Enit. Right now though, they were both staring at me with hooded, lust-filled eyes.

I kissed her thigh, scraping my teeth down the sensitive flesh. "This is fucking heaven. I'm never leaving. You can pry my cold dead body out from between these glorious thighs with a crowbar," I announced to the room, moving back to her sensitive clit and circling it with the tip of my tongue. Bohdie grabbed my hair again, and I might have purred against her clit, making Enit groan.

He turned my head and licked my face from chin to cheekbone.

The noise I made was guttural. Still, I couldn't help but ask, "I thought you didn't bend that way?"

He just grinned down at me, his fist in my hair keeping my head pulled all the way back. "Never say never, but right now? You're coated in my favorite flavor in the world."

We both looked at Enit, whose pale skin was now flushed the prettiest pink. Kell still looked hesitant, so I crawled my way back up Enit's body, my cock still trapped behind the meatlocker masquerading as my Levi's.

When I reached her face though, I leaned into Kell, swiping my tongue against his lips, and he pulled me in tight. Enit moaned, and it appeared that our sweet little Omega was a bit of a closet voyeur. He licked every last ounce of her cum off my face, and my pants were getting painful.

Enit reached out, grabbing my face. "I need you," she said, surprising the hell out of me.

I'd expected her to want Kell or Bohdie, and I was more than happy to be relegated to the background this first time. Later, I would have made her fall in love with my dick as well, but this time, especially with all the uncertainty, I'd figured she'd have gravitated to an Alpha. I nearly cried at the thought that she wanted me instead.

She grinned at me. "Get naked, Cedric."

I couldn't take my pants off fast enough.

Kell

Frost nearly fell on his face trying to peel himself out of his jeans. If I wasn't so achingly hard, I would have laughed.

I looked down at Enit, who was languid with her orgasm, draped against my chest as she watched Frost's truly awful strip tease. She stole the breath from my lungs, and not for the first time, I wondered whether it was the bond or my heart making me feel these things. In the end, like always, I decided I didn't give a fuck.

The chance to feel this? The bubbling, giddy rush that burned through my veins, the absolute elation of seeing her smile at Frost's antics?

I'd pay for this feeling. Find a way to crush it down and into a pill? I would have been an addict. Instead, she spread that joy around like she was an endless well of it and god, it hurt my heart so good.

I pulled her onto my chest, her breasts pressed against my own. When I felt the hard press of her nipples, I was so glad I'd taken off my shirt and jeans before climbing into the bed beside her. We kissed, and I left Enit in complete control, surrendering to her. I'd attempt to make up for the bullshit of our past even if it took forever. I hoped it took forever because that would mean she would be with me forever too.

I met Frost's eyes over her shoulder, but then my gaze skittered around the room. The other girl, Stacey, sat in the corner, her chin resting on her palm as she watched what was going on with almost a clinical eye.

On the other side was the shifter, and meeting his eyes still made panic surge in my chest. He wasn't watching me though, he was watching her. The center of this ragtag group. The nucleus of our atom.

Frost knelt between my thighs too, running a hand down Enit's spine, and she curled against me, making a happy little hum even as she kissed me. He plucked at her hips, raising them slightly, but not attempting to take her from me. I knew I could easily share with Frost. I loved him, even though the first few months had been rough. We were both fucked up, and combined, we had more emotional baggage than an airport. Frost had looked at me like I was meant to save him, and I was just an epic fucking failure. But we'd settled into a routine, made a life together, and became a couple.

Though Enit was always that missing piece for me. For Frost, I knew he'd missed all of them. Told me stories of what it was like to be a part of their Pack when he was on house arrest. I'd heard more from the calls and messages I'd had with Enit over the last two years. But stories weren't the same as real people.

Luckily, step one of being better was not being a jealous fuck.

I felt the moment Frost pushed inside her—it was like the reality snapped into place. She threw her head back and I kissed her. Her body slipped along mine with his thrust, the friction delicious on the hard length of my dick pressed between us. Sandwiched between me and Frost, it was perfect, and my hands slipped around, stroking the places where Enit and Frost met and became one.

Frost made love to her with slow, easy movements that made her moan against my lips, going deep until he was driving her into my body and fucking us both. Her body started to shake as I lightly thrust up toward her, nudging her clit until she was writhing between us.

The sound of her coming was like fucking coming home, and I held them both as Frost thrust shallowly, coming not long after her, as her body milked his. I'd felt that sensation, remembered vividly the indescribable pull of her hot little cunt. Still dreamed about it.

Frost pulled out and rolled off us, dragging Enit with him until she was sandwiched between us even now.

She reached for the aching hardness in my boxers, but I grabbed her wrists. "No, little monster. I am going to woo you properly. Make you fall in love with me. Then I'll make love to you. Not before."

She looked at me softly, opening her lips like she was going to protest, before shutting it again. "Okay."

The silence rolled around the room, muffled only by Frost's panting. "I need to do more cardio. Work on my core."

Bohdie burst out laughing, and even I grinned. Stacey shook her head from the corner. Enit just leaned up and kissed Frost's chin.

Bohdie looked at me approvingly, and something passed between us. Not respect, but at least an understanding. The rest would come.

"A good orgy deserves pizza. What does everyone want?"

With that, the rest of our lives began.

ABOUT THE AUTHOR

Grace McGinty is eclectic. She has worked as a chocolatier, a librarian, a forensic accountant and finally a writer. Like her professional career, the genres she writes are also eclectic. She writes romance, reverse harem romance, fantasy, contemporary young adult and new adult books.

She lives in rural Australia with her crazy family, an entire menagerie of pets, and will one day be crushed by her giant piles of books that litter every room.

Head over to www.gracemcginty.com and join my mailing list for sneak previews into what I am working on and to stay up-to-date with new releases and giveaways!

Not ready to leave Eden Academy yet? *Secrets and Strays, Eden Academy Book 3*, is coming in this winter!

Join my Facebook group Grace's Bookish Angels to stay up to date!

Want to see where Bohdie came from? Check out Hunting Isla (Black Mountain Mates Book One) on the next page!

Grace McGinty

HUNTING ISLA

ISLA

My stomach bulged from an overload of pizza, but I resisted the urge to pop the top button of my jeans. The guys laughed as the comedian on the tv made another dick joke, and I rolled my eyes. Teenage boys all had the same sense of humor. I checked my phone again, hoping Cara had messaged.

I looked over at Axel, who wasn't outright laughing at the movie, though his lips were curled in a rare smile. He was too cool to laugh at dick jokes. "She still isn't answering her calls. You think I should go over to her place and check she's okay?"

His eyes shot to my face, and he shook his head. "Don't go to her place, ever. Her parents aren't nice people."

He frowned, a solitary wrinkle creasing his smooth forehead. That wrinkle was the reason I knew he'd had a hard life, maybe as difficult as mine. That, and the fact that he was the legal guardian of Archer and Wyatt, his younger cousins, even though he was barely eighteen. They all lived in this tiny apartment together, not an adult in sight. How they escaped the notice of Child Protective Services was beyond me. But I wasn't going to ask too many questions. They gave me a key the week after I moved here and let me come and go as I pleased so I didn't have to be at my foster home more than I needed to be.

If you added Cara, my flighty best friend who was pregnant at sixteen, we made quite the little band of misfits.

"She'll be fine, Isla. Her parents probably have her grounded or something."

He was probably right, but I chewed my thumbnail all the same, a nervous habit I'd had for as long as I could remember. Wyatt reached over and grabbed my hand, popping my thumb from my mouth.

"Stop, Lala, or you'll make it bleed."

I huffed but dropped my hand back into my lap. Wyatt was the only one I let call me Lala because let's face it, it made me sound like a five-year-old. But I had a soft spot for Wyatt, who was the baby of our group at sixteen, a year younger than me and a few months younger than Cara.

I tossed and turned a little more, trying to get comfy on the guy's lumpy couch, before I gave up. "I'm gonna head home," I said, getting to my feet. The guys all stood. It was a weird, old school thing they did every time I got to my feet, even if I was just going to pee.

They came over and kissed my cheek one by one, another weird ritual they did, but I wasn't complaining. It made me feel special, and besides, it wasn't romantic or anything like that between us. We were friends, completely platonic, and it had been that way since I moved to town a year ago. They didn't have any interest in me other than as a friend.

I looked them all over. They looked related, that's for sure, each one had beautiful olive skin that shone almost bronze in the sunlight, and deep golden hair, though Axel's was a little darker than Wyatt and Archer's. But they were all different too; Axel was tall and built like a Greek statue and had a gruff attitude that hid his soft center. Whenever we went down swimming at Geronimo's Bend, I basically had to pick my jaw up off the ground whenever he took his shirt off.

Archer was just as tall, and his shoulders were just as wide but his body was leaner, probably because he worked as a mechanic rather than a tree-feller like Axel. The girls loved him and he was a terrible flirt, but there was a serious side to him that I'm not sure anyone else saw.

Wyatt was tall but rake thin. He definitely hadn't

grown into his limbs yet, but I thought that in the next couple of years he might get bigger than even Axel.

"Archer will walk you home," Axel stated. It wasn't an offer. It was fact. In the beginning, I'd tried to argue that I was fine. I basically lived on the streets before I moved to Chatsville. But no matter how I argued, I always got an escort to walk me home through the sleepy streets of my new hometown.

Archer held out an arm to me. "You want a ride home on my bike?" he asked, grinning, already knowing my answer. It was a resounding HELL NO! I'd seen that thing when it was just rusted pieces of metal that looked like it belonged in a dumpster. He'd restored it by hand, and now it was a beautiful piece of machinery, but I did not want to be a road fatality statistic, thank you very much. I didn't even care that I only lived three blocks away, so the likelihood of us going over twenty miles an hour was pretty slim.

"One day I'll get you on the back of my bike, Isla, and you will fall in love with riding forever," he promised in that flirty way he had, like what he was saying was part joke, part promise.

"Not in this lifetime, Archie." I slipped my backpack onto my shoulders and leaned in to give Wyatt one last kiss on the head. We were an affectionate bunch, Cara included, and while it had taken me a while to adjust to their need for physical contact, I reveled in it now. I knew that human contact was part of what I had been missing all my life. I was so lucky now.

Archer held out an elbow, and like an old-fashioned gentleman, he escorted me out of their apartment and down the stairs.

In a last-ditch effort, I tried to call Cara again. It went straight to voicemail. "Do you think Cara is okay? What if there's something wrong with the baby?"

Archer's face hardened. "I don't know. But there's nothing we can do to help. She'll find us when she needs us."

Cara had gotten pregnant after I'd been in town a couple of weeks. Cara had instantly befriended me at school, ignoring my "fuck off" face. She just sat down opposite me in the cafeteria, and declared that we would be friends. She was right. Her joy was infectious. But there were only highs and lows with Cara, there were no ordinary days. Every day was as wild as a party, or as somber as a funeral. Eventually, she'd dragged a shy Wyatt over to meet me, and we'd become our own little clique. When she'd gotten pregnant, I'd been shocked. I hadn't realized she'd even been seeing anyone, although at first, I thought that perhaps it was one of the guys. Axel, in particular, doted on her, but I soon realized it was more familial than sexual. No, I was positive the baby's father wasn't one of my guys, but she wouldn't tell any of us who it was. Well, she wouldn't tell me. The guys didn't even try to guess.

We were silent as we walked down the street, past the sweet little rows of houses with manicured lawns, or landscaped rock gardens. Chatsville was quaint, and on the surface, it looked like a postcard. But for some reason, something always felt a little off about the town, something that made the hair on the back of my neck tingle, but I could never pinpoint why I felt that way. I shivered and stepped closer to Archer. I complained about my escorts home, but sometimes I was secretly glad they were there.

He took the opportunity to wrap an arm around my shoulders. "What are we doing for you eighteenth birthday, Sweet Cheeks?"

As the icy wind that promised winter swirled around us, I pressed closer to his side. "I don't know. I've never had a party. I don't think I'm the party girl type. Maybe I'll do what normal teens do when they turn eighteen. Vote. Get my driver's license. Get blackout drunk. Maybe I'll finally get rid of my V-Card."

I grinned when Archer let out a choking sound. "Don't even joke about it, Isla. You'll give me a heart attack, and Axel will be forced to beat the unfortunate soul to a pulp for sullying his perfect Isla."

I elbowed him in the ribs. "I was kidding, doofus. Have you seen the quality of guys at my high school? Wyatt excluded, of course, but it's not like I could lose my virginity to Wyatt."

"Don't want to be a cougar?" Archer laughed, though he was pulling a weird face.

"No, I don't want to mess up what we have. He means too much to screw it up with sex. Sex ruins everything." I'd seen my mother, and her Johns, and the drugs. Sex was a commodity, and nothing I'd seen since convinced me that it would be any different for me. The guys meant too much to me to even chance fucking it all up.

"We'll figure something out for your birthday, Isla. You just leave it to me. I have a whole week to come up with an extravaganza that will make you forget every other birthday you've ever had."

I grinned at him. He would too, I had no doubt. But in all honesty, pizza and movies with the guys and Cara were all I needed. I didn't need an extravaganza. I just needed my family.

We stopped in front of my foster parent's house, and I sighed. It wasn't that it was bad. I'd had way, way worse. It was just like stepping from a warm hug into a barren wasteland.

I leaned over and kissed Archer's cheek. "Night, Archie. I'll see you guys tomorrow?"

He hugged me tight. "Yeah, we'll pick you up on the way to school. Night Isla."

He stood on the path and waited until I walked around to the side of the house, letting myself in the back door. I gave him a finger wave and snuck into the house on silent feet. I could hear Tony and Lorraine fighting in the front room, so I made my way to my small bedroom in the back of the house. I switched on the light and slid the chair under the doorknob.

When I'd first arrived, their fights had scared me. Too often foster kids were a convenient punching bag. But I'd eventually gotten used to the raised voices and the sound of Tony's fist hitting the drywall. I was pretty sure they hated each other. But they just ignored me, and I was okay with that.

I texted the guys to tell them I was safe and sound in bed, and laid down on top of my comforter, staring at the crumbling moldings on my ceiling. I plugged my phone into its charger, giving Cara one last call. If she didn't answer tomorrow, I was going over there, to hell with what Axel said.

A knock at my window made me jump off my bed, my heart pounding. I pulled back my curtain and jerked away in shock as a wild-eyed Cara appeared in the glass like a ghost.

I opened up my window.

"Cara, what's wrong? What are you doing here?"

She reached through the window and tugged on my arm. "You have to come with me, Lala. I need you. Please." She tugged harder on my hooded sweatshirt. "Please."

The level of desperation in her tone scared me. "Hey, okay. Just let me grab my phone."

She shook her head. "No. Leave it. Please, you have to hurry. Grab anything important to you. But hurry." She was crying now, her arms wrapped around her belly. Her flat belly.

"Cara, the baby..." I couldn't ask. She cried harder.

"I'll explain. Please, Isla, now." Her tears clinched it for me. I ran to my dresser, pulling out the few things that meant anything to me. A silver chain that my grandmother gave me before she died when I was six. A picture of my mother, before she got hooked on heroin. A picture of me, Cara and the guys down by the river. I also stuffed in my converse sneakers, all my underwear and a change of clothes.

I was halfway out the window when I heard a heavy thumping on the front door. Cara was vibrating with terror as she dragged me through the backyard, into the woods behind the house. "Come on, you have to run," she whispered, pulling me with a speed I didn't know she possessed.

"Cara, what's going on?" She was freaking me out now. My heart was thudding with fear. We stopped in front of a beat-up old car.

"I don't have time to explain, Isla. But I need you to do this for me, okay? I'm so sorry, but you're the only one. The only one I can trust. The only one they can't track. There's so much you don't know and I can't tell you now, but I'll find you, okay? I just need you to run now. Go as far away as you can tonight, then ditch the car and go further. Don't stop, okay? You can't stop because they'll find you."

She pushed me into the driver's seat and shut my door as quietly as she could. "You are the only one I can trust with this," she repeated as tears streamed down her cheeks.

"Cara, come with me, or we can go see the guys. Axel will help with whatever this is. You're scaring me right now."

She grabbed my arm too tight. "You should be scared, Isla. God, I hate that I have to do this to you. I love you like a sister, you're the only one. I'll tell the guys, okay? I promise. Then we will all come and find you. But you need to go now. There's a suitcase in the back with everything you need, as much money as I could get. It'll help. Now go. Please go."

I started the car and did what she asked, pulling off the fire trail where she'd parked and onto the dirt road that would lead to the main highway. I watched as Cara got smaller and smaller in the red glow of my tail lights, and my heart thumped with terror.

I pulled onto the highway, and Cara's beater mixed in with the trucks and nighttime travelers. I realized the banged-up old car had no radio, so I hummed to myself in an effort to block out the thoughts that kept swirling in my head like a hurricane.

Then I heard it. The tiniest sound from the back of the car.

I swerved onto the shoulder, making gravel spray up against the side panels. Unbuckling my seatbelt, I whipped to stare at the rear seats. In the back of the car, hidden by the darkness, was a baby car seat. Inside the car seat was an infant, who couldn't have been more than a day or two old. It let out a tiny mewl, and the sound cracked my heart in two.

"Oh Cara, what have you done?"

I missed my phone so badly. I was desperate to google 'how to take care of a newborn' but I made do. I wanted to call the guys and see what was happening because I had a feeling that it was nothing good.

In the suitcase, I found baby bottles and newborn formula, diapers, onesies and a basic assortment of other baby stuff, including a parenting book. Also about five thousand dollars in cash. Two birth certificates that listed his birth for two days ago. She'd named him Bohdie, after the lead singer in her favorite band. Both birth certificates were exactly the same except for one small detail. I'd almost thrown up when I saw that the mother's name on one of the certificates was listed as mine. When had she had the time to create a false birth certificate? For someone in such a state of terror, Cara had been super prepared. It made me wonder how long she had been planning this.

I made the baby a bottle from water heated in a coffee cup at a gas station. He was a quiet little thing, his face screwed up and wrinkly, and he spent most of his time sleeping. I was jittery, partly because I'd drank four cups of coffee already, and partly because every shadow made me think someone was about to jump out and take the baby from me. Or maybe the cops would show up and accuse me of kidnapping. But I had the birth certificate and my ID, and by all accounts, I was Bohdie's mother. I bought an armful of snacks, energy drinks, some oversized sunglasses. I dumped it all on the counter, smiling pleasantly but not making eye-contact with the bored dude behind the counter. Above his head was a shelf of toys, probably for people who traveled too much and forgot their kid's birthdays and stuff. But one of the toys was a stuffed lion in a soft lemon color.

"I'll get the lion too," I said to the gas station attendant, who swiveled on his chair and grabbed down the toy. It looked like a baby toy, with little tags and rubbery bits for them to rattle and chew on. It was perfect. There'd been no room for toys in a suitcase packed with diapers and wads of cash.

I paid up and hefted the baby carrier back to the car. It took me ten minutes to work out how the baby carrier clipped back into the car seat bit, but eventually I worked it out. However, by the time I was done, the baby was crying and tears streamed down my face too.

I couldn't do this. I was seventeen. I'd never even held a baby in my life. I couldn't do this. I sat in the backseat and cried along with the baby for another minute, then I wiped my arm across my face and pulled the bottle from my backpack. I tested it on my wrist to check it wasn't too hot like I'd seen them do in the movies, and gave him the bottle. His crying stopped instantly. His big golden eyes stared into mine as he drank, completely trusting despite the fact I was a stranger.

I could do this. I would do it. I made a promise and I intended to keep it.

I'd done what Cara had said, I'd driven through the night, and I hadn't stopped until I hit Omaha. Now, we were waiting at the bus depot, the old beater parked in the mall across the street. With the baby car seat, including all the attachments, resting at my feet, the suitcase beside me, we sat in the waiting room. I pulled the hood of my sweatshirt further over my face and tried not to close my eyes. I was exhausted. Mentally and physically drained. Every time I nodded off, I'd imagine something happening to the baby, and that kept me awake. I stared down at Bohdie. Was he supposed to sleep this much? I pulled out the parenting book and went back to the part about bringing your newborn home.

Glancing up at the tv, the headline ticking across the bottom of the screen caught my eye. Then a photo of a face that was all too familiar flashed on the screen, along with almost a dozen others.

I strained forward to hear what the newsreader was saying.

"It was a tragic scene in Chatsville this morning, as a dozen bodies were pulled from the remains of a fire that killed a local family, including five children. Police described the scene as horrific when they arrived early this morning to find the house completely consumed by flames. The family of six that resided here, as well as extended family and friends who were staying for a celebration, all perished."

Cara.

My fist wrapped around the bar of the baby seat, my knuckles turning white. She'd been murdered, along with her whole family. I knew that in my gut. Her terror had been too palpable for it to be anything else.

I choked back my sobs and stood as they called for my bus. I straightened my shoulders and looked down at my charge. He would have been the thirteenth victim last night.

I was more resolute than ever. I would do what his Mama asked. I would never stop running. I just hoped that the guys would find me eventually as Cara said. Because I needed them more than ever right now.